Dinner was quite an event. It made me feel wanted. Even though I was sure it was all in my head, and that I was imagining things, it still made me feel good.

It all started when Ashley and Trisha both wanted to sit next to me, then there was the little scene over the broccoli salad in which both women tried to serve me from the same bowl at the same time.

Trisha *accidentally* spilled her drink down Ashley's back while she was walking by.

I was torn between disbelief and suggesting a three-way.

"I think we should sit around the fire and tell ghost stories!" Kevin suggested, trying to lighten the mood. Trisha and Ashley were still growling at each other, although they had apparently decided to take turns with me. Who'd a thunk that? Me, being shared by two right beauties!

Titles by Therese Szymanski

Available from Bella Books

The Brett Higgins Motor City Thrillers (in order)
When the Dancing Stops
When the Dead Speak
When Some Body Disappears
When Evil Changes Face
When Good Girls Go Bad
When the Corpse Lies
When First We Practice

The Chronicles of Shawn Donnelly
It's All Smoke & Mirrors

New Exploits
Once Upon a Dyke: New Exploits of Fairy Tale Lesbians
Bell, Book and Dyke: New Exploits of Magical Lesbians
Stake Through the Heart: New Exploits of Twilight Lesbians
Tall in the Saddle: New Exploits of Wild West Lesbians

Edited by
Back to Basics: A Butch-Femme Anthology
Call of the Dark: Erotic Lesbian Tales of the Supernatural
The Perfect Valentine
Wild Nights: (Mostly) True Stories of Women Loving Women
Fantasy: UnTrue Stories of Lesbian Passion

THE FIRST CHRONICLES OF SHAWN DONNELLY

It's All SMOKE & MIRRORS

Therese Szymanski

Bella
BOOKS

2007

Bella Books, Inc.
P.O. Box 10543
Tallahassee, FL 32302

Printed in the United States of America on acid-free paper

First Edition

Editor: Cindy Cresap
Cover designer: Stephanie Solomon-Lopez

ISBN-10: 1-931513-117-8
ISBN-13: 978-1-931513-117-8

For Stacia

Acknowledgments

Thanks to Effey, 'cause she was SO whacked cool enough to help me SO much with all the Irishisms and Irish myth and legend and all!

Thanks also to Marianne K. Martin, who wanted to see a "little imp of a dyke" in print; Effey's wife, for allowing some very valuable Effey time to be used in helping me with this book; Beth and Julia, who gave an initial thumbs up to this project, back before . . . much major mucho rewriting; and, of course, to Cindy, who called me on some of my cheap shortcuts and made me work even harder.

The old woman sat in front of the fire, one night, some twenty-eight years ago, rocking the wee babe in her lap in front of the open turf fire. Her frail body was covered by a homemade shawl. Her daughter and her daughter's husband were in the kitchen, making tea.

Her son-in-law, Brian, was American, but Eileen didn't reckon that was too awful a thing. He seemed sensible enough, and willing enough to listen to her and her daughter, as well as their other powers and forces. This was a fine thing, as she couldn't abide by some bog stupid eejit who'd not understand when his offspring came to inherit her gifts. That is, if he lived to see her come into her own.

Not that her little grandbaby would ever be a direct threat to him or anyone else. It was just, with the way that man ate, by the time her wee one came into hers, he'd just as like to have keeled over from a heart attack or some such.

"Eh, my wee one," Eileen said to the baby. "As your Seanmhathair. I need to tell you some things. You likely won't remember anything I say—or at least not for a very, very long time. But it's important, so you must listen very carefully."

The baby stopped cooing and stared intently at her, as if she knew the import of that which was about to be spoken to her.

It was indeed a fine thing that this far-apart daughter of Lir would cross the ocean to continue the strong maternal linkage in a different country.

Part One:

They Do It With Mirrors

1

Whence My Story Begins

I looked up at the dark and roiling clouds overhead and thought about turning back.

When I left work in Southfield early to head up to Lexington for the reunion of my best college friends at Karen's place, Michigan had already begun her little trick of changing the weather. You see, in Michigan, if you don't like the weather, all you have to do is wait fifteen minutes and it'll change. The problem with this is that even if you like the weather the way it is, it'll still change in fifteen minutes. Of course, after growing up in Ireland I was accustomed to such frequent and fast changes of climate.

For instance, this morning when I got up, the day was disgustingly bright, sunny and shiny, yet when I left work early to drive up north for the weekend, it was dark and brooding, and you could virtually see Mother Nature wondering what to do next, like a vindictive ex-girlfriend plotting how to destroy your life.

Unfortunately, Mother Nature is considerably more powerful than any ex. After an initial foray into snowflakes, she dropped something that resembled Mt. Everest.

I hoped Karen's remote cottage on a secluded shore of Lake Huron would have all the regular conveniences, and that those things, like heat, running toilets, electric outlets and lighting, would be up and running. I really didn't care much for the idea of going out in this weather to take a dump, let alone be forced to do something butch like chopping wood for the stove. Especially because I had never hefted an ax in my entire life. I'd hate to learn something like that at twenty-eight.

When I drove through Lexington Village it seemed like something out of some sort of cheesy horror flick—the sort where hapless folk go to some small town, are immediately surrounded by people saying "the Others are here," "the Bates Motel always has a vacancy" or "we have need of a ritual sacrifice," and are never heard from again.

I glanced down at my directions and continued merrily along, trying to avoid thinking of anything much, like what I would do out here in the middle of nowhere if my car slid off the road and into a pole.

I was thankful there were no poles anywhere in sight.

Every bad movie I had ever seen about stranded motorists suddenly flew through my mind. Fortunately, there was no corn for children to hide their prey in, nor were there any cops to haul me to a jail from whence I'd never reappear. What there was was plenty of snow.

Well, I thought there was also a road somewhere beneath the snow, but I wasn't exactly sure about that.

It didn't help that the sense of foreboding I had awoken with that morning was still with me—and my old granny always did tell me I'd inherited the ability to see the future.

Unfortunately, this ability did not help me to foresee that on my first try, I would drive right by Karen's place. I only realized that I had done so, when I managed, somehow, to see a number on a place a bit beyond it, a creepy place with an ominous totem-pole reaching into the sky in front of it, reaching as if it were beseeching, praying toward an other-worldly power. (Frankly, it sent shivers down my back.)

I turned around and inch by inch, foot by foot, yard by yard, slowly headed back toward town.

All the houses were a good half-mile off the road, located much nearer the lake than the road on their lengthy lots. When I figured out which place was Karen's I really wasn't surprised I had missed it on my first try—there was a wall of firs right on the road, blocking the house proper from all but the sharpest eye.

The white-crusted trees loomed like ghosts around my car as I crept slowly down the snow-covered driveway, carefully trying to follow in the deeply embedded path of the last vehicle that must've just gone down the drive.

A big, red Explorer was parked beside the attached garage, engine still ticking as it cooled, so I pulled next to it, grabbed my bags and followed the footprints to the house. I'd go back for my skis if the weather improved enough to make use of them. Karen was at the front door, trying a variety of keys from an expansive key ring on it, to no avail.

Snow poured from the sky directly into my collar. I was thankful the weekend hadn't been called off, but still Karen seemingly unable to gain access to the house did not give me good feelings. It in fact gave me shivery visions of sleeping in my car during a blizzard.

"What the fuck?" Karen was obviously thrown by my bundling within parka, black turtle headband, gloves and boots. "Irish!" she cried after she got a good look at my helpless grin.

"Nobody's called me that since college." My rebuke was said with a laugh, because I'll take *Irish* over *the little Irishwoman*,

7

which I had also endured all through college because of my red hair and impish (or so I've been told) green eyes. And *Irish* was also heaps better than bad leprechaun remarks—doubly insulting as real Irish didn't believe in them. Beyond that, leprechauns were *ugly* and evil. Now faeries, the true little people (not fagboys who had a tendency toward saying "Fabulous" and doing three-snaps), could be really evil, especially if you pissed them off by cutting down their tree or something, but at least they weren't *ugly*.

"Please tell me you have the key," I said, shivering slightly as Karen continued her assault on the door. Of course, they probably also called me Irish 'cause my family'd just hopped to this side of the pond when I was thirteen, so I was still, well, really Irish when I'd hit college.

"Yes, as a matter of fact, I do. Unfortunately, I think it's in the top drawer of my desk. At home."

"You are taking the piss, right?" It'd be just like Karen, one of the ringleaders of our little crew, to do such a thing. After all, she'd orchestrated a great many practical jokes and ridiculous stunts back in our days at Uni—as had we all. But we were more often than not her merry little gang of pranksters.

"Don't worry about it, we can get in, I'm sure."

"Are you talking about breaking and entering? Because you know I try to keep my criminal activities confined to between the hours of two and three on alternating Jewish holidays in odd-numbered years during the full moon."

"What's illegal?" Karen asked, leading me around the house to the deck. "I own the place. It's not like it'd be a criminal activity."

"Well, let's see. Obviously you'd need to break in order to get in, so we have the 'breaking,' beyond that, the entire point of this escapade would be to enter, and thus we have the 'entering' portion of the entire phraseology. Thus, you have every intention in the world of involving me in the criminal activity of breaking and entering." I knew this would get Karen's goat and a wicked little grin slid across my freezing lips.

Karen turned to me in exasperation. "Fine. Then we'll just freeze to death out here."

"So which window are we gonna break?"

We ended up fudging with the sliding door that led out to the deck on the lake side of the cottage, lifting it up till we could slide it open.

I went through the house to the side door, mentally making a note to discuss with Karen the minor security measure of putting a bar across the deck door. I grabbed my gear and was almost inside again when a baby blue Beemer came sliding down the driveway.

The BMW made my cheap little Sundance look exactly what it was: cheap and little—but it was what I could afford, given my meager Assistant Media Buyer/Planner salary. Kevin Dinello's lean, six-four body came bounding out the passenger's door, a big grin plastered across his face as he leapt through the snow like a little puppy dog being told he gets to finish the Thanksgiving Day turkey all by himself.

Kevin lifted me up off the ground by more than the foot that separated us in height, swinging me around in a circle, heedless of the slippery footing. I could've told him how this would end up, which is exactly how it did—a jumble of arms and legs on the cold, frozen ground.

A burly man I assumed was Kevin's boyfriend gave me a hand in extracting myself from Kevin.

"Hi. I'm George Lewis," he said, a wide grin peeking out from behind his gray-splattered black beard. Kevin was probably in seventh heaven now because he had always been massively attracted to older, bearish men who were big and covered in coarse, thick hair—but he had hated the interpersonal dynamics caused by the combination of his and his tricks' ages. They always looked at him as a chicken and themselves as the chicken hawks. He just wanted an ordinary relationship, even though he was attracted to such men.

And George Lewis definitely fit the bill.

"I should just leave you lying there," George said, looking at where Kevin lay in the virginally white snow. Kevin stuck out his tongue and proceeded to make a snow angel.

While I was getting all the snow off me, George labored inside with his and Kevin's multitudinous bags (I was willing to bet I could guess which set of luggage belonged to whom—especially because there was only one bag from one set and four from the other), when I heard a massive rumbling.

I would have recognized the big blue economy Ford van anywhere. Granted, the paint was a little more chipped, the muffler a little louder (if there actually was still a muffler on the vehicle), and the odometer even higher, but I'd recognize Jamie Reed's love machine anywhere. As would most of the other lesbians who had been on-campus with us.

Jamie's arrival most assuredly ensured an interesting evening.

2

Where There Are Flames . . .

There were several bedrooms upstairs, each with some bare
furnishings, including a double bed. Karen led me to the one I'd
been assigned to, but then I had to dash back down to greet my
ex, Trisha, with a good and proper bear hug.

"Some joint, huh, Irish?" Trisha said as we toured the cottage.

"Too right." The cozy main room was dominated by a large
Franklin stove. Trisha was every bit as beautiful, poised and
groomed as ever. "You're looking good." I already knew she'd
grown up to be a Realtor, and by everything I could see (and all
I'd heard through the years), she was a very successful one at
that.

She smirked at me. "I *am* good."

Stairs led up from the living/dining room, which was separated from the kitchen by a counter. Down the hallway were a
bathroom and what I expected was the master bedroom, which

led into the breezeway and the garage. A sliding door led from the living room out onto the deck.

"Oh, thank God! I never thought I'd make it!" a woman I didn't know said, coming in via the breezeway and stomping her snow-encrusted feet on the floor.

"It's a mess out there," Don Taylor-Williams, Karen's fiancé, said, coming in right behind the other woman. He carried several bags.

"I wasn't sure you two were going to make it!" Karen said, running up and hugging Don. She hugged the other woman and, with her arm about her waist, said, "Denise, this mixed cast of characters are Kevin Dinello, George Lewis, Jamie Reed, Trisha Laskowski, Shawn Donnelly and Robert Jackson. Everyone, this is Denise Teisman. She's a fellow accountant I met at work. She's heard so much about all of you, she wrangled an invite from me for this weekend. Oh, and of course, you all know my guy, Don."

"Robert?" I said, quickly finding him. "You must've sneaked in when I wasn't looking!" He'd been the only straight boy in our class, but had since turned queer as the proverbial three-dollar bill.

"Girlfriend," Robert said to Karen, "you need some professional decorating advice here, stat!"

I looked about the main room and realized just how correct Robert was. Colorful throw rugs brought some life to the rather plain linoleum, tiled floors and paneling I normally would've thought tacky (its main color was yellow and there were little flowers in it, but it seemed quaint in this setting). Some of the furnishings looked like things that might've been picked up at garage sales, and it was all done at a relatively low cost—from the shelves hung on the walls with their collection of Reader's Digest Condensed Books, an old radio and an assortment of board games, to the '70s-style couch and table, with the plastic-padded chairs. A few modern touches, like a stereo, TV and cordless phone made it just off-balance enough to amuse me.

Something about it all took me back to my childhood. I could imagine my *Seanmhathair* living in a place like this, or maybe one of her friends. Well, without the CD player, that is.

"Okay, so everyone to your rooms—" Karen started.

Don said, "We've only got six rooms, so a few people had to double-up besides the couples—"

"I'll show the newbies to their rooms," Karen said. "Don, get settled and help everyone else. Shawn, man the bar and build up the fire!"

We all lounged by the fire, drinks in hand, and I took a thankful sip from my Bailey's-spiked cocoa. I pulled my chair a little closer to the Franklin stove, which was the sort of thing that sat away from the wall so all the heat stayed in the room, instead of blowing up and out the flue.

"I hate to disappoint you, Shawnie, in case you were looking forward to some quality alone time," Karen said. "But I remembered how cold-blooded you are, so I put you and Ashley in the room the flue runs through."

My heart plummeted to the floor when I thought of Ashley with her long, blond hair and vivid green eyes. "Me and Ashley?" I stopped to think of the setting—the room would be the warmest in the house.

Karen sounded like the perfect hostess, but the smirk on her face belied her innocent expression. "I remembered you two like things a bit warmer than anybody else here."

I heard the word "warmer" in conjunction with Ashley and my mind went crazy. It didn't go to merely warmer but went all the way up to hot-enough-to-burn-the-feet-off-a-fire-walker. I hadn't realized I'd be sharing the double bed in my room with anyone else. Let alone Ashley.

A double bed. Just one double bed. And two of us. Me.

Ashley. Me and Ashley in a bed together. In a warm room. Under the covers. Alone. Together.

Of course, Ashley wasn't here yet, and it was still snowing, so it was quite likely she wouldn't make it at all. But she hadn't called to cancel yet, either.

"Hmmm . . . And just what does that look mean, Irish?" Kevin teased from across the room. "Do we have a thing for blondes?"

Trying to cover my blush, I quickly retorted, "I don't know, do we?"

"Uh-huh, I remember how you used to hang on her every word during class."

"Sure, sure," Trisha said. "Have her room with Ashley and stick me with Jamie."

"I resemble that remark!" Jamie called, coming into the room with another drink. She had brought her own bottle of Jack Daniel's, and I was somehow certain that there was a lot more where that came from.

"Girls, girls, girls," Kevin said, "please, let's not get too graphic here. Remember there are some present who are simply *not* interested in all the nasty details of who puts what where and why."

"Hold on, I thought you said Ashley was straight?" Denise said.

Karen said, "I figured I could trust Shawn more than either Trisha or Jamie," she referred to the other two lesbians, "and thought Ashley might be uncomfortable rooming with a boy."

"Oh, and I'm just too weird to room with her," Denise said, her short brown hair swaying with the movement of her head.

"Oh, sweetie." Karen left her comfortable perch against Don's shoulder and wrapped an arm around her. "You know I love you to death, it's just that I figured you weren't in that feminist drama class with us when we all started hanging out together . . ."

"So I should just be ostracized, like a head of lettuce that's been forgotten for several months in the veggie drawer."

Karen grinned and went back to Don. "You know perfectly well that's not it. I just thought we might have some fun reminiscing, y'know." We'd all seen each other off and on again in the years since college, sometimes complete with college-style pranks, but this was our first big, all of us together, reunion.

Robert sat beside Denise. "Oh, sweetie, we can room together if you think you're gonna be too lonely," he said. The flames from the fire brought out the richness in his chocolate brown skin.

Denise swatted him. "Mr. Queer as of last year, like you could really keep me company anyway! A straight girl has no use for you except as fashion consultant."

"Well, we all know you and Ash wear those straight-girl shoes." Robert mugged for the guaranteed laugh with a Queer Eye swish I was certain he never got to do during the week. Contractors aren't allowed to swish.

"Yeah, but I'm not *your* type anyway."

As they bantered I was grateful that Karen had recently told me about Robert and his brother. Had I not known I might have teased him for those years in college he'd played it very straight. But it was really no wonder that Robert couldn't come out during college—not only had his gay older brother killed himself before Robert was old enough to shave, he'd also left a note saying that he'd done it because he was gay.

I was glad Robert had finally made enough peace to accept himself, and knowing the truth behind things kept me from the most annoying and embarrassing habit I have of firmly sticking my foot in my mouth.

Of course, sometimes knowing the back story didn't help one wee bit—I'd still stick that foot right down my throat regardless.

When I got up to refill my drink, Jamie followed me to the kitchen. We hadn't had much of a chance to talk so far tonight—

what with Jamie doing the big, butch thing of bringing in lumber and building the fire while I lugged my luggage upstairs and tried to be helpful as Karen made everyone snacks and drinks.

"Hey you, long time no see." I put my mug on the counter and reached over to grab the hot cocoa mix and mini marshmallows.

"Hey, *you* know where to find *me*. Have known for quite a while."

"I'm sorry, I just don't have time to get out much anymore." I swirled water and hot cocoa mix in my mug and—

It all foamed up into a snow-like substance. Well, if snowflakes were made of fiber or Styrofoam. Regardless, I couldn't drink it.

"So what you been up to?" Jamie asked nonchalantly. Studiously nonchalantly. With studied nonchalantness, even.

I stared at her.

She shrugged. "Hey, you can't blame me for taking advantage of an opportunity like that. You put your cup down and walked away from it."

"What is this shite anyway?"

"Insta Snow. Pretty cool, isn't it?"

Jamie'd always liked playing with props and toys like flash paper and such. I put my cup in my sink, pulled a new one from the cupboard and prepared a new cup of hot cocoa, which I never took my eyes off of, even when it was in the microwave.

Jamie frowned at how closely I was watching my cocoa. "So, really, what you been up to?"

"About five-foot-four."

Jamie slammed the heel of her hand into her forehead. "When will I ever learn? You've been using that line since college. Fine, then what're you doing with yourself these days?" I shrugged, so Jamie grinned and shrugged back. "One day at a time, huh?"

"Yeah, something like that. What about you?"

"Well, ya know, keeping busy. Between the plays and the bar, I'm meeting so many women even I can't keep track of 'em."

"Same old Jamie, huh? Always on the chase. I never could understand how you could keep up with them all."

Jamie grinned and shrugged. "If ya got it, ya got it." She ran her hand over the stubble on the side of her head. She wore her blondish-brown hair long in the back and almost shaved on the sides.

I dumped the weird snow-like substance into the trash, since it was totally dry, cleaned up the counter and added a shot to my cup before I headed into the living room, where a clatter from the front door announced Ashley's arrival. She carried a briefcase in one hand and a worn, compact dark blue suitcase with wheels in the other.

Karen hung up Ashley's snow-covered coat and everyone gathered around her, going on about how long it'd been since anyone had seen her.

Feeling more than slightly tongue-tied, I grabbed Ashley's suitcase and briefcase. Of course, when I took it upstairs I realized how much I was being an absolute wimp, trailing after Ashley with her tightly packed, heavy bag up to our room.

But I'd been a big girl's blouse from the moment she whipped my arse at Trivial Pursuit years before—and it wasn't just luck either. She boasted she was going to annihilate me and then she unleashed a shark attack from the first roll.

Dear God in heaven, that made me hot. I *never* lost at Trivial Pursuit.

Ashley was still every bit as beautiful as I remembered. Even though her long blond hair was soaked from the short trek from her car to the house, even though her bright eyes didn't flash so brilliantly in the dim light of the hallway because of the long, nerve-wracking journey to the cottage in the blizzard, even though her creamy skin was beet red from the cold outside, she was still drop-dead gorgeous. And the smile she gave me when I

17

took her bag was enough to send a warm current running through my entire body. Hell, it wasn't just warm, it was . . . *electric.*

'Course, the Bailey's in my hot chocolate probably didn't hurt any on that last count. I really liked Bailey's, and if my sweet tooth was really acting up, I'd mix Kahlúa with my Bailey's and put it on ice. That was something I really yearned for at a certain time each month. If that didn't fulfill my chocolate craving, nothing would.

I put her suitcase on the bed. I longed to open the suitcase and smell Ashley. I longed to bury my face in her clothing, knowing her scent would be on every piece of it.

I stared at the suitcase for a moment, then realized how sick and twisted that thought was. I really needed to get laid.

When I returned to the living room, Karen and Don were cuddling together at one end of the long, plaid sofa, while Kevin and George were at the other. Trisha sat in one of the chairs at either end of the oak coffee table, while Robert mirrored her position on the other end.

Jamie, who had always been a lesbian activist, wasn't too surprising in how she turned out—she was now a bartender at a local wimmin's bar and worked with a theater troupe on the side. A lesbian theater troupe, nonetheless. But that was just so Jamie—she'd always had us doing theater and staged readings together at school, even if it was just to break out into a scene or other such caper suddenly in the study lounge. She even got us all into a few theater classes together, convincing us the public-speaking sorts of elements of it would help us out no matter what line of work we went into after university. *All the world's a stage, and all the men and women merely players: they have their exits and their entrances; and one man in his time plays many parts.*

Jamie truly lived the Bard's old saying.

And now, of course, Jamie was acting like she always had—she was leaning against a wall near Ashley, already trying to make time.

Ashley was warming her extremely cute butt and elegant, long hands in front of the fireplace. Red on her nails made those incredible fingers look even more elegant and exciting.

Oh, God, I was really losing it, I was thinking of fingers as exciting. Well, okay fine, fingers can be exciting when you think of what they are used for. Or can be used for. Hm.

The loose, cream-colored sweater over snug blue jeans that accentuated the swell of her hips and the fine line of that oh-so-nice butt—it all made my palms sweat. Her arse was a thing of beauty, firm and just right to fill your hands when you cupped it. It was high and tight and you just knew it would be smooth and soft.

She had left her western-cut boots at the door when she came in, and was now sporting stockinged feet. Argyle socks. She always liked those, I remembered with a smile. She said everything else about her was so boring and humdrum that she didn't need her socks to be as well.

I found absolutely nothing about Ashley boring.

"God, the roads are such a mess," she said, running her hands over her shapely butt. "I thought I was just going to fall off the side and not even know it!" I was really stuck on her butt. And her hands. Her fingers. Her.

"I know I barely saw the roads at all when I was driving up," Jamie said. "It was like playing a fun game of 'Guess where the lane's at.'"

"Days like today I wish I had a big truck like yours," Ashley said.

"Ashley! I never knew you to be such a size queen!" Robert said, getting up and going over to the stereo to find some music. "Any preferences?" he asked us all in general.

While Robert put on some dance music and Karen refreshed

everyone's drinks, we all did a brief catch-up on each other's lives. As it turned out, the two in the group who were coupled off had done very well for themselves: George Lewis, Kevin Dinello's catch, was a software engineer, and I could only guess that he made six-digits a year; and Karen had caught herself Don Taylor-Williams, a very upwardly rising attorney.

What I found most humorous and unexpected thus far about how everyone turned out was that Kevin, a cute lil' flaming fagboy, was a successful writer of Harlequin romances.

"The most exciting part about it," Kevin said, "is that when I'm blocked, George helps me out by dressing up in all these pirate and heathen costumes and ravishes me so I can get in touch with my heroines and their bold, handsome," he ran his hand across George's rough cheek and then grabbed his crotch, "well-hung heroes."

George jumped back, grabbing Kevin by the wrists, and said, "Now don't go telling them all about me without explaining why those books you write are known as bodice rippers."

Apparently the world was a stage to all of us.

An abrupt banging from upstairs brought Don and me to our feet.

Karen burst out laughing, stopping the two of us from charging toward the stairs. "Oh, I'm sorry about that. I think a couple of critters found their way into the attic. You can't really blame them on a night like this."

Kevin pulled his hands free from George's grasp and began dancing with him, moving to the fast beat of the music. I noticed with some distaste that Jamie went to the kitchen for another drink. Although I myself was on my second, Jamie must've had four by now, and knowing Jamie, they were pretty stiff ones. That was probably what most concerned me about Jamie being a bartender—she always seemed to be a bit of an alco.

The lights flickered. "Ooo, scary," Denise said with a definitely lop-sided grin. I realized everyone was drinking a bit, so I shouldn't be too hard on Jamie. I took another long sip of my drink, wanting to catch up with the others and lose myself in the gaiety of the moment. After all, I was here in a quaint cottage with some of my best friends, and the snow outside made me feel snug and secure, like I was in a cocoon.

When the lights flickered again Karen frowned. "I'd better find the candles and flashlights just in case the power goes out." She hurried to the kitchen.

Trisha said with a worried look, "Does that happen a lot here?" I had always loved running my fingers through Trisha's long, thick curly hair that hung loosely from her head, providing a perfect frame for her coffee-and-cream complexion. Sometimes Trisha would complain about those who said she wasn't black enough and I would pull her into my arms, telling her she looked like wonderfully creamy milk chocolate I wanted to eat up whole.

I knew it was totally politically incorrect, but it always led to some really hot sex. What can I say? I don't excel at political correctness, but I've been told I excel at hot sex. In fact, girls say that all the time.

I wish.

My mind seemed to keep focusing on sex tonight. Perhaps I should stop drinking. Or else get laid.

I glanced around at the women present and realized my chances for the latter were practically nil. Chance would be a fine thing. I could entertain fantasies all night about Ashley, but nothing was going to happen. I downed my drink, deciding if I couldn't have one, I didn't want the other either.

Karen shrugged in reply to Trisha's concern. "I don't know. I mean, it only happened occasionally when I was growing up, but that was during the summer. We really didn't use this place much during the winter, so I don't know how likely it is tonight."

"Well that's a reassuring thought," Trisha replied. I allowed my gaze to follow her hair down to her arse, which was every bit

21

as nice as it ever was. Was it really such a big mistake to sleep with an ex?

Yuppers, I thought, I should stop drinking while I was ahead. I always got horny when I was drinking and that was the last thing I'd need tonight when I was in bed with Ashley.

In bed, alone, with Ashley. I glanced surreptitiously around the room and decided Ashley had the nicest arse, and fingers, in the room. At least I thought I was discreet about it, till I looked at Trisha.

"Checking out asses and hands again, huh?" she murmured so that I was the only one who heard it when our eyes met.

"Oh, don't worry, baby," Jamie said, sitting next to her on the none-too-spacious chair. "I'll keep the boogey-man away if the lights go out." Obviously, Jamie had something in common with me as far as the effects of alcohol went.

Ashley rubbed her arms as if still chilled. "But won't it get awfully cold if the power goes out?"

Jamie looked at Trisha, then glanced suggestively across the room at Ashley. "I could keep you both warm."

I bolted upright. Robert said, with a slight leer at me, "Oh, but I believe keeping Ashley warm should be up to her roomie."

Kevin grinned. "Now that will be a homework assignment Shawn'll enjoy."

Ashley turned to me as a slow smile danced its way unbidden across my lips. My gaze slowly slid up her long body, stopping at a few crucial points along the way. By the time my eyes met hers, I was sure my face was the kind of red that totally clashed with my carrot-top of unruly locks.

"Care to let me in on the joke?" Ashley said in a near purr, her gaze locked on mine.

My gaze dropped to the floor almost as quickly as it would've had I been hit in the back of the head with a frying pan. "We're roomies—there's only six rooms in the house so some of us who aren't in couples have to share even though all the rooms only got double beds and Karen figured you'd rather room with me than with Denise 'cause we were both in class together and might wanna reminisce and—"

"Shawn," Kevin said.

I allowed a breath into my choking lungs and looked up to find Ashley smiling at me. "What?"

"You still do it, huh?"

"What?" I repeated, panic swelling in my chest as I realized everyone in the room was grinning at me.

"Ramble," Ashley said.

"Blither," Kevin added.

"Especially when she's nervous," Karen said, coming into the room with several candles, a few books of matches and a couple of flashlights.

I growled and Ashley burst out in laughter. "You're adorable." She smiled and went into the kitchen for a refill on her white wine.

I met every gaze that was left in the room and allowed a slow growl to build in my chest and rumble on out.

Karen ruffled my hair. "Face it, Irish. You weren't born to be ferocious."

I growled my reply.

When Ashley came back into the room, Karen looked at me. "By the way, you don't have to worry about heat, Ashley—this old Franklin stove can keep the whole place pretty toasty so long as it's kept well-stocked."

Jamie's gaze dropped rather stupidly to the timber next to the fireplace. If nothing else, she was definitely getting toasty. Or toasted. Whatever.

"I suppose that means we gotta bring some more in," she said.

"Well," Karen said, sidling up close to Jamie. She was always a notorious flirt, not ever worrying about flirting with lesbians because she was also a notorious het. "Jamie, if you butch types are volunteering to bring more in . . ."

The lights flickered, this time staying out.

"Y'know, we should tell ghost stories," Kevin said, breaking the silence in the unexpected blackness.

There was the sudden sound of a slap.

"Jamie!" Karen yelled. "Keep your hands to yourself!"

"Hey, you started it!"

I felt around for one of the candles or flashlights Karen had brought over. I heard the featherlight padding of stockinged feet and my hand found someone's denim-covered leg. I paused, knowing I should move my hand and look elsewhere, but instead I slid my hand up the long, slender limb until a soft hand slowly enveloped mine and drew my hand higher up the shapely thigh.

I looked up toward where the woman's face would be. I knew it was a woman. No man, no matter how flamey, would have a hand so soft or a leg so shapely.

Lips as soft as the kiss of night brushed over mine while a swirl of the softest, most feminine scent I had ever encountered wafted around me.

My hands were suddenly empty, as empty as the air that surrounded me. A burst of light broke the darkness.

"It was a dark and stormy night," Kevin said, turning a flashlight on his face.

I looked around. Every single woman in the room was the same distance from me and they were all wearing jeans. It could've been any of them. The only way to know would be to sniff them all out, like a dog searching for the scent of another on its master.

But my heart told me who it was, although my head tried to explain, rather eloquently, that that was simply wishful thinking and not at all possible. Ashley was straight. At least she *had* been. Okay, Robert had been straight too, but now he screamed "gay," while nothing about Ashley seemed in the least different.

"We should leave that sort of thing up to Jamie," Karen said, taking the flashlight from Kevin, cutting off his story, and aiming the beam toward Jamie. "After all, she is the theatrical one of us." She played the flashlight around the group, aiming it like a spotlight.

"Hey, hey, hey," Jamie said, "I'm just backstage help. A behind-the-scenes sorta gal."

"C'mon," Don said, tugging on George's shirt sleeve. "We butch-types don't have time for all this nonsense, we gotta bring in the wood."

"Just so long's we don't have to fry it up in a pan," George said. When no one got it, he explained, "Oh, c'mon—bring home the bacon, bring in the wood—fry it up in a pan?"

Yup. He was an engineer all right. The only thing he lacked was a pocket protector. It must be hard to be a geeky fagboy—torn between the stylish and wearing one's pants two inches too short.

Jamie joined George and Don, as did I, until Jamie stopped me. "C'mon, you ain't butch. Why don't you stay in the kitchen with the rest of the girly-girls?"

" 'Scuse me?"

"I jes' called you a girly-girl. I'm just surprised you ain't wearing makeup and heels and plucking your eyebrows."

I grabbed my parka and gloves and led the way to the woodpile.

"Oh my God," I heard Ashley say as I left. "She is *such* a butch. Jamie just used the oldest femme trick in the books on her—and it worked!"

I wouldn't let just anyone get away with saying something like that, but then again, Ashley wasn't just anyone. It's so nice to be utterly transparent to your friends. I decided I was not yet having sufficient fun, but I didn't know what I was going to do about that.

3

Can Dreams Come True?

I buried my nose in Ashley's hair, pulling her closer in my arms, spooning our bodies together. Ashley's body was so soft, so smooth, her hair like silk against my face. Nothing really mattered. This was a wonderful dream and I wanted it to last forever. I buried my nose in her hair, inhaling deeply of her wonderful, intoxicating scent. I molded myself to her, one arm draped casually over her waist, the other under her head.

She moaned softly, rolling onto her back. I ran my hand down to her hip, finding the line where her panties met her T-shirt. I had never before experienced such a fully tactile dream. I could feel the texture of her T-shirt, the smoothness of her satin panties, the silk of her skin, the warmth of her.

She moaned again, arching her hips, then rolling slightly toward me. I fit our bodies together automatically, as if we were two pieces of a puzzle. I slid my hand around to her arse, barely sliding my hand down her panties.

"Oh, Shawn."

And that was when it hit me: *This was not a dream.*

SHITE!

I suddenly realized I was lying in bed holding Ashley. We were buried beneath handmade quilts that Karen's granny probably made years ago, and the flue had kept the room nice and toasty all night long.

I gently pried myself free, trying not to wake Ashley, who was apparently oblivious to our position.

This was not good. I am not a morning person, and the last thing I needed to wake to was Ashley freaking because she found herself entwined with me. All but snogging me. Granted, Ashley was extremely cool for a breeder, but I really didn't want to test the limits of that, even though I was tempted to momentarily take advantage of this oh-so-luscious but oh-so-forbidden fruit. Probably even more tempted than Eve had been with that bloody apple.

Of course, I had already gone to a bad place just in waking up with Ashley and seeing her normally beautiful, aristocratic features calmed by sleep into a deep peace that was even more beautiful and alluring. I wanted to hold this golden-haired woman for the rest of my life.

What was I thinking? A long line of ex-lovers were laughing at me in my mind. They'd all heard forever-after talk from me. Fortunately—or not—I was the only one who ever believed I meant it. The way I felt just looking at her, after not seeing her for seven years (we always seemed to keep missing each other. Well, okay, yes, we had seen each other that time in Ann Arbor, then there was that group coffee in Fashionable Ferndale), was different. This time I knew it.

Shut up and get out of bed, I told myself. You always think this time is different.

Ashley moaned and rolled into me again. I allowed myself a

few more moments against her soft body, feeling her silken hair against my cheek, letting her breath warm my neck, and then finally, reluctantly, extricated myself from the bed.

Was this time different?

Damned if I'd find out before I'd had coffee, anyway. I had to get away from her. She was obviously dreaming I was someone else. That had to be it.

I glanced once more at her sleeping form on the bed. For all her brains and aggressiveness, she looked like an angel when asleep. Her face was relaxed in peace, her hair a tousled mess spilling over her face and the pillow, her arms and legs akimbo in sleepy abandon.

This was different.

Ashley rolled over in the bed as if searching for the warmth of my body—or someone's body. Then she actually did reach her arms out, searching for me. I felt light-headed. It had to be someone else she was thinking of, dreaming of, being with. Even though it was my name she had breathed out.

Shawn Donnelly does not panic. It's a law.

With deliberate haste, I pulled off my pajama bottoms and picked up my discarded jeans from the night before. I quietly donned them and pulled my gray-and-black flannel on over the plain white T-shirt I had slept in. I looked in the mirror and brushed my fingers quickly back through my hair and then realized that with the flannel and the jeans all I was lacking were Birkenstocks to truly look like a stereotypical dyke.

I thought about changing, then decided I liked my jeans and flannel no matter what they made me look like. I looked at Ashley's appealing and wanton body, then changed the flannel for a satiny green-and-white MSU sweatshirt that was soft to the touch.

After all, she was a fancy-pants banker, one who went from bank to bank, all over the country—maybe even all over the world, for all I knew. (She'd told us something of what she did the night before. Karen and Jamie had had some problems tracking her down for this get-together, but they did. Eventually.)

Downstairs, Karen was fussing around the Franklin stove. "We'll have coffee in a few," she said, noticing me. "And we've got cereal with milk for breakfast." She shrugged apologetically. "Sorry we don't have more, but the power's still out. We've got to be careful not to open the fridge too much until it comes back on."

"Just so long's we got coffee," Don rumbled, in nothing but boxer shorts and a T-shirt, regardless of the chilly floor. Apparently, he shared my passion for mornings.

Kevin and George showed up next—together, like the perfect lil' couple they were—and the five of us gathered around the dining room table that had been expanded to its greatest possible seating capacity.

"So did you and Ashley have a good night?" Kevin asked with a raised eyebrow. I elbowed his ribs while making a low growling noise to show my disapproval of his insinuations.

"Right now it hardly seems possible that you were one of the best writers in our class," Karen said. She probably wasn't even sure how to spell the growl I emitted. Actually, neither was I. Thank God I didn't have to spell my own noises whenever I wrote something. Or tried to write something.

"Shawn just gets a little lost when it comes to being spontaneous and getting the words out of her mouth," Kevin said. "If she has the time to write them down, then she's fine, just fine."

Trisha came downstairs rubbing the sleep from her eyes. She was clad in green-and-white MSU sweats. I knew she slept in the nude, so I wondered if she had slept in the sweats in honor of Jamie's presence in her bed, or if she had put them on to come downstairs and join the rest. I knew Jamie and Trisha had been together before, so either scenario really wouldn't surprise me.

"Jamie in the bathroom?" Trisha asked, pulling her long hair back. I was envious of her. After all, dreadlocks really didn't have the problem with morning head I did.

29

Denise emerged from the bathroom.

"We haven't seen the Jamester yet this morning," Karen said, bringing more bowls and spoons to the table and putting more water in the pot on the stove so we could continue our coffeefest.

I stared around, wanting to help, but wasn't sure what I could do.

"Wasn't she in bed with you?" Kevin asked with a grin.

"No, and actually, I slept like a log. I don't remember anything."

"Uh-huh," Kevin said with a great deal of intimation.

Robert appeared in the doorway. "Did you do anything in particular to scare her off?"

"Whips, chains, handcuffs, leather slings, hot candle wax?" Kevin asked.

"That wouldn't scare Jamie, that would get her excited," I said. I had a brief remembrance of the way Trisha's smooth, dark skin looked in tight, black leather. 'Course, at the time I had not thought it nearly so erotic as I did now.

I recalled that at that point Trisha had made several rather deprecating, quite racist statements about my ghostly white appearance when she was attired in black leather. God, if only I had known then what I knew now.

"I would've thought she'd stay in bed late," Karen said. "What with how much she was drinking last night and all, besides whatever else went on after you two went to bed."

"You're sure she's not somewhere in your room?" I asked, getting worried. I knew Jamie had a bad habit of wandering around and not thinking right when she was bolloxed.

She thought some of her stunts were funny, but they never were to me. Jamie was the sort that, when we were out messing about, drinking in the woods, would say that she was off to take a piss, and add, "I'll be right back," the infamous horror movie line characters say just before they're never seen again. No matter how often Jamie insisted she belonged behind the scenes, not on stage, she was a true actress—but one who made the world her stage, in the truest Shakespearean fashion.

We'd always end up searching for Jamie about a half-hour later, only to find her either back at the campsite drinking or smoking a joint, or she'd jump out to scare the living shite out of someone.

"Didn't you say she was the practical joker of your bunch?" George asked.

"And that's saying something," Denise said. "From what I've heard, they were always playing jokes on each other. I mean, did you hear about that time Trisha and Jamie set up a day-long series of pranks on a prof?"

"I vote we eat our cereal and drink our coffee," Robert said, pouring himself a cuppa. "We just encouraged Jamie before by going after her." He wasn't quite so flamey this morning—he was probably in contractor mode. Either that or hungover.

"Wait her out, you mean?" Trisha said.

"Yes, she'll show up. She's just hiding out somewhere."

"I'd think she'd be too hungover for such games," Don said.

"That's one of the most annoying things about Jamie," Trisha said. "She never seems to be as hungover as she should be."

I walked over to look out on the morning. Impossibly, it was still snowing. This was easily a first-class blizzard we had on our hands. It had snowed a couple of feet since yesterday afternoon. The accumulation from prior snows had brought the level to waist-deep, probably neck-deep in areas.

I decided not to worry about Jamie, because not even she was stupid enough to go out in this. She was just holed up somewhere, waiting to spring on us as soon as we went looking. What had I ever seen in her? Even to go along with her for such a short time? To buy into her games and be attracted to her? I had thought it was forever after, with her, and that just made me think of how I had felt looking at Ashley this morning. *Was* it different? My palms were sweating. It had to be.

31

"Whatcha thinking?" a soft voice asked from my right.

With a start, I turned to meet Ashley's incredibly piercing gaze. "We're snowed in. No electric, probably no phone, and there's no way we're going anywhere through this. This is definitely a blizzard."

"Good thing this weekend's a bank holiday, huh?"

"'Bank holiday'?" I asked. "Must be nice. But normal working slobs like me have to go to work on Monday."

Ashley ran a long nail down the back of my neck and raised one fine eyebrow. "You don't look like a slob to me," she observed in a sultry whisper.

I felt a flush rush to my cheeks and I glanced quickly about, knowing I wasn't quite understanding whatever was going on. Or perhaps I *was* understanding—that Ashley had lost her mind or was experiencing temporary snow-induced insanity.

"You're mumbling to yourself again, Irish," Ashley said.

Trisha walked up on my other side and said, "I've always found it so adorable when she does that."

"It's almost as if she's speaking her own language." Although I was studiously looking out the window, I could almost feel Ashley's gaze upon me. The warmth of her hand was still sitting possessively against my neck.

"But not too many can understand it," Trisha said.

I was sandwiched by two beautiful women. I did what I always do in such situations, I pretended not to notice the array of thighs and hair and lips.

The property beyond the sliding door and deck extended perhaps another fifty to a hundred feet before it gave way to a tree-lined cliff, which, I supposed, led down to a beach and the lake. Well, there would be a beach during the summer. Of course, as it wasn't summer, there wouldn't be a beach now, just a ledge of snow and ice.

"I always wonder what she's thinking when she stares off like this," Trisha said. "You wonder if she's contemplating the greater thoughts of life, or just thinking about lunch."

Part of my mind was aware of what she was saying, knowing she was looking for a rise, but there was something wrong outside, and the back of my neck would not stop tingling until I knew what it was.

Or was that just Ashley's hand playing with the back of my neck?

"Knowing her, it's none of the above," Ashley said. "She's probably wondering about why pants are plural, as are shoes, but shirt and blouse are singular."

Trisha gave a deep, throaty chuckle.

Through the glass door I could see snow that was making the sky seem to be falling down in chunks, in such a way as would've made Chicken Little totally insane, and I was just able to discern the tree line, the greens and browns of the trees . . . The greens, browns and reds of the tree line. *Reds*?

Oh no. I ran my hand back through my unruly hair, adding to the already massive case of bed head.

"Well, Shawn?" Ashley asked. Apparently a response to something was expected of me. God, I hated when that happened.

I held up a finger. "Ah, umm." I pointed out toward the bit of red. "Did you happen to notice that?"

"What?" Trisha asked, glancing out.

"Is there something out of place out there?"

Trisha now squinted out the window. "Oh, shit. Tell me that's not Jamie's scarf."

"The one she was wearing last night?" Ashley asked, also seeing it.

"Yeah, that one," I said. "That is it, isn't it?"

"What are you guys looking at?" Karen said, walking up next to us.

"Jamie's scarf. It's out by the trees," I said. "It looks like Jamie *was* stupid enough to go outside last night."

4

C'mon In, the Water's Fine!

I was right, the snow was just about up to my waist as I tried to make my way out to the beacon of red scarf in the distance. If it was any farther of a walk, I might've tried to get my cross-country skis out of my car. It would be much easier to traverse territory on top of the snow, instead of sinking down to my belt with each trudging step.

Like most of the rest of the others, I'd pulled on half the clothes I had brought anticipating the cold without expecting the exertion. Karen and Denise had stayed at the house in order to search it and the attached garage from top to bottom for any sign of Jamie. They were still hoping for the best.

I, on the other hand, was sure searching the house was futile. I knew deep down that Jamie had wandered out into the blizzard sometime during the night. It wasn't surprising she had lost her scarf, considering how much she had had to drink, but I didn't like it. It gave me the chills, regardless of how much I was sweating. It showed just how careless she had become. The same carelessness that showed in her reckless drinking.

I had my turtle on, as well as a scarf around my neck. My parka was zipped all the way to the top, which covered the lower half of my face, and all the snaps were done up as well, in an attempt to keep the cold air out. Of course, it wasn't that cold out, because if it had been one of Michigan's famous negative-zero days, it would've been too cold to snow, and the quantity of the white stuff around certainly attested to the ability of snow to proliferate today.

Still, the snow landed on me, inside my coat, in my short hair, and melted, but I was working up a sweat making my way through it. I only wished I had my skiing goggles, because the snow kept blinding me.

I was trying to focus on the weather, because that was a much more pleasant thought pattern than the other obvious choice. When I'd left the house I'd wanted to reassure everyone it would be all right, except for most of my life I've had an odd sixth sense that tells me when the outcome would not be what anyone wished for. I couldn't say a word now, what with all the confusion in my head.

I wasn't getting any feelings about this, except foreboding. I couldn't accept that anything untoward had happened to Jamie, but I had only ever once before lost a friend—one of my old employees from the fast-food restaurant I had managed when I was just finishing high school.

But I didn't want to think about that now. I unsnapped my jacket so a bit of a breeze could cut through the zipper to help cool me off. I knew it wasn't good for me, but I have been known to run with scissors.

I got to the tree first and reached one gloved hand out to grab the scarf. It was tightly tangled among the smaller branches of the tree, so I had to use both hands to gently unwind it.

The three boys quickly showed up beside me, huffing in the frigid air. Robert gave me a worried frown while Don peered through the trees.

"Is it hers?" George asked.

"Yeah, it is," I said, noticing the frayed edges and fading color. Jamie'd had it since college. I remembered Jamie using it to tie my hands behind my back one drunken night after the bar. Allowing her to do that had been a huge step for me at the time. I hoped no one noticed the deep breath I took.

The same sense of foreboding I had when I woke from the ominous dream of the night before last suddenly struck me, chilling me all the way down to the bone, through the layers of clothes and the sheen of sweat that coated my body. I'd been worried at the time that the dream had been some sort of portent indicating I should not come on this trip—it'd been the sort of dream where you kept running from some unknown terror until help finally comes with loud sirens as you're treading water in a cold Atlantic, but the sirens are just your alarm clock signaling that it was time to wake up.

Robert stepped a little into the tree line. The snow wasn't quite so deep between the conifers. Even the deciduous trees kept some of the snow from the ground.

"There aren't any tracks in here," he said. "No broken branches or other signs that she cut through this way. There's no telling for sure, but . . ." He shook his head.

There was a fence along the property line farther along this way, so I was willing to guess that Jamie had gone down to the lake along the established path instead of going to the trouble of getting through or over the fence. By the time Ashley and Trisha caught up to us, I was already heading toward the makeshift stairs I presumed led down to the lake.

"She didn't go through there," I said, instinctively knowing she wouldn't have gone through the trees. "Even drunk, Jamie would've seen the right way to go down. She would've taken the staircase." I again led the way.

Calling the route down to the beach a *staircase* was an exaggeration, actually. Along the downward curve of the cliff were old railroad ties positioned like steps, but they functioned more as a retaining wall than viable stairs. Still, in good weather they would be serviceable. In this blizzard it remained to be seen. I was guessing unseen rocks lay between the ties because I couldn't actually see the ground in most places. The entire path was partially sheltered by the trees overhead. The naked branches had let through enough snow, though, to require careful treading on my part. Once or twice, I almost wiped out when I lost my footing, but I managed to recover without breaking my neck.

The snow was still too deep and too much had fallen in the past few hours to be able to discern whether or not Jamie had come this way for sure. Except I knew she had. I just *felt* it.

I took the very end of the stairway in one step. One really big step. One really big step that was really hard on my arse. I had been so intent on getting safely down that I hadn't realized the steep change in the terrain at the bottom of the staircase. My foot went out from under me, leaving me to slide the rest of the way on my dignity.

"Watch out for that last step—it's a doozy!" I yelled up to the rest. My only other choice, when they broke out in applause at my gymnastic act, would've been to take a bow, but I wasn't feeling that bold.

I briefly wondered if whoever had built this place had put in such a stairway, if that's what you would call it, to preserve the aura of nature, or because they were too much of a cheapskate to put in something less deadly.

I glanced around. As I had expected, the slip of shoreline wasn't really a beach, and it was covered with snow, very deep snow. At least this was packed much more solidly than the snow up top was.

What I found interesting was that there were larger snow piles closer to shore. I guessed it was that the water pushed up against it before it froze, thus forming the hills. Nature could do incredible things when left to itself.

As the others joined me I carefully worked my way up one of the hills. The last thing I needed today was to pull another fast move like I had coming down the cliff and fall into the lake because of it. The temp hadn't been so cold for so long that I could count on the ice holding me if I slipped.

I looked out across the vastness of frozen water. This was one of the Great Lakes, Lake Huron, the fourth-largest lake in the world. In fact, all the Great Lakes were ranked among the thirteen largest lakes in the world, and it was in one of these lakes, Lake Superior, that the *Edmund Fitzgerald* had met with its most tragic ending. These weren't the sorts of lakes most folks are accustomed to. Bloody hell, Nessie herself could've gotten lost in one of these massive bastards.

At the shore its possible brutality was quiet because ice and snow covered its furor.

Except . . .

My gaze fell to a patch of ice several feet out from shore that wasn't covered with snow. In fact, the ice didn't look too thick at all in that area.

"Wow," Ashley said, coming up beside me. "It's so peaceful. So untouched I'd almost call it pristine."

I wiped the flakes from my lashes and looked back toward the beach. Everyone seemed to be wandering around a bit, as if either unsure of what they should do, or uncertain as to what they were looking for. I could definitely relate with that.

I looked at the clear spot on the ice, and the feet between it and the snow bank I was standing on.

And that was when I noticed the almost-empty bottle of Jack Daniel's buried in the snow just a few feet from me.

"What is it?" Ashley asked, then a soft, "oh," when she followed my gaze to the bottle.

I looked from her to the telltale ice. I balanced Ashley with my hands on her soft shoulders as I went around her to get to the bottle. I felt like I was mucking through quicksand pavement.

"Did you find something?" Don asked as he and Trisha came up next to Ashley. I pointed out to the lake, then to the bottle.

Kevin came up from the beach side of the hill just as I picked up the bottle. The quarter-inch or so of rust-colored alcohol in the bottom of the bottle was frozen solid. I lifted the bottle to my nose to take a whiff. The smell was even frozen.

"Shit, she drank the whole thing," Kevin said, taking the bottle from me.

"Look out there," I said, pointing at the spot on the lake where there wasn't so much snow. "Something happened there recently."

We were all quiet for a moment, but I had to get a closer look at the ice before I put my horrible fears into words.

"Be careful, Irish," Kevin said when I slowly worked my way down to the snow-covered ice.

"Better me than anyone else. Oh, the endless rewards of being the smallest." I gently felt the solidity with one foot while the other stayed firmly on solid ground. Ashley kept a steadying hand on me. This was especially treacherous because I couldn't actually see the snow-laden ice, but going out to inspect the suspicious-looking area was the only way I knew of to tell if someone could've fallen through. "This isn't all that thick. All of you just stay on the shore."

Slowly I crept forward. Inch-by-inch, step-by-step. I imagined a drunken Jamie falling through the ice, taking with her the snow that had accumulated on that spot. It would be a while before the ice would refreeze enough to support the falling snow.

I knelt to brush the little bit of accumulated snow from the area and examined the unevenness of the freeze. Whatever had broken the surface had cut through the ice quite a while ago, maybe even a dozen hours earlier. It could have been a deer, I told myself.

"What do you see?" George yelled out from the shore.

If Jamie had fallen through here, it had been so long ago that it had already frozen over, just like her body would if she were immersed in the water for that long. Wasn't that how Houdini had finally met his untimely demise? Under iced-over water?

"Hey! You guys gotta check this out!"

We all turned around to see Jamie running toward us, covered in snow with a tire tossed over her shoulder.

"Jamie!" I yelled with relief. I forgot where I was. My mind just jumped to realizing how very typical of her this all was—to make us think she was dead while she was off doing—

It happened in a split-second that seemed to take forever. One moment I was on the ice, the next I was spluttering in freezing water, and during the eternity between those two moments I was trying to keep the second moment from following the first— to no avail.

The water hit my skin like a thousand needle pricks, cutting deep into me.

5

What, No Lap Dances?

"We need to get you out of those clothes." Ashley was already working on my zippers and layering.

"I . . . I . . . didn't know you cared," I stuttered while shaking uncontrollably. A pit of warmth had started in my stomach and was spreading through my body from the touch of Ashley's soft and gentle hands. Alas, it wasn't enough to cut through the residual freeze from the lake.

Karen ran to get a warm blanket while Ashley and Trisha pulled me out of my freezing wet clothes. I suddenly realized I'd really enjoy this if I weren't quite so worried about freezing to death. I tried to get them to stop at my underwear, but they wouldn't have anything to do with it.

"Give it up, Shawn, they're wet as well," Ashley said, kneeling at my feet. Trisha wrapped her arms around me, latching her fingers under the elastic on the bottom front of my sports bra so she could pull it over my head. The only reason she got away with it so easily was that I was rather preoccupied.

Just as Trisha reached around me to pull off my sports bra, Ashley hooked her thumbs into the elastic of my silk boxers and looked up into my eyes, distracting me from Trisha's further movements.

"Silk boxers?" Ashley asked. "For anyone special?"

I quickly covered myself with my goose-pimpled arms and Ashley yanked my knickers off.

And that was how I ended up naked between two beautiful women. It was one of the great ironies in life that back in college, when I would've been more likely to get into this sort of situation, I would've run like hell—kinda like I did when Trisha mentioned trying something different with some ropes.

But now that I was older and mellower, enough so that I might be intrigued by such a situation, I could no longer find anyone as interested as I was. But here I was nonetheless—just when I was frozen solid and unable to do a damned thing about it.

Okay, fine, I was probably as frozen by the cold as I was with fear. Trapped naked between two gorgeous women, and unable to take advantage of it in the least.

Karen reappeared with a big, fuzzy blue blanket, which Ashley took from her and wrapped around my bare shoulders. "We'll get you all nice and warm," she whispered into my ear when she was leaning close to me, tucking the blanket in around me. I was surprised the warmth of her breath against my ear alone wasn't enough to defrost me.

I was glad the underthings I had put on today were in good shape. It would've been embarrassing to be caught with holey things.

Ma always told me to wear clean underwear in case I got hit by a car. Right now, there wasn't a chance in hell I'd get hit by a car, so I was glad yet again that I never listened to her.

"Here, drink this," Karen said, placing a warm mug between

my hands.

I took a sip of the hot tea and it burned its way down my throat, filling my body with its warmth. "What, no whiskey?" I stammered, holding the cup up.

"Drink that first. Whiskey takes the warmth from your body and that's the last thing you need," Karen said.

"Damned pragmatists," I murmured into my cup. "Doncha know whiskey means *water of life* in Gaelic?" I said, affecting my very best Irish brogue, which really wasn't all that difficult, considering I'd been born with it.

"I'm sure I could get you all nice and warm in no time," Trisha said, sitting on the arm of my chair in front of the Franklin stove and snaking her arm around my shoulders.

Ashley stalked off, mumbling something about telling the guys it was okay to come back in.

"How're you doing?" Trisha whispered into my ear after watching Ashley depart. She rubbed my shoulders through the blanket.

Although my head was still rather fuzzy, I was pretty damned sure Trisha was coming onto me. Ah, what the hell, I thought, leaning back against her soft body. She gently ran her fingers over my hair, caressing it.

I remembered the first time I met Trisha, back when we were suitemates in Hubbard Hall, the primarily freshmen dormitory at MSU. Neither of us were out to ourselves at that point, but still I found Trisha to be truly gorgeous. I kept finding reasons to look at her. Especially when she changed clothing. She was so different and exciting, both regardless and because of it. Of course, I was intrigued by her many piercings.

I heard people entering with a loud racket of tapping boots and shaking of jackets. As I tumbled down a long, dark, slide into slumber, I heard Jamie talking about the perfect snow run she had found. She had been using the tire as a sled to ride down the cliff and onto the beach and lake since early morning.

There were questions about whether or not they should allow me to sleep or if they should keep me awake, and who else wanted to try the snow slide, but I didn't catch it all because I was busy drifting off to a warm, safe place full of beautiful women who were all lesbians.

"Hey, honey," a silky voice whispered into my ear. Trisha. I rolled over in bed.

"Fire!" I yelled, jumping to my feet. Fire in our dorm room! "Yiii!" I screamed, realizing the blanket, which was all I was wearing, was falling off me. How was Trisha waking me up and where was I and what was I doing here and just how much trouble was I getting into doing it anyway?

"Shawn, calm down, you need to put on some clothes and then come eat some supper," Trisha said.

Still disoriented, I looked around. Karen was in the kitchen, cutting up helpless things far too quickly with a lethal-looking knife. Denise was stirring something menacing in a pot on the Franklin stove. George and Don were bringing in more wood, letting in a cold draft. Kevin was carrying a pan from the Franklin over to the table. Ashley was setting the table.

Toto, we're not in Kansas anymore.

And that was just the sort of dream I had when something really bad was about to happen. Or something truly weird was about to happen. But then again, sometimes a bad, or weird, dream, is just that: A bad or weird dream.

Ashley's eyes reflected the fire from the stove as she glanced up at me, illuminating the devil I'd always known was inside of her.

"I'm a grown girl, Trisha," I said as she tried to lead me up to my room. "I can get dressed by myself." As I stomped up the stairs on my own, I recalled that Trisha had always been rather motherly toward me. That was part of the reason we'd broken up. I never thought I'd want to grow up, but I knew for certain I didn't want to be followed around for the rest of my life by my mother, or any mother for that matter, not even some Star-Trekian alien Moogie-mother.

Trisha had rolled my socks up into neat little balls in the drawer, for chrissakes! No telling what a woman like that would do in the long run—probably want to have cute little girls she could raise to be Girl Guides while totally giving up on any ideas of black leather and whips. If I had to choose between those extremes, I was leaning toward the leather and recreational equipment for sure.

But then I remembered the way Trisha's long, black hair used to reach down to her arse, the ends curling around her hips, which filled out the jeans and slacks she always wore. A perfect curve, all the way down her shapely legs.

Whoa, Nellie, I chided myself. I dug in my suitcase and recalled the primary reason we had broken up. Trisha had decided to have an affair with Jamie, an affair she dumped me for, an affair that lasted exactly one night.

Jamie was the sort who liked the thrill of the chase, the excitement of the flirtation and the joy of getting what she wanted. She lived for that, and, of course, she needed to consummate the chase, prove to everyone, including herself, that she did have what it took. That the women did want her, enough so they'd give up whomever they were currently dating for her.

The only way to be sure about everything was for Jamie to sleep with them. That was also her way of signaling victory, of putting an end to the chase. After all, it couldn't last forever. I knew I didn't want to be yet another woman who realized her worth by sleeping with others. I didn't want to judge myself by my conquests.

Anyway, Trisha dumped me for Jamie, even when I warned her that the Jamester really wasn't up to much. That she'd just use her and leave her, like she did all the others.

As I pulled on clean underthings, I wondered where they had put my wet clothes. I hoped I didn't have to go outside any time in the near future because I had only brought the one pair of boots and one coat.

I had spent a while with Jamie eons ago, and it had been an eye-opening experience.

I was sitting on the edge of the bed with socks in hand when Ashley appeared in the doorway.

"Hey," Ashley said while I mumbled to myself and lunged for more clothing. "I think I packed more than you." She pointed at her suitcase. "If you need anything just let me know and I might be able to help you."

Pants! I know I packed pants! "Um, I should be fine, I brought this T-shirt to sleep in, though, so I might have to sleep naked—"

Ashley grinned. "Now that's a thought."

Trisha popped in next to Ashley, pushing her out of the way. "You'd better hurry up," she said to me, "or else dinner'll be cold."

"I could probably get ready a bit quicker without an audience," I said, trying to cover myself with the bedspread.

Given how prone to prankage the entire group was, I could only wonder if this'd all been set up for the sole purpose of confounding, confusing and embarrassing me.

I just didn't know what to think anymore.

Ashley and Trisha hitting on me had just thrown the world off its axis, after all.

Dinner was quite an event. It made me feel wanted. Even though I was sure it was all in my head, and that I was imagining things, it still made me feel good.

It all started when Ashley and Trisha both wanted to sit next to me, then there was the little scene over the broccoli salad in which both women tried to serve me from the same bowl at the same time.

Trisha *accidentally* spilled her drink down Ashley's back while she was walking by.

I was torn between disbelief and suggesting a three-way.

"I think we should sit around the fire and tell ghost stories!" Kevin suggested, trying to lighten the mood. Trisha and Ashley were still growling at each other, although they had apparently decided to take turns with me. Who'd a thunk that? Me, being shared by two right beauties!

"I like that idea! What a perfect time for it, too!" Karen exclaimed, replying to Kevin's suggestion. "Besides, it'll help us conserve the candles."

"We need one, though, or a flashlight, for the storyteller to shine on their face," Kevin said. "C'mon, everybody, get in a circle out here."

Kevin and Karen quickly shepherded everyone into a rough circle in the living room, with people stretched out on the floor, chairs and couch. I found myself sitting next to Ashley in front of the fire. Jamie again had her ever-present drink, which I assumed was poured from her new bottle of Jack.

"It was a dark and stormy night," Kevin began, the flashlight in his hands casting an eerie glow upon his usually smiling face. "The wind whistled through the trees in its own macabre melody—"

"Hold on, I don't know this one," Karen said.

"And your point is?" Denise said.

"Well, everybody knows all the ghost stories!"

"Shh!" George ordered.

"—and the wind whistled its own macabre melody," Kevin repeated, trying to take control of the situation. "I remember the night vividly. It was the sort of night that you wanted to curl up in front of a fire with a hot, muscular, hairy man or bury yourself under the covers with your favorite teddy bear—not the sort of night during which you'd want to be out, no matter with whom! That night Steve and Julie were all alone." He quickly flicked the light on and off, adding to the mood.

47

The snow had finally stopped falling, but the weight and thickness of it on the roof and against the walls dampened all sounds from outside. The full moon reflecting from the piles of snow cast a glow of white on everything it touched, but it did nothing to placate the feelings of being alone and trapped that were building up within me. It reminded me, yet again, of the evil/awful dream I'd had that I was now, ever increasingly, sure meant I wasn't supposed to come up here this weekend.

Also, something wasn't right. And this time, I was pretty damned sure of it.

"The radio crackled when Steve turned it on." Kevin was losing himself in the part. "Instead of romantic music, they heard the heavy voice of an announcer: 'We interrupt this program to bring you a special news bulletin.'"

I began to giggle nervously at how into it Kevin was, but quickly turned my nervous and very unbutchly giggling into a cough.

With a quick, nasty look at me, Kevin continued. "Steve immediately wanted to change the station but Julie stopped him. She said she wanted to hear." Kevin again flicked the light. "'A maniacal man has escaped from the local asylum.'"

"A maniacal man?" Denise said. "I've never heard an announcer use words like that."

Kevin ignored her. "'Everybody is advised to stay inside tonight until the police apprehend mass-murderer John Kelso. Asylum officials confirm that the most brutal of Kelso's acts was committed exactly twenty years ago today!'"

I abruptly realized what was wrong. "Where's Trisha?" She'd been gone a while.

Kevin ignored me, too. "'Steve, let's go home,' Julie said. 'I don't like this one bit.' She pulled her jacket tighter and redid the buttons on her blouse."

"I don't know," Karen said, looking around for Trisha.

"Maybe she went to bed early," Don suggested.

" 'Oh baby,' Steve said, trying to pull her close again. 'Don't worry. I can take care of us.' 'Steve, I'm serious,' Julie said, pulling away again, 'I want to go home, right now.'"

"Without saying good night?" Karen said about Trisha.

I got up. "I'll go check."

"I'll come with you," Karen said, then whispered in my ear, "I don't like scary stories. I hid behind my popcorn for most of *Scream*. Or some sequel of it."

As Karen lit a candle, I stole a glance at Ashley. Flickers of firelight danced through her hair, making her look like an angel, or some enchanted creature from a beautiful, faraway land. She met my gaze and I turned away, feeling my face heat up.

Much to my consternation, Ashley said, "I think I might turn in early," and followed closely behind me while Karen led the way up the staircase.

This was truly a scene from some scary movie—three women moving in a column slowly up the darkened staircase to the darkened floor above, the snow muffling any sounds from outside while Kevin's spooky voice followed us. I wondered if his tale was to be the one where the boyfriend leaves the car to investigate a noise, only to be found by the girl hours later, dead, hanging upside down from a tree over the car, with his fingernails dragging along the top of the car, making an eerie *scritch-scratch* noise? Or perhaps it was to be the one where no one died, but the two teenagers arrived home to find the madman's hand, complete with hook, attached to the car.

We all knew all of them, of that I was sure. So he must be weaving a new tale.

The light of the tiny candle Karen carried flickered across the walls of the long, dark hallway. Why hadn't I thought to bring a light of my own? I liked some measure of control in my life, and being able to light my own way would grant me some of that.

All the upstairs doors were open, and we briefly peeked into each room as we passed.

"Trisha?" Karen's usually bold voice was dampened, perhaps by the same sudden fear I felt.

All the rooms were vacant. Some of my friends were neat and tidy. Others were not—at least from what I could tell from quick glimpses into empty rooms. If this were a scary movie, this entire scene would be perfect—because our dallying about in the hallway built suspense and tension. I could almost hear the music swelling, and swelling some more, in the background. I couldn't help but wonder what had to happen before it would fade.

The clot thickened.

Knowing that the clot was thickening and the tension building and the music swelling meant that it was all happening for a reason—that it was escalating toward something. So therefore, there was probably something we ought to be avoiding. I didn't quite know what it was we should be avoiding, but there was something truly wrong with this entire setup. Dreadfully wrong.

Music on Radio Donnelly doesn't build for no reason.

We came to Trisha and Jamie's room at the far end of the hall. This one door was closed.

Karen first knocked, several times. There was no reply. We stood outside for a moment, and then Karen knocked yet again. "Trisha? Are you in there?"

I don't know what she expected to happen—it wasn't like one moment Trisha wouldn't be there but the next moment she would.

I reached past Karen to open the door. The squeak of hinges was long and deep against the silence of the night. "Trisha?" I said softly, cautiously. I hesitantly took a step into the room and then reached behind me for Karen's candle.

The breath froze in my lungs. I was frozen. Couldn't quite take it in. Couldn't move. Cold all over.

My mind just didn't want to accept what I was seeing. I wanted to focus on anything but what I was seeing—I wanted to turn around, to Karen and Ashley, and walk with them back downstairs, back to normality, reality, a world that was sane. A world where I could sit, drink and joke with Trisha.

We probably all saw it at the same time; if not, there was only a fraction of a second separating each of us from our first sight of what lay behind door number one: Trisha. Oh yes, there was no question, it was Trisha. *Was* being the operative word.

I was going to be sick.

Trisha's neck was slashed all the way across. I wasn't sure how many pints of blood the human body had in it, but it seemed a good deal more than I thought possible when it was all spread across the bed, the floor and all of her clothes. There was even some painted on the walls.

The slow dripping of blood onto the floor was the only sound that broke the silence. Drip. Drip. Drip. It glistened greasily in the dim candlelight.

Ashley screamed and backed toward the stairs. She ran into the wall, fell down, found her feet again and clawed her way to the stairs. I had been frozen in place, but when Ashley fell, I turned to help her, only Karen collapsed on me instead, nearly taking me down with her.

A moment later the rest of the group came charging upstairs. Don held them back and helped Karen to her feet. She pulled away from him and slowly ventured into the silent room, using Kevin's flashlight instead of the flickering candle.

I couldn't breathe.

"She's dead," Karen said a moment later, after closely inspecting the body, including reaching a tentative hand out to feel for a pulse, as if there were any question. Karen's eyes were so wide I could see the whites in them. She walked stiffly back out of the room, trying to shepherd everyone back out ahead of her. Leave it to Karen to take being the proper host so far—all the way to trying to protect her guests from . . .

. . . good God, it was murder.

6

Serial's Not Just for Breakfast Anymore

"I can't believe we're cut off from the world," Don yelled, snapping his cell phone shut. The main phone lines were down. Ashley's cell needed to be recharged, but she didn't have the recharging unit. Karen's, Don's and George's weren't getting a signal, and Robert's was missing. And of course, no one had a recharging unit compatible with Ashley's phone.

Let them make fun of me for not having a cell phone now.

"There's no way any of us can go anywhere in this," Karen said, looking out through the drapes. The snow was starting to slow down, but there was no way any of our vehicles could make it through the accumulation, let alone any one of us on foot.

"Who did it and when?" George asked, pacing back and forth across the room, apparently deciding that we had to think about what we could do, instead of what we couldn't. "We've all been together all night."

"Obviously not," Ashley said, crossing her arms over her green wool sweater, "or else Trisha never would've been alone long enough to be killed."

"Maybe it wasn't one of us?" Don asked hesitantly. I was surprised at how timid he suddenly seemed.

"Then who the hell else could it have been?" George said. "Look outside—where could anybody have come from?"

"Maybe they've been here the entire time," Karen said.

"Maybe there really aren't any animals in the attic after all," Denise said.

Everyone looked around—especially up, toward the attic. We were all standing around the living room, with plenty of distance between each of us. George shivered and threw a few more logs on the fire—apparently he was feeling the same extreme chill that was penetrating deep into me. I was frozen solid. But still I shivered uncontrollably.

"I've seen animals in the attic, I've heard them," Karen finally said, breaking the hard, cold silence.

"I have, too," Don meekly offered. The logs George had thrown onto the fire crackled. I could feel the added warmth, but it didn't seem to touch the coldness permeating the room. Every element was adding its own bit to the scene that was playing out, just like a good TV show. Or, rather, a good mystery.

"But none of us have," Denise said.

"Why would they lie about something like that?" I said, shivering. I moved closer to the fire.

"Maybe they're hiding someone up there," Denise said.

Nothing made any sense anymore. Silence ensued.

"We need to search the house," I said. I'm not quite sure how I managed to get the words out of my mouth, especially since I didn't have a copy of the script. I didn't quite know what I was feeling—sad, scared, shocked, confused . . . Everyone was starting to freak out, you could see it in their eyes. The coldness that sliced through me like an old broadsword, the type the Vikings used, wasn't because the temperature was low, it was from the suspicious glares, the dark looks, and the meanings behind the words that were being exchanged. We were supposed to be friends, but everyone was turning against each other.

It was like the very worst nightmare, where nothing was possible, where everything that happened couldn't be happening and no one was acting like they were supposed to, like they always had.

I looked at each of my friends: Karen, Kevin, Robert, Jamie, Ashley. I couldn't imagine any of them picking up a knife and . . . and doing that.

Then it must be Don, George or Denise. I looked at each of them in turn, trying to imagine one of my friends having such bad judgment about friends or mates. I tried to picture any of them picking up a knife and slashing, thrusting, cutting with it. I just couldn't do it. I couldn't see any of the people in this room purposely slicing the life from another.

Plus, there were simply a lot of logistical problems to one of us being the murderer. For instance, clothes. Really, with the mess upstairs, with what had happened, there was . . .

. . . there was no way whoever did it did not get blood splattered.

I couldn't believe I was thinking so calmly and coldly about one of my friends being dead. But it was necessary. For now. And would help me continue. And no one had time to commit the murder, shower and change. Frankly, since we'd last seen Trisha, we'd not been outside of each other's sight long enough for any of us to do all that.

So that meant there was someone else in the house with us. I shivered and wrapped my arms around myself, though they did nothing to cut the cold.

There was no telling who he'd kill next.

But everything was so plotted, so scripted, down to the cell phones not working. Even I knew there were cell phone jammers on the market . . . We always used to prank each other, do things to each other, plot and plan against each other, with all sorts of toys like those, after all!

But this was here and now, real life.

Everyone was by themselves, or with their partner, as if no one outside of their own pairing or selves could be trusted. We had known each other for years, had shared many things together, but now we were all strangers trapped together, when we were really friends trapped together with a stranger. I was regretting my sophomore-year obsession with Hitchcock. We'd started with ten and now there were nine.

Anger was covering fear, and fear left no room for grieving. Right now, we could not afford to properly grieve for Trisha because first we had to save ourselves. We had to figure out, find, whoever was responsible.

"Shawn's right," Ashley finally said, taking my arm, unifying us. "We need to search the house. We need to find out who's responsible for this." She was good at playing her role.

"I just can't believe this!" Karen screamed, throwing her hands into the air and throwing herself onto the sofa behind her.

"It's gonna be all right." Don dropped next to her and wrapped her in a protective arm.

"Okay, everybody." Robert's hands were visibly shaking. "We should start at one end and work our way through the house methodically. In a method and manner that is . . . that is . . . methodical!"

Jamie, who had been pacing like a caged animal, took another slug from her bottle. "We need to stay together. This needs to be an organized search to be effective."

Ashley looked into my eyes. She understood that everyone was losing it, and was hoping I wasn't, so the two of us could hold everyone together.

"Robert and Jamie are right. Let's start in the garage," George said, holding Kevin close.

The nine of us agreed to a temporary truce and we grouped together tightly, beginning the search in the garage on the west end of the house. We tried to stay close enough together so we were safe, if there was indeed someone else in the house.

Don and George went up into the garage's attic while I stayed on the stairs and the other six spread out through the main floor of the area. A boat and a work area occupied most of the space. Numerous wrenches and hand tools, such as hammers, T-squares, drills and handsaws, hung on the walls, with further tools, I guessed, in the drawers. A fine coating of dust lay over all the tools, shelves and drawers, making me pretty sure the murder weapon had not come from here.

There was also a distinct and utter lack of any sign of anyone trying to stay warm out here.

I peeked up into the attic, which seemed to be used primarily for storage. Don and George were making sure no one was there or using it as a home base. Any sort of recently used sleeping bags or food items would be a sure clue as to another presence in the cottage with us. This search might've been part of a fun murder mystery game, except that my hands were shaking and I couldn't believe one of my friends was dead and I was scared for my life and the lives of my friends even while I was scared of my friends and—

"All clear in here," Jamie said, peeking out from under the tarp that covered the boat. I couldn't believe she could drink so much yet still be able to climb into the boat without a ladder.

The breezeway, which attached the garage to the house, had a spare bathroom, complete with a shower, and there were a wide variety of model rockets hanging from the ceiling—including replicas of the Starship *Enterprise* and various military planes. I noticed a broom just inside of the outside door, standing in a small puddle of water. I would've thought any water from when we'd entered the last time would've dried by now.

It looked as if the garage and breezeway had been built quite

56

a while after the main building was finished. There were three entrances/exits from the garage/breezeway area: the garage door, a door leading outside from the breezeway and the door leading into the house. My soaked clothes from earlier were hanging on a clothesline that stretched across the space. I hated that they were there—not only was my rather intimate apparel now on display for everyone to see and comment upon, it also created a bit of a mask through which we had to go in order to fully search the room. And going through clothes drying on a line into a dark space was something no one really wanted to do. The clothing cast shadows in human form—unless there really was someone back there.

We looked at each other, then at the clothesline. Then at the shadows behind it.

"Did something move back there?" Robert asked, staring wide-eyed at Don.

"No, it was just a . . . just a breeze blowing through here," Jamie said, not at all confidently.

"Uh," I said, "how can there be a breeze if we're in a sealed house?"

"Our movements are causing it! We're . . . we're disrupting the air, causing currents and stuff, causing this breeze." Jamie boldly stepped through the clothesline. "See there's nothing here." She turned around in circles, her arms wide. "Nada. Zilch."

There really wasn't anything there.

Don went into the bathroom. "Nothing in here either."

I looked slowly from face to face, meeting each set of eyes in turn. I could feel my heart beating in my throat.

Flashlight in hand, I turned away from everyone to lead the way back into the house. I opened the door into the house's original breezeway. I paused just long enough to shine the light around the small enclosure, ensuring no one was in there with us.

I led the way into the hallway, with everyone behind me.

"No, wait, stop," Karen said, her voice making her sound at the edge of a nervous breakdown. "The crawl space." She was clinging to Don's arm.

Don and George hesitantly made their way toward the handle in the floor Karen was pointing at.

George pulled the handle up and shone his light into the darkness before slowly stepping into the ground. Even at this distance I could smell the cold, hard clay that lined that part of the building. It smelled like a cemetery. I glanced around nervously, the minutes seeming like hours, days, before George finally reappeared.

"It's clean," he said in his authoritative voice. As if such an area could ever really be clean. I shuddered at the thought of the bugs and creatures that were surely down there, even in the winter, in this coldness.

We again gathered together, and I took the lead this time, stepping into the bathroom on the left and looking into the shower and under the sink while everyone waited in the hallway.

I could feel my heart pounding in my throat, see my hands shaking, and wanted to jump at every minute shadow, but I knew I couldn't scream. I had never, ever screamed in fear, and I wouldn't start now, no matter how much I wanted to, I just couldn't.

(Okay, fine, I sometimes screamed in embarrassment or mortification, like that time when my mother told the neighbor that her daughter had reached her womanhood, but that's another story entirely.)

I had to be strong. Strong and butch and brave. Robert was about ready to dissolve into a puddle on the floor, Kevin was shaking so badly I thought he might start falling apart, and although Karen outwardly looked like she was coping, I could tell by her eyes that she was about to lose it as well. We were falling apart. I knew I had to be strong, at least for Ashley, who looked at me with worshipful eyes.

I had to be her rock in the storm.

"Two of us should stay here," I said. "We need to watch this door so no one can sneak by us."

"Irish is right," George said. "And it *should* be two of us. Strength in numbers and all that. Kevin and I will do it."

Don nodded, and we all stood outside his and Karen's bedroom while he went in, searching meticulously under the bed, in the closet, behind the door, and through each nook and cranny. He rejoined us, and I again took the lead, bringing us into the darkened main area of the first floor. I almost jumped out of my skin when the fire crackled menacingly, throwing light and shadows across the rooms.

"Spread out, don't leave any area unchecked," I ordered. Ashley's hand on my arm gave me strength and courage as I flashed my light briefly over the furniture.

Don went into the kitchen with Karen, and I could hear them opening and closing all the cupboard doors, even the oven. Robert and Denise went through the dining room, while Ashley and I combed the living room, carefully examining behind each piece of furniture and Jamie searched the slight hallway that brought it all together.

"All clear?" Don asked, coming up behind me and Ashley.

"Dining room's clear," Denise said, her voice small and scared.

"We're fine here," I said. "George! Kevin!" I called, "We're clear in here, come on!" I wanted them to keep watching our tail. If they stayed in their position, the sliding door off the dining room wouldn't be guarded.

We'd know if anyone came from outside, regardless, because they'd leave footprints in the snow, but I wanted our rear guarded, and there just weren't enough of us left to watch all the exits.

I found myself again going up the stairs to the second floor. My blood was pounding in my ears. The only sound I could hear was the eerie cadence of everyone breathing.

We made it to the top of the stairs unscathed.

I looked down the hall and was reminded of the whirling special effects in Hitchcock's *Vertigo*.

I stopped, and everyone ran into me, sending me to my knees. "Watch out!" I said. It would've been funny, like something from *Scooby Doo*, except . . . it wasn't.

A glance behind me revealed Ashley's lips trembling, her body shaking in fright.

I took her hand once I was on my feet. "It's okay." She smiled tentatively at me, holding on to my hand as if her life depended on us not losing our connection. I led us into the first bedroom, leaving Don and Karen in the hallway while the rest of us searched the room.

"All clear," I said, stepping back into the hall. I glanced up at the ceiling, studying the attic door in the ceiling at the end of the hall. I found myself straining to hear any noise that might come from there, but there was nothing. I wondered what had happened to the animals Karen said lived up there, or even the ones that strolled through, looking for food.

Was the house haunted? Was there some logical explanation (or rationally illogical?) for the noises that had been there and now weren't? Something wasn't right here, and I felt stuck in the mud, trying to fight my way out when I tried to focus my brain to think about it. It was like something was on the tip of my tongue and I couldn't get it out, or more like a thought unthought, but wanting to be thought. Waiting to be thought.

This sometimes happened when something wasn't right—it'd get stuck like a skipping record in my brain until I figured it out.

Great, now I was blithering inside my own head. By the time this was all through, they'd need to lock me up.

The sense of foreboding again swelled through my body, becoming one with my heartbeat. I was again in that dream world from the night before last where nothing I did made any sense, any difference. No matter what, I couldn't get out of it or even save myself. Every which way I turned lay another precipice.

We continued our trek down the hall, slowly spreading out to cover more territory in less time. We were all on edge and wanted to finish our search as quickly as possible. I was alone in George and Kevin's room, and had just realized I was alone, all alone, when I heard Ashley's gasp.

I raced out into the hall and she ran right into my arms, so we tumbled to the ground together.

"Omigod," I panted.

I had a fleeting, inappropriate thought of just how damned good Ashley felt lying on top of me, but I quickly helped her to her feet. Wrapping my arms around her, I tried to give her my strength, as she had given me hers. For comfort, of course. I looked over Ashley's shoulder into Trisha and Jamie's room to see what had shaken her up so badly. Don, looking white as a ghost, was leaning against a wall just outside the room.

I peered into the room by the light of Don's flashlight. I didn't see anything. It took a moment for that to sink in: I didn't see anything.

Trisha's body was gone. It took a moment to take that in and realize the blood was still there on the sheets and walls and floor, all artfully staged. It was just the body that was missing.

A chill ran down my spine. Actually, it more than ran down my spine, it stampeded like horses down my spine, then stopped, said, "that was fun" and went racing back up to do it all over again.

I looked at the rest of the group. "We have one more room. Don, you, Ashley and Karen wait here. Robert, Denise, Jamie and I are going up to the attic to check out the animals." I could almost hear the eerie spikes of music swelling and fading in the background.

The attic had no windows through which the moon and snow could shine light. It was pitch black. Horrid shapes loomed around us, preying on us like ghosts from some old story, some horrible nightmare given to wee children.

I girded myself and stepped from the ladder into the attic. I confronted the phantoms of the attic and my dreams and stepped forth into the realm of nightmares. I hurled myself toward the first ghastly shape and yanked the cloth from it revealing it to be a . . . a . . . a piece of furniture. I ran to the next, and the next, and not until every other-worldly shape had taken on the form of something from this world—a lamp here, an overstuffed chair there, and a filing cabinet and loveseat in the far corner—did I stop.

When I was done, and still hadn't heard a sound, I stomped hard and pounded against walls, trying to disturb any creature, great or small. I wanted to know that whatever we had heard was of this planet.

Ashley, Robert and Denise were still on the staircase when I was finished with my frantic search-and-destroy mission. They stared at me as if I were some troll or dwarf, some being from elsewhere that was bent on destruction and had very little mind.

"What?" I asked.

"N . . . nothing," Ashley said, reaching a tentative hand out to me. "Are you all right?"

"I'm a little freaked, okay?" How could I ever explain to her that although I was an American, schooled in these here United States of America since I was thirteen, creatures from the old country were imbued in my blood? That goblins, trolls, demons, banshee and things that went bump in the night (other than buildings settling and rodents in the attic) were part of my blood? Part of me?

I cupped her face in my hand and looked into her eyes, where the world was a rational and plausible space. "It's okay," I whispered. Then I looked at the others. "There's nothing up here that shouldn't be. No ghosties or goblins, and no rats or opossums." I took Ashley's hand and squeezed us down the stairs past the other two.

"Nothing?" Don asked when we put the staircase back into

the ceiling.

"Nothing," I said, firmly closing the latch on the stair. On the one hand, it was a relief that there was no mystery outsider stalking us, but on the other hand, it meant one of us was the killer.

"We need to talk with the others," Don said somberly, intently studying all of our faces and leading the way down to the living room.

"You didn't find anything up there, I take it?" George asked when we got back down to the main floor.

"Trisha's body is gone," Don said.

"Oh fuck me," George said, leading Kevin to the couch.

Everyone followed, taking a position, standing, sitting or pacing, while watching the others.

"We're all thinking it," George said from where he was sitting near the fire. "So why doesn't anybody just say it?"

"Say what?" Karen asked. I was standing by the window looking out toward the lake. "That I feel like a trapped rat? We have absolutely no contact with the outside world and there's a killer loose here!"

"What we're thinking," George replied, "is that one of us must be the killer. We're alone, so that's the only explanation."

"So then who the fuck is it?" Kevin yelled, pulling away from George. "I can't fucking take this!"

"It's okay, baby, I won't let anything happen to you," George said, pulling his lover down into his arms and quietly soothing him.

"If we're alone, what happened to the body?" Ashley whispered from our spot on the end of the couch. I had my arms wrapped around a pillow, keeping it as close as a lover or a teddy bear.

"It couldn't have just disappeared," Don said. "It has to be somewhere."

"So either we missed someplace during our search," I began, trying to be the voice of reason, although I knew I was less than two steps and a hop from panicking myself. In other words, I was trying to keep the shrill edge of panic out of my voice. I wasn't sure I was succeeding. "Or else it's been taken somewhere. We only searched inside the house."

"What're we supposed to do? Search the entire world?" Robert yelled. He was obviously nearing the fry-point. "Bodies don't just disappear!"

"Look outside the house for footprints," I said. "If anyone's come or gone, their footprints will let us know."

"But we were all out there earlier," Ashley whispered.

"Hours ago. Our prints would be at least somewhat covered up. Even though it's stopped snowing now, it snowed for a while after we came in, and the wind's still going, which would mean our paths are just about gone." I looked around at the somber faces surrounding me. "Robert, let me have that flashlight. We'll at least be able to tell if a set of prints are fresh."

"You're not going out there alone," Karen said. "What if he's out there?"

"Then who's going to go with me?" Staying in here meant losing my mind. We had to do something, figure something out. Take action. I tried to stay my shaking body with that thought.

"Why don't we all go?" Karen finally asked into the darkness.

"We can't," I replied.

"No, Shawn's right," George said. "If we all go we'll destroy any tracks that are there. With so many people traipsing around it won't matter how careful we are, something'll happen."

Don gestured helplessly at George. "Why don't you and I go?"

"No. You stay here and Shawn and I'll go," George said with finality. "One of us needs to stay inside in case anything happens in here."

"I'll go with you two," Jamie said, glancing at us.

Outside the night was quiet. The snow was deep, so we had to work to get through it, and much of our earlier tracking *was* still visible—but we were each armed with a flashlight to try to discern the difference between old and new tracks. The snow had drifted in closely around the house when it was falling, and the wind was forming huge mounds of snow against the western walls of the building. The torch beams brought some illumination to the scene, but still it was difficult to figure it all out because we had spent quite a bit of time around the house this morning looking for Jamie, and those tracks were still visible, though softened by new snow.

I knew George had left Don inside because they were obviously the two biggest and strongest, so the task of offering protection against whomever, or whatever, we were dealing with logically fell to them. Still, I could tell by his voice that he was a little scared about actually finding anything, or anyone, out here.

All the same, I was glad Jamie was with us. If George was the murderer, I didn't want to be alone with him out here.

"These all look like old tracks to me," George said, with a slight tremor in his voice, as he scanned the light around behind the garage. We were slowly making a circuit of the place, going all the way around. If someone else came or went from the house, they would need a magic carpet not to leave signs within a few feet of it. Even with just flashlights, we would see *something*.

Karen had found an old coat and boots for me to wear. Although both were a little too big for me, I could already feel a trickle of sweat making its way down my back, caused, I was sure, as much by the nerve-racking fear as by the strenuous trek through the deep snowdrifts. In some areas, because the drifts were so deep and soft, we had had to follow our circuit of the house several feet, or yards, away from the actual building.

I hated those times because I didn't have the building to ensure there was at least one direction from which I could not be attacked. I wished I had inspected Trisha and Jamie's room better, even though the thought of spending much time in the same room with Trisha's corpse or her blood made bile rise up in my throat. I couldn't believe anyone could slash a body so much. I couldn't believe the body contained so much blood.

I kept expecting someone in a hockey mask, in a Father Death costume or with knives for fingers to sneak up behind me. I suddenly realized how often knives were the chosen weapons of horror movie villains and wondered if that was Hitchcock's *Psycho* influence. Maybe it was just because knives were so much more *fun*? The more gore, the more fun—how bloody and disgusting can we make it?

I chuckled. Then I laughed. It was disgustingly funny.

"Irish? Irish?" George said. "Are you okay?"

I leaned my head against George and let him wrap his bearish arms around me as the laughter convulsed into tears.

Jamie turned around and joined us. "Are you all right?"

I wiped my eyes. "Sometimes it seems to me that things go so far in one direction they pop out the other side. Like liberals who have so many rules about just how liberal you have to be in order to be one of them. They become so restrictive, they might as well be conservative."

George smiled a sad little smile and nodded. "And now things have gotten so bad, and so gruesome, they popped out the other side and became funny."

I wiped at my eyes with my wet gloves. "Yeah."

The gore of it all made my stomach turn as I envisioned Trisha's mutilated corpse, and experienced again the fear I had felt when I'd seen her body was gone. Amazing how the sudden absence of something that had struck terrible fear into your heart could cause you to become even more afraid.

I remembered the chill I felt when I realized Trisha's body was gone. And realized it hadn't been just fear. *Thick*, I cursed myself. Stupid and slow for not noticing sooner. *There was an open window in the room.*

7

See No Evil, Hear No Evil

"Did you find anything?" Karen asked us when we came through the deck door and pounded the snow off our boots so it formed little puddles on the tiles. I stared at the tiny pools of water, feeling a sense of déjà vu.

George shook his head dolefully. "Nothing. No new tracks, no blood, nothing."

Jamie sighed. "We were alone out there."

Karen sighed and said, "Um, before you take off your boots, would you mind bringing in some more wood? I don't think anybody's going to want to go out by themselves during the night in order to stoke the fire."

While the three of us made a few trips to the woodpile, the others took the wood from us at the door so we could bring more. Apparently they decided that as long as we were already hanging around outside in the Arctic temperatures, we wouldn't mind freezing ourselves a wee more and making further targets of ourselves as we wandered around outside where there might likely be a raving lunatic with a really sharp knife. Of course, since we hadn't found anything outside, or inside, maybe it really was one of us who was the murderer, so we would be just as safe bringing in the wood as anyone inside was. Unless it was George or Jamie who was the maniacal murderer, then the other two of us could end up dead meat. But I didn't think anyone would be so obvious as to kill the two of us, since, as the sole survivor he, or she, would have to be the murderer.

Unless of course the murderer said we had either disappeared or wandered off to investigate a strange noise, or perhaps that someone had come up and grabbed us, and the guy was either too big to take on, or the snow was too deep to be able to chase him.

Stop blithering, I told myself, but it didn't help.

Well, okay, fine, scratch investigating a noise. Not even I could be that much of a fucking eejit and I hoped none of my friends would believe I could be that much of a gobshite, either. And I didn't think Jamie'd be that much a muppet, either, no matter how pissed she was, which is to say *drunk* in American.

I stopped and stared at George, a shiver racing up and down my spine.

"Irish?" George said, "Are you all right?"

"Uh, yeah, yeah, I am." I made sure to keep him in sight, so that if he did anything, I'd at least be able to anticipate his next moves. How fast could such a big man be anyway?

But how could anyone do that to Trisha? How could one of *us* do that to Trisha? I realized I was thinking about Trisha almost as if she was an object—I wasn't yet really understanding that a friend—hell, more than a friend, an ex-lover—was now gone from my life forever. I could never again call her late at night to discuss our amorous misadventures, to exchange brownie recipes, or even to talk about the latest bondage techniques and whether or not you can use a silicone-based lube with a latex dildo. Granted, we never talked about those things late at night, or at all, but we could have.

Now we couldn't.

I should be grieving, but I couldn't. I was afraid. I didn't have time to grieve for Trisha, to remember all the good things or to think about everything that might've been.

Trisha would understand. Survival was what was important right now. Staying alive. I'd miss her when we made it through this alive.

But still, how could some son-of-a-bitch kill her in cold blood?

And yet . . .

And yet . . .

Well . . .

"What's going on?" Jamie asked, walking up to us.

I whipped around to face her, and wondered just how sloshed she was.

Don and Kevin took the wood from us at the door and we turned to get some more.

"Just one more trip should do it," Karen said.

George, Jamie and I carefully inched our way to the wood-pile, separating a bit a ways from each other. We were halfway there by the time I realized they were each eyeing me and each other. Which meant neither of them was the murderer, or else one of them was a terribly good actor.

But I just really couldn't imagine this friendly, big bear of a man killing anyone.

I was sure some people might be able to imagine it, but that would be a reaction based solely on his appearance, an appearance that could also cause one to change one's mind if you really considered it—after all, he was an engineer, and as such, a bit of a geek.

It would be like crossing your teddy bear with Bill Gates and expecting to come up with Jeffrey Dahmer.

Nor could I imagine my old friend Jamie intentionally hurting anyone.

But wasn't that what the neighbors always said? "I just can't imagine it. He was always so nice and friendly. Kind to small children and dogs. I just can't picture him sucking the blood out of the neighborhood squirrels, then barbecuing them and saying, 'Secret's in the sauce.'" Who cared what he was like with small children and dogs—it was his attitude about adults that was in question here. "He helped little old ladies across the street, always said hello to everyone. But that was just before he snapped their necks till their bodies drooped with a sickening lack of life."

"George," I finally said when we stopped at the woodpile to load up again. "Do you ever help little old ladies across the street?"

"No. With the way I look, they'd probably think I was a mugger."

"Oh. Well, I'm glad."

"Y'know, Kevin warned me about you."

"Warned you? What do you mean?" They couldn't possibly think *I* was the killer!

George gazed at me, looking a bit like Santa as the wind painted his beard and mustache white with snow. "He said you were weird."

"Weird how?"

"Different. Strange," Jamie interpreted. "Oh, for chrissakes, Irish, everybody's blowing everything out of proportion. Knowing Kevin, he meant it in a good way. And I, for one, don't think either of you are any more capable of what's going on around here than I am."

Oh my, wasn't that a relief?

"Just one more load should do it," Karen said, again, as she, Denise and Ashley took the wood from us. When I growled at her, she continued, "Well, you keep carrying less and less!"

"Only because we're bloody well exhausted and half-frozen!" Ashley smiled at me, and even threw in a wink, and, just like any well-trained butch, I turned tail to get some more.

"Sure, sure," I mumbled to myself, "I wasn't butch enough last night for them, but suddenly I'm now Miss Studly when there's a maniacal man on the loose."

Jamie laughed out loud. "She's got you pegged!"

"Karen has always been able to play anyone."

"It's not Karen I'm talking about."

A few minutes later, I again took my snowy boots off, and immediately stepped into a puddle of water where the snow had melted since a few minutes before when I had first stamped, thus soaking my bloody socks.

Then . . .

. . . it reminded me of something, but I had no idea what.

Robert looked wide-eyed around him when George, Jamie and I rejoined the group. He seemed to be terribly nervous and on edge, like he had drunk about sixty-nine pots of coffee in the past hour. He kept inching away from me.

"The phone's still dead," Karen said. "And the electric's still out." I wondered what they had all been talking about while the wood gatherers were outside.

"I still can't believe none of the cell phones work," Don said, folding his up as if he had been trying again.

"Can I have some hot chocolate?" I asked. Everyone who had stayed inside was drinking something out of steaming mugs and I wanted some too.

"Oh, I'm sorry, of course," Karen said. They must've been talking about something really important that was able to throw her off her role of perfect hostess so much that she could forget to offer something to warm us up.

But I would really rather have Ashley offer something to warm me up. Oh great, now my libido was back in action, with its usual

71

perfect sense of timing.

"We didn't see anything out there," George said, sitting on the couch next to Kevin. "Nothing made it look like anybody besides us has been out there doing anything."

"What do you think the chances are of us going anywhere now that the snow has stopped?" Don asked.

George shook his head.

"There's no telling what condition the roads will be in if we could even get a car up the driveway, which we can't," I said. George and I had briefly discussed this when we were out near the cars. We were all perfectly snowed in and out of communication with the world. The cars were mere mounds of snow, you couldn't see the driveway, and it looked as if the road hadn't even heard of a snowplow or salt yet. The only car with a chance, Karen's gigantic Explorer, was surrounded by all the other vehicles. But even if we could get it free, even it didn't have a chance in drifts this size.

"So we're trapped—trapped like mice in a cage," Robert said. He still looked like someone who'd drunk a case of Jolt. He was pacing back and forth, constantly looking around, as if unsure whom to trust.

I couldn't really blame him. I sat down with my back to the stove. Somehow, it felt safer to know there were only three directions from which someone could surprise me with a knife, scissors, cleaver, rope or big fisherman's hook.

Kevin looked first at Robert, then at me. "If nobody else has come near here, and we've searched the house, then it must be one of us." He said it quite matter-of-factly. There was no sign of his wisecracking fagboy arse now.

Karen returned with mugs of hot chocolate. I took mine gratefully. I was suddenly feeling quite chilled again. I thought about poison—as in someone might have poisoned it—but I was cold. *Fuck it.*

After a large, comforting swallow, something in my head suddenly clicked. I could almost feel the light bulb blinking over my head. I stood. "We saw that Trisha was dead and we've searched the house. Now her body is missing—but *we've searched the house*."

Ashley jumped up from her seat on the chair. "She's got to be somewhere!"

"We were all together during the search," I said. "Weren't we?"

Everyone looked at each other, as if mentally checking to ensure no one had been absent for any period during the search.

"So where's Trisha's body?" Ashley slowly said.

Suddenly, from out of nowhere, Robert said, while looking directly at me, "Trisha was your ex."

"What?" I said, amazed.

"Oh, for God's sake, Robert, haven't you ever heard about lesbians and their exes?" Ashley said.

"Lesbians are always *friends* with their exes," Kevin explained to Robert. "They lose their ID card if they aren't."

"You might as well be saying that Kevin and I weren't with the rest of you during the search," George said, "after all, we were watching all your asses."

I wasn't sure what I should be feeling right now—grief over Trisha, confusion as to what was happening, anger that someone was trying to point a finger at me, hurt that I was being questioned, or fear that death might strike again. Not even death. It was more than mere death. It was a person who was killing us. A cold-blooded killer. A murderer. Perhaps even serial killer.

What I knew was that my mind was all over the place because I had to push away ridiculous images of mutilated cartons of breakfast food. Poor little cereal.

I stood up. I couldn't believe my friends were trying to place blame on me, but I knew they must've discussed it while George, Jamie and I were outside because of the way they were looking at me, the way they were acting toward me. They discussed it when

I wasn't here to defend myself, and apparently no one else had stood up for my honor.

I thought about mentioning that Jamie had also slept with Trisha, but decided against it. "This doesn't make any sense," I said. "What happened to Trisha's body?" I looked around the group, then got up and grabbed a flashlight.

"Where're you going?" Ashley asked, touching my wrist.

"Upstairs. I want to look over Trisha and Jamie's room." I hated the thought that one of my friends was a murderer, and I couldn't bear that any one of them thought I was a murderer. I needed to figure this out. It was a puzzle to solve, that was it. That was what I had to do—solve this puzzle. Any other way of looking at it was unbearable, though I knew in the days, weeks, months and years to come I would do it quite often enough.

"We decided that nobody should be alone at any time," Ashley said. I looked around the group, as if searching for a volunteer, before Ashley said, "I'll go with you."

I again looked at the others. "Karen? Denise? Jamie? Anyone else coming with?"

I didn't wait for an answer, instead I headed upstairs. Apparently the feelings against me ran pretty deep, because Ashley was alone in joining me. Great, so now I wasn't just grieving or afraid, I was hurt. I even forgot about Ashley's nearness to me because I was too damned busy being overwhelmed, and when that was nigh unbearable, a swarm of dark faerie ran over my grave.

Everything seemed magnified—the silence, the creaks in the floorboards as the house settled, the darkness that pervaded everything but the path of my flashlight.

I found myself opening doors as I passed them—not only to peer inside the other rooms briefly, in order to ensure that nothing was out of place, but also so the light coming in the windows from outside could help alleviate some of the darkness in the hallway.

Once inside Jamie and Trisha's room, I again noticed how the light glistened off the not-quite-dried blood. I also again noticed the chill that crept up my spine.

Followed by Ashley, I went to take a closer look at the bed. The blood had already soaked into the quilt and sheets, and apparently there had been quite a bit of it, judging by how it had spread. Some had even dripped or spattered down to the floor and was oily on the bottom of my socks.

There was a strange odor in the room, something that was familiar, but I couldn't quite place. It was so faint, I was sure I was only noticing it because of my other senses feeling deadened. The darkness threatened my sight, and the peculiar muffling effects of the snow surrounding the house deadened all outside noise till there were only the sounds of Ashley and me breathing.

I sniffed again. "What type of perfume are you wearing?"

"My perfume?"

"Yeah. What is it?"

"Shawn. We're in the room where a woman died and that's all you can think of?"

I was surprised the blood hadn't dried yet, but of course, cold floors took a long time to dry during the winter.

I felt Ashley's gaze on me, but I couldn't tell if she was surprised or grossed out by my next actions. What can I say, I'm a very tactile person. I held my breath and tried not to throw up as I put my finger into the blood. I had to breathe to sniff it. The bright red stuff on my finger didn't smell like I expected. It didn't feel like I expected, either. Though I resented it as a lesbian, every month I had a lesson in what blood looked, felt and smelled like. Apparently, what's in our veins is a little different.

I wiped my finger on one of the clean spots of the sheets, and it left a vague, greasy red shine on my finger. I felt the bile rise in my throat and knew why I hadn't ever gone beyond that first biology class when they made me dissect a poor, helpless little frog.

I could feel Ashley's presence in the room. It was so quiet I thought I could hear her heart beating.

Maybe it wasn't a murderer after all, but maybe a vampire who was a really messy eater. Of course, this silly thought made me wonder what Buffy would do.

I looked around the room. Like ours, it was small and cozy, but it wasn't as warm. A lamp that had once been on the bedside table was now on the floor, and the bedding was tossed around a bit, as if Trisha had fought against her attacker, at least briefly. When I went to right the lamp I was nearer to the window, and the chill was unmistakable.

I was right.

No way would this window have been open earlier, not with the heat and electric down. Everyone was trying to make sure the place stayed warm because we weren't sure how long we'd be trapped here.

I shone the flashlight out the window. This particular room looked out toward the road—over the garage. There were footsteps in the snow on top of the garage, which wasn't as deep as it was on the ground. The tilted roof common in snow country took care of that.

I looked down to the ground. It looked a long way off. It also looked very cold outside and I was just wearing socks on my feet.

"What is it, Shawn?"

I again played the flashlight around the room.

"Irish, what are you looking for?" Ashley asked when I began digging through Jamie's and Trisha's things.

"Shoes and a jacket or something."

"You're not going out there, are you?"

"I need to check this out. There are footsteps on the roof of the garage."

"Is that what you were looking at?"

I found a pair of Trisha's tennis shoes. Fortunately, we were both the same size. While I put those on, Ashley found a pair of

Jamie's boots and donned them, then a jacket as well.

"You're not coming with me, are you?" I asked.

"Remember our little talk earlier about nobody being left alone? We just discussed it a few minutes ago. I know your mind's not what it used to be, Shawn dear, but . . ." I stopped to look at her, and all I could do was realize that she had just called me *dear*.

I quickly pulled myself together. "Ashley, no one's going to attack me when I'm on the roof—I mean, where would they come from? Anyway, it could be slippery and stuff out there."

"Who's worried about you? I'm worried about being left alone in here, okay? This place gives me the creeps."

I lifted the window the rest of the way and a cold breeze came in to surround me. I was hit with the sudden chilling thought that if a deep freeze came right now, we could be trapped for quite a while alone out in the middle of nowhere.

I stepped out onto the roof, working to get a good footing with my first foot before following with the other. I leaned up toward the roof's apex, to balance my weight on the slope, while I played my flashlight over the surrounding ground. It was more difficult from this distance to discern the differences in older and newer footprints down on the ground, but I could tell there weren't any disruptions in the pure snow farther from the house.

What I had thought were footprints on the rooftop weren't. What they were I couldn't quite make out, but I was sure someone had been out here. It looked almost as if someone had tried to obliterate their footprints as they made their way across the roof.

While Ashley watched, I carefully inched forward to a clear place with untouched snow. I walked a few feet, then drew my foot across my prints to obliterate them. All in all, it looked pretty much like the older path across the roof looked like.

"What are you doing?" Ashley asked.

"Look at this." I pointed to my recently made trail and then to the original. "Someone's intentionally trying to cover something up. They couldn't totally cover their tracks, so they did the next best thing." But it didn't make sense—why would someone do such a poor job of covering their tracks—or go to so much trouble to do so when it was still just as apparent that someone had been there?

Ashley bent down to her haunches and examined the earlier prints. "They didn't want us to see their prints—they covered up the size and brand of their boots."

I saw that Ashley was right. Those two key clues were totally obliterated by the brush job. Whoever had done this was being very careful.

I slowly moved across the snowy roof with my feet sliding just a bit with each step. It took me a moment to realize Ashley had a grip on the back of my jeans, as if that would really help either of us if we fell.

Realistically, the roof was only about a dozen feet off the ground. And all the snow on the ground would provide a lot of padding if one of us were to slide. Regardless, I wasn't real excited by heights, so I could feel the blood pumping through my body and in my ears as I carefully moved along.

Suddenly, Ashley gasped and I felt a rough tug at the back of my jeans. I whipped around and cost Ashley her grip on my trousers, but I was able to grab her by the wrist even as I slipped on the slick roofing. I threw my weight up and away from the edge, losing my footing but grinding my shoes into the roof so as to hold us briefly in this precarious position.

Ashley's eyes were wide with fear and shock. The snow was melting coldly against my back, down my clothes, soaking me through again as I slowly inched us away from the edge. Balancing against the slickness of the roof required every ounce of my energy, as well as all the leverage, strength and balance I could put into it. It took Ashley a moment to get her feet back on the roof so she could help with the effort, but she was pretty quick in realizing I wasn't going to let her fall.

Once we were both sitting securely on the roof, Ashley glanced down toward the ground. "I guess it's not so far away after all."

"No, it's not. But it would still hurt."

"Thanks."

"No problem. Just remember you owe me one now," I said with a grin, trying to lighten the mood.

"Hmm, and how would you like me to repay you?" Ashley asked with an almost natural wink. "Take it out in trade?"

Ashley simply wasn't getting it. She must not know just how attractive I found her, and was just acting like Kevin always did—constantly flirting with anyone within flirting distance without worrying about the consequences.

At the end of the roof, the farthest point from the house, I stopped and shone the light out across the surrounding area.

I couldn't believe it but a good twelve feet from the garage was something in the snow that looked like a weird, deformed snow angel, highlighted with bits of red. Leading away from that were footsteps going away from the garage and out into the snowy night.

I couldn't believe George and I hadn't noticed the markings when we went around the house, let alone that anyone was able to heave Trisha's body so far. Unless there was more than one person involved. Which could be another reason the tracks had been obliterated—so the number of people involved couldn't be discerned either. Because, from what I had seen, there really could have been more than one person.

I started crawling down to the edge of the roof, wondering if the snow was deep enough to cushion me if I jumped.

"Shawn? Shawn? What are you doing?"

I wanted to jump off the bloody roof and track down my ex's murderer, but my torch suddenly flickered and dimmed. I banged it against my hand.

"Shawn, you can't jump down there," Ashley said, sliding down the roof toward me. How did she know me so well?

"Dammit," I said, banging the torch against my palm yet again. It went out.

"There you go. You can't track down anything without a flashlight."

I glared up at her.

She cupped her hand around mine and the flashlight. "You don't have a light and you might hurt yourself jumping. You have to be realistic." She slowly pulled me to my feet and together, holding hands all the way, we trekked carefully back across the treacherous rooftop.

I noticed a few red blotches in the snow along the roof. Someone had indeed dragged a bloody corpse from the room, across the roof, and heaved it into the snow a ways away from the house. The little bit of time between the murder and the moving of the body hadn't been enough to stanch the flow of blood. Well, even I knew blood didn't pump in a dead body, but all the blood on it would've spread as it was dragged along.

I let Ashley crawl in through the window ahead of me as I looked back over the rooftop. My fists clenched in anger. How could anyone drag Trisha's body out like so much trash? How could anyone destroy that beautiful, vivacious woman?

I slammed my fist against the wall. "Goddammit, Trish, he's not gonna get away with it."

8

Maniacal Maniacs Make Much Mayhem

"Great, so there was a maniac in the house with us," Kevin said once Ashley and I told everyone what we had seen.

"Then that's good news," Karen said. Everyone looked at her as if she were nuts. "It means it wasn't—isn't—one of us."

"Well, gee, that's such a relief, Karen," Robert said. "One of our friends is dead, but one of us didn't kill her. Somebody has been in the house with us, somebody who doesn't belong has been freely coming and going, but at least we now know it's a stranger." He was obviously still on edge. "That's such a god-damned fucking relief!"

"Freaking out isn't gonna do us any good." I clenched my fist again. "We need to work out what we're gonna do." I wanted to follow the tracks from the snow angel. I wanted to follow the trail of my ex-lover's blood.

"How do we know there's only one of them?" Jamie asked.

"Or that one of us isn't involved? I mean, what reason would a complete stranger have for coming in here and killing Trisha?" I noticed she had finally put down her bottle of Jack. It was almost empty.

Once again, we were all gathered in the living room, which was the warmest room in the house. I did have a chill in my bones that I couldn't quite seem to get rid of, but I didn't think it had anything to do with the temperature. Regardless, no matter how ugly the furniture here was, it really was rather warm and cozy, especially with the firelight casting a glow over everything.

I sat in my usual place near the stove with Ashley next to me. Even the nearness of this incredible woman couldn't cut the coldness I felt inside. Ashley had been keeping close to me, usually making some sort of physical contact, so I was beginning to feel a little like Linus's security blanket. I didn't mind because I needed any measure of safety and security I could get as well. Not to mention the occasional cheap thrill. The only thing that could touch the cold running through me was the warmth of Ashley's body, no matter how sick and twisted it seemed with all that was happening around us.

"Can I get anybody some hot chocolate? Something stronger?" Karen asked suddenly, rising from her cozy position against Don.

When nobody said anything, Kevin said, "Why don't I help you make us all some hot cocoa? I don't think anybody really needs anything stronger. We need to keep our senses straight, so to speak, but I know I've got a chill I can't get rid of."

"We need to see where those tracks lead to," Don said. He looked at me. "You said you saw tracks outside. We need to follow them, see where they go."

"You want to go out there in the dark?" Jamie said. "With barely any candles left and so little juice in the flashlights?"

He shrugged. "It's probably lighter out there than it is in here. And I don't think any of us are going to be able to sleep tonight. I know I need something to keep me from going crazy." He glanced suggestively at Robert. "We need to follow whatever clues we've got."

"Count me in," I said.

"But who's going to watch the house while we're outside?" Ashley asked. "I mean, somebody could just sneak in—"

"Someone already has full run of the place," I said.

"*We* don't even have a key," Karen solemnly reminded them.

"What?" Don said. "Then how'd you get in?"

"We broke in," I said. "Karen left the key at home." I looked over at Karen. "This *is* your place, right?"

"Yes, yes it is," Karen said. "I wouldn't pull a stunt like that these days."

"So we can either break up and leave some here while the rest go follow the tracks—" I began.

"Robert, Denise, George and Kevin stay here," Jamie said, looking us over. "Ashley, Shawn, Don, Karen and I will go out."

I didn't care that my toes were still blue. "Come on. I want to see where those tracks lead."

"I can go out again," George said.

"No, you can't—you're staying here with me!" Kevin said.

"You okay?" Ashley asked, touching my arm. I knew I had to stay with her.

I grimaced at Karen. "Can you find me yet another set of dry clothing?"

When we were all thoroughly insulated against the increasingly cold Michigan winter night, we went through the breezeway and out the side door of the garage. The wind had picked up even more, and the coldness of the night was freezing the top layer of snow so that with every step my feet broke through to become swamped in the soft powder beneath.

"Hang on a sec," I said, "I want to get something from my car!" I had to raise my voice to be heard across the wind, which whipped my words away from the group.

"We'll go to the spot," Don yelled back. "You said it was just beyond the garage?"

"Yes!"

"I'll go with Shawn," Ashley said, still staying close to me. We fenceposted over to the pile of snow that was my car.

"Shit," I mumbled, surveying the heap. I brushed my arm over the area I thought was a door, and got a better idea of where the lock was at from that. Fortunately, the lock did not appear to be frozen, so I gave the key a try. It turned fine.

Alas, the *door* was frozen. I tugged on it, and pulled, and cursed, all to no avail.

"Let me try," Ashley said. "You go try the other side."

I trudged through the snow to the other side, cleared it off, unlocked it and began the fight to get it open. I wondered if all the cars were in such shape and if any of them would even start at this point. I hadn't thought it was cold enough to freeze them, but then again, it really was cold out, and it was no longer snowing, which meant it could be below freezing.

I brought my foot up against the car, got a good grip on the handle, and pulled back with all my might, leveraging myself with my propped foot. The door didn't give, but I lost my grip and flew backward into the snow. Ashley came into view a moment later and burst into laughter.

"You think this is funny?" I said in my most serious voice as I brushed uselessly at my clothes. I approached Ashley with a grim look, trying to cover my stupid accident with something else. I hated looking like a fool, especially since Ashley was looking so very beautiful in the moonlight of this shockingly clear night. Such a shockingly clear night meant it could get very cold indeed.

Ashley looked at my white form, then broke out into more laughter.

"You think this is funny?" I repeated. Ashley didn't stop laughing, but she did meet my gaze, looking deep into me with those beautiful eyes. I took the final step to her, closing the gap between us and pulled her into my arms, bringing our lips together.

Ashley stopped laughing. First her hands were against my chest, as if she meant to push me away, but then she wrapped her arms around my neck, molding our bodies together.

Her soft lips parted under mine, inviting me into the warmth of her mouth. My tongue shyly touched hers, and I felt as if I were going to melt from the incredible softness of it. I felt my pulse quicken and my knees weaken. Ashley fell back against the car, moaning softly, spurring me on. Our lips explored each other's softness, with our tongues flicking out to occasionally brush and caress.

Breathlessly, I pulled back and gazed at Ashley's soft features. I smiled, pulled off a glove, and tenderly let my fingers caress Ashley's face. "I've wanted to do that, really do that, for so long," I said.

Ashley brushed her lips over my fingers. "So have I," she said, bringing up a hand to guide one of my fingertips into the warmth of her mouth, where she gently sucked and licked it for a moment, causing a fire to break out somewhere below my stomach.

Still meeting Ashley's gaze, I said, "My skis. I came here to get my skis."

"So?" That lovely tongue, those incredible lips . . .

"I brought my cross-country skis with me and thought they might be useful right about now." I knew we had to get down to the business at hand, because that had to be taken care of before we could get to the other business currently occupying most of my mind and senses. God, I wanted this woman.

"Can I ride on the back?"

I grinned. "I'm not sure if that'd work, but we can try."

A few more tugs on the door later it finally gave and I was able to unload the skis and equipment, then sit down in the car to change into my cross-country boots and the knee-high Gore-Tex gaiters that would keep snow from slipping down to my ankles.

Once I was done I locked the car, not wanting anyone but myself to mess with it, and then Ashley and I headed toward the spot where we had seen the markings in the snow.

Ashley tried to stand on the back of my skis for the trip, but her boots kept sliding off the slick surface. Also, her additional weight caused the backs of the skis to sink into the snow. I had thought about offering my boots to Ashley to wear, but I had donned them with something particular in mind, something that might be a bit dangerous. I wanted to be the one taking the chances.

With the skis, I would be the fastest of the group, and something farther off might need to be investigated. Although I was foolhardy enough to volunteer for such a mission away from the rest, I didn't want to risk Ashley to such a thing.

Don, Karen and Jamie were pacing around the markings in the snow, and had been for some time, which, of course, meant that they had totally ruined any chance anyone had to identify much at all from the initial, red-spotted area.

But I was still able to decipher a colored area that wasn't pure snow, but wasn't red or yellow, either. I bent down and picked up some of the snow in my gloved hand and sniffed it. Then I tasted it.

"What the heck are you doing, Irish?" Jamie asked, bending down beside me.

"God, I hope that wasn't yellow snow I just saw you eating," Karen said, coming closer.

I looked up at them and shook my head. The snow had tasted a bit like tea. I stood and looked around. Leading away from this spot was a single trail. It looked as if whoever had made it thought about doing the same trick they had done on the roof: The tracks were somewhat smudged, as if they had dragged a

86

foot over them after making them. In snow this deep, however, this did not work. The smudging only covered the top surface of the snow, but the actual footsteps were much deeper. Apparently they had also realized this because this apparent tactic stopped just a few feet from where we stood. They apparently didn't want to waste time with things that didn't work.

The night was silent. No sounds came from the distant road. Our isolation was complete.

I aimed a flashlight toward where the footprints disappeared into a tree line. "We need to go in that direction," I said. No one moved.

"At least now it looks like there's only one of them," Ashley said, again coming to my side.

"Not necessarily," I said. "One could go in front and the other followed in the same prints. Because of the way the boot shifts on its way down through the snow, whatever its real size is, it leaves a pretty big print, which means no big in trying to walk in those manly sized prints." I knelt, glad of the flexibility of cross-country boots.

"Still, if it was more than one person, how could they have jumped off the roof and into the same place as the first person?" Karen asked.

"Look at the size of this area," I said, pointing out the large vicinity that had been totally ransacked so no footprints were identifiable.

"I just thought of something," Ashley said. "Shouldn't we watch what we do? After all, isn't all of this now a crime scene, and cops are going to need to go over it?"

"I think the snow's already covered it up pretty well."

"I guess you've got a point."

"And that's where whoever it was went," I pointed the flashlight toward the trees. I looked around at my reluctant mates and headed in that direction myself, reasoning I could move the most quickly of all of us. Move and run, that was. In case something evil suddenly launched itself at me, intending to do me dire. Plus, somebody had to go first, and it didn't look like any of them were going to be moving anytime soon.

The other three trudged in my wake, sinking up to their hips with each step. I knew it couldn't be that deep everywhere, they were just in the midst of some really bad drifts caused by the proximity of the buildings, vehicles, fences and trees.

I followed the old footprints, quietly shooshing over the top of the snow on my skis. My senses were on alert, rather like they were whenever I had walked on the Michigan State University campus alone at night. MSU was one of the top places in the country to be raped, so I had always been listening with a keen ear and watching for anything happening around me when I walked alone there after dark.

I did the same now, listening and watching for anyone in the trees, trees that brought sudden darkness to the moonlit night. I heard a quiet sound somewhere in the distance in front of me, so I shone the light in that direction. All was quiet, all seemed natural enough. The wind blew through the trees, or what was left of them without their summertime finery. Even here there were enough firs and other evergreens to prevent me from easily seeing through them.

I paused, waiting for the others to catch up. Really, I just didn't want to venture into the darkness alone, or at least not without the others nearby. Especially not with that sound up ahead. I knew I recognized it, knew it, but I couldn't for the life of me figure out what it was.

I turned around just in time to see Ashley get her foot stuck in the snow and take a nosedive into it. She resurfaced a moment later, looking quite a bit like Frosty the Snowman. I might've been amused or empathized with her, but I was too busy noticing just how lovely she was.

I turned back toward the trees. The sound was still there—a low sound, going on continuously with few variations in it. What went on continuously, not stopping? Besides the Energizer Bunny?

"What's going on?" Don asked when they caught up with me.

"Shh," I commanded. "Listen."

"What is that?" Ashley asked a moment later, after they had all heard the noise I was referring to.

I shrugged. Well, I shrugged as well as anyone in an oversized parka and sweatshirt could shrug. "I dunno."

"Well, lead on," Don said, a slight trepidation in his voice.

I slowly moved forward, even more aware of my surroundings than before, if that was at all possible. When I got into the trees, I had to move my skis around a bit to maneuver, but it wasn't as if I were going downhill at a high rate of speed while I did it. I was on fairly level terrain, and cross-country skis did quite well at this sort of thing.

The sound was definitely familiar, and I was fairly certain it was not man-made. No one would make such a sound continuously for so long without a machine of some sort, and it really wouldn't make any sense to bring a machine out here just to make a weird noise. When I realized this, my confidence rose, and I sped up.

I abruptly halted in my tracks. Fortunately no one was directly behind me to push me forward. But still, all I could think was, "Bollocks."

In front of me was a fairly shallow stream.

The tracks went right into it. It looked as if perhaps the person, or people, who had gone this way had dawdled a bit at this point, as if deciding what to do. But again it was impossible to determine how many people there were because, with the trees granting some amount of cover, less snow had fallen here and whoever I was tracking had realized this and again obliterated most identifying portions of their tracks.

I shone the light along the opposite side, but just as I suspected, whoever it was didn't go right across. They either waded through the water up or down stream for a bit, or hopscotched along the branches and rocks that poked their heads up through it. There was no telling how far they went in this manner before making the cross to the other side.

The rest of the group came up behind me.

"There's no telling where they went," I said.

"We've got five sets of eyes," Don said. "Let's work our way down toward the lake first. We know it's not that far. We just need to keep our eyes peeled for anything."

Whoever did this knew the lay of the land. They had known there was no way to cover their tracks totally, but they managed to avoid detection for as long as possible—sweeping up behind themselves on the roof, and making the deformed snow angel on their landing spot. I had no doubt there was another such ruse going on here.

I could sense that tensions were high because of all we had been through. Fear was the adrenaline keeping us all going for so many hours without sleep. That fear deepened with the flickering of the flashlights, a bold statement that the batteries would not last much longer. The woods, protected as they were by the branches from the moonlight, could be even darker and spookier when overactive imaginations were added into the mix.

And we definitely had those. Every branch and bramble was an unknown attacker coming from behind, every noise was the murderer stalking us. I could practically hear the banshee crying in the distance. A distance that lessened with every moment.

I was going to lose my mind.

9

Every One for Her/Himself

When the batteries on one flashlight gave out, and it was apparent that those in the others were almost gone, we had to give in and realize we couldn't spot any tracks in the dark. Inside the house, the fire was almost out. I could see it as we walked around it to the back door.

We hadn't even been able to make it all the way to the lake.

"I still can't believe you only have a handful of candles and a few half-dead flashlights around here," Ashley said as we trudged through the snow.

"Ashley," Karen replied. "How many candles do you keep at your place? And I will have you know that these flashlights were fine till we used them so much."

"Ash," I said into her ear, wrapping an arm around her waist. "We're all going through a lot right now. Taking it out on Karen isn't going to help anything." Tempers were running high, getting even worse than they had already been.

The only thing holding me together was trying to hold us all together.

"I'm going to bed," I finally said, unable to take this any longer. With that, I picked up a candle and went to the stairs. As I was going up, I slowed down to hear anything that was said.

"She's guilty," Robert said. "It's her. Otherwise, she wouldn't be willing to go upstairs all by herself."

"But if it's somebody from outside—" Karen started.

"Then they're coming and going as they please and we're all still in danger!"

"Or there's somebody here who's helping them," Don said in a low voice.

I went upstairs to my bedroom where I angrily began pulling off my shirt and jeans. I heard a noise behind me and whipped around to see what it was. My nerves were on edge, and I was trying to shut out everything I was feeling.

Ashley stood in the doorway, framed by the subtle light that was falling indoors from the outdoors. That snow/mirror effect again. She slowly closed the door behind her and stood with her back to it.

"I don't think you did it," she said in a low voice.

I turned my back to her, lifted my T-shirt around my neck, pulled off my bra and then put my T-shirt back on.

"And I didn't mean what I said. I'm just scared like everybody else. I'm sorry, Shawn." She put her hands softly on my shoulders from behind.

Hot, angry, tears began to run down my face. I tried to keep them in, but they were stubborn little bastards. "You can go back down with the rest. I'll be fine, Ash."

Ashley turned me to face her. "I know you, Shawnie, you try to bottle everything up inside. You're so afraid of letting people know they've hurt you or made you angry." She took my head in her hands and gently brushed away my tears with her thumbs, which made them come all the harder.

"Why—how could they think that about me?" I managed to gasp out between sobs. Ashley's kindness was making it all the harder. I was hurting—not only for what had just happened, but because it looked like one of my friends was dead and I had been refusing to accept it so it was just hitting me now. Granted, I still had to hold it together to get out of here safe myself, so I couldn't really grieve, but still I did. Some. I hurt deep down inside and I just wanted Ashley to pull me into her arms and hold me. Mother me like Trisha always had.

Ashley pulled my head down to her shoulder and held me, gently stroking my hair. Her hair was soft against my face, her perfume an intoxicating musky scent with just a hint of sweetness. I allowed my arms to circle her slender waist and bring me in a bit closer, pressing our bodies together even tighter. Just this moment was all I wanted, all I asked for.

"Huh, I'm getting your shirt all wet," I said, raising my head from her shoulder. My face was still wet, although the tears had just about stopped.

"It's all right, honey," Ashley said, pulling my head back to her shoulder.

I knew something had to happen. Ashley was far too near, my body feeling way too good against hers. If something didn't happen, I was going to do something even stupider than one of my trademarked Stupid Moves.

I raised my head to meet Ashley's gaze. Even in the dim light, I could see their shining depths. "What's going on, Ashley?"

"Oh, Irish," Ashley said, tousling my hair lightly. "Can I just give you the *Reader's Digest* condensed version?" Her expression suddenly seemed much deeper and less teasing. "Basically I came out right after the last time we saw each other, and have been living in a very deep and very tight closet ever since. Jamie's been after me to come out for quite a while now, and all this just seems to support the reasons I was staying in."

I was dumbfounded, knocked almost speechless. Almost. "How did Jamie know?"

Ashley shrugged. "She guessed it somehow. She wanted to be my first—y'know how Jamie is."

"Yeah, I do." I never could figure out what Jamie got from lesbian virgins, because so much of being good in bed as a dyke came from experience, and if you were someone's first they didn't have any experience so . . . It just really didn't make any sense.

Finally it dawned on me. I was sometimes a little slow. Especially if someone did actually try to change the subject or utilize any other clever distractionary techniques.

"So you're a lesbian," I said. "And Jamie knew this. And Jamie wanted to be your first. But she wasn't—"

Somehow Ashley cut me off with a mere grin—a small, slow one that worked its way across her features, beginning with her lips and ending with her eyes. "I wanted you to be my first."

"—And you have a whole hell-of-a-lot of internalized homophobia," I finished my sentence, pushing it out with a deep breath so we wouldn't be thrown into a really incredibly awkward silence when I melted into the ground and became a disgustingly gooey puddle on the floor. Ashley had wanted me to be her first. *Wanted* me to be her first.

"Shawn, did you hear what I said?" she murmured lowly, so softly I had to strain to hear her. I could see she was suddenly very nervous.

Sometimes when you hear something you've dreamt and fantasized about for years, if it suddenly becomes more than a dream, escalates to a remote possibility, you are faced with the incredible power to be of an unsurpassed stupidity. At least, if your name's Shawn Donnelly, you are.

"Uh. Yeah. I did," I prosaically replied. Why would this goddess want a prat like me? That is, if she still wanted me. Oh, God, what if she didn't?

It was almost as if Ashley could read my mind. "You are so adorable." She again tousled my hair. "You make me laugh." She moved impossibly closer to me, and my stomach decided that this would be the perfect moment to fall right out of me and to the ground. "You're sweet and kind and intelligent and a good listener." She brushed her hand along my cheek. "And I like the way you look at me. The way you've always looked at me. You make me feel sexy, beautiful and brilliant."

I had to remind myself to breathe when I gazed into the unguarded depths of her beautiful eyes. I knew I should grab this moment, before it passed, and kiss her, but I wasn't one of those women who could be so bold and brazen. So instead I chose a classic Shawn Donnelly move and whimpered deep in my throat and backed up against the nightstand, tipping the lamp off it.

Ashley suddenly looked uncertain. "I'm sorry, Irish, it's just that I thought . . . I thought you liked me. I mean, with the way you look at me and all."

It took me what seemed like an eternity to screw up the courage to actually say anything, me being the queen of the gobshites and all. "I do like you, Ash."

She took a deep breath and kept her distance. "Is there someone else?"

"Uh, no, no there isn't."

"You're not attracted to me?"

"Oh God, Ashley, you are the most incredibly attractive, beautiful, sensuous woman I've ever met."

"Then why are you running away from me?"

"I'm scared."

"Of what?" Ashley said in surprise, or was that amazement?

I had to work to meet her gaze. Not just because the rest of her was so pleasing to the eye, but because I was so timid about actually admitting to my crush. "Of making a fool of myself," I finally murmured.

"So I've got to take all the chances here?" she said. She took a step forward and I couldn't back up anymore. The nightstand was already tight against the backs of my knees.

I had never before considered that Ashley was taking any chances. I thought what I wanted was clearer than the way my mother used to wash the glasses before we got a dishwasher and they all ended up spotted. My mother had never heard of Cascade, and of course, I didn't have a clue as to whether or not it actually worked, with its cascading action and all, and I also didn't have a clue what I should do with Ashley, except maybe kiss those soft lips I had dreamt about for so long. Kiss them again, that is.

I *was* a right prat.

I lifted my butt off the nightstand, moving ever so slight a fraction of an inch closer to her while I took a deep breath to prepare myself and then . . .

I wondered how Jamie had drunk so much Jack Daniel's and yet remained so sober. But at the same moment I realized that she was in theater, and I knew that thespians often used cold tea as a prop for whiskey.

The little voice inside my head suddenly sat up, tapped me on the shoulder and said, "I told you so."

10

There Doesn't Seem to Be Anyone Around

"C'mon," I said to Ashley, taking her hands and pulling her back into the hallway. I could hear voices downstairs, where everyone was still gathered around the fire.

"Where are we going?" she asked, but I answered that by dragging her to Jamie and Trisha's room. "Are you nuts? I'm not going back in there!"

I left her standing in the hallway as I felt my way through the room to the bed. The blood was still wet.

I felt around until I found a book of matches in Jamie's backpack. She was always prepared for everything. I bet if I looked, I'd even find duct tape, which Jamie was sure could fix anything. Under the light from the match, I carefully inspected the bedspread, and then, after the match went out, I went through the rest of the contents of the room, my eyes gradually acclimating to the wan moonlight.

It was still slow going, though, in the relative darkness, but it sped up once I discovered the torch in Jamie's belongings.

"What are you doing in there?" Ashley whispered from the hallway.

"Soddin' bastards," I said, then, "Finding a few things."

"Where did you get that?" she asked, referring to the flashlight.

"In Jamie's things. Along with these." I held up a bottle of canola oil and a little container of what I was sure was red food coloring.

"What's going on?"

"We've been hoodwinked," I said, leading the way downstairs, where everyone was still gathered around the fireplace. "Where is she?" I demanded of Jamie.

"What do you mean?" Jamie replied, while everyone else looked up at me. I tried to tell who was truly surprised and who was in on it.

I looked over at Karen. "This would be a lot easier if you'd turn the lights back on."

"Irish, are you feeling okay?"

"No, I'm not. I'm actually rather pissed. As in angry—not drunk." I again looked at all of the faces around me, and then focused on Jamie. "So, how long have you been sober?" I picked up her now-empty bottle of Jack and ran my finger along the rim, bringing it up to my mouth to taste what I knew now was merely the tea it had contained earlier.

"What are you talking about?" Ashley asked.

I tossed the canola oil and red food coloring I had found in Jamie and Trisha's room onto the couch. "Jamie's favorite recipe for theatrical blood—except it's a bit oilier than real blood, and never coagulates. Earlier tonight I noticed the broom in the breezeway was sitting in a puddle of water, from when you used it to obliterate the footprints on the roof and around the area outside."

"So is that all?" Jamie asked with a smirk.

"Hold on," Denise said, standing. "What the fuck's going on?"

"Just about," I said to Jamie. "All I'm wondering now is where Trisha really is, and whether you spilled the Jack outside by where the body was tossed on purpose or on accident."

"On purpose, of course," Jamie said with a wink.

Don looked at me. "Damn well took you long enough, Irish."

"What's going on?" Ashley said, staring around at everyone.

"Got ya!" Karen said, tweaking the tip of Ashley's nose.

"What the hell is going on here?" Ashley whispered, her face pale, her entire body trembling. Her gaze darted back and forth across the room and Don, Karen, Jamie and me.

I looked at Ashley, about to reach over to reassure her, let her know everything was all right, that it had all been a great, warped game . . .

But it hadn't been. They'd royally fucked with me and I realized I didn't know who all was involved to what extent—Ashley could be involved as well. There was no telling to what extent her actions had been pre-scripted. She and Denise and who knew who else could just be acting as well.

I backed away from Ashley. My excitement at figuring it out was gone, my relief to realize no one was dead and no one was a murderer vanished in a puff of rage. They had scared me, they had put me through the worst hours of my life, made me question everything I had ever held dear, everything I had ever thought or felt.

I had been living in a hell imposed upon me by those I had thought to be my friends. The betrayal was complete.

"You're all fucking assholes," Ashley whispered at Jamie and Karen.

"Are you telling me nobody got killed here?" Denise asked in apparent outrage. "Are you telling me you were all just putting us on?"

"C'mon, Irish, we used to put each other on all the time in college," Robert said.

"This is different," I said. "We're adults now. I thought this was all real." But throughout it all I had kept remembering all the pranks and stunts we used to pull on each other all the time. Maybe somewhere deep inside I'd known this wasn't real. Believing I'd thought this wasn't real made it easier to explain why I hadn't truly mourned Trisha fully and earlier. Why I'd worried so much about me and forgot about her. "It was real this time."

"No, no, it wasn't," Karen said, looking at me with sorrow-filled eyes. "It was just like everything we used to do. We didn't think you'd have a problem with it." She turned to face Ashley and me. "We thought once you knew, you'd realize we'd just had you like we used to do." She looked at Ashley. "I'm sorry if we hurt you."

"So this was all a put-on," Ashley said.

"I just cannot fucking believe this!" Denise said, waving her hands in the air.

"Okay, will someone please walk me through this?" Ashley said, putting on her most patient voice.

I was having none of it. I left the room. Behind me I heard Ashley angrily asking again what was happening, then I heard Karen tell Don to fill Ashley in.

"Listen, Irish, it's not what you think," Karen said, following me.

"And just how the *fuck* do you have any *soddin'* idea what the *feck* I'm thinking?"

I had turned to face Karen, and now Karen backed away, a mixture of emotions crossing her face. "We wanted to put together a mystery weekend sort of thing but we needed to do some things first—"

"Like what? See how badly you could make friends turn against each other? See how many of us you could drive insane?

See how much you could fuck with all of us?"

"Like test out some of the stunts, do a sort of dry run. And we also needed to get some professionals involved."

"Professionals?" I had figured out that no one had actually died, that it was all props and stunts, but I hadn't been sure what the purpose of it was. "What sort of professionals are you talking about?"

"Well, for example, somebody in say, advertising."

"Karen, for fuck's sake, I'm a media person. I buy and plan media."

"Yeah, well we discussed it and wanted to get you to help us out. C'mon, Irish, remember some of the stuff you used to do in college? You're not just a media person—you did some great ads for that one class you had, and put together some killer plans for your senior project. You're the one we want to market this."

"You're not talking about a job, are you?"

"No, c'mon, we're talking about a hobby. Something fun to do, and if we make a coupla bucks . . ." Her sentence trailed off and she shrugged. "It'll be a chance to work together again, and, well, remember how much fun we used to have together?" Karen could be quite persuasive, especially when she started flirting, which she did now. She walked up to me and straightened my collar, looking into my eyes with a teasing grin. "I know I miss it, so do Robert, Jamie and Kevin. And it's a lot more fun as a hobby than some other things people have been known to do—like basket weaving or model rocketry."

"Hey, model rocketry is fun. Especially blowing them up." I had often put together the little rockets during the winter in my dorm room so we could all launch them spring term. But that was beside the point. The bitch was just trying to get me un-mad.

"And think of all the cute lesbians you could meet."

"But who's actually going to run this thing?"

"Mostly me," Jamie said, entering. "We've got all of that

worked out. I'm definitely in charge of all the makeup and theatrical effects—"

"And they enlisted me for some special construction projects," Robert said, coming in behind her.

I gave up and led the posse back into the living room, figuring we ought to all have it out at once. "So you four and Don?" I asked. "That's all?"

"Yeah, I was just as shocked as you were, if you couldn't tell." Denise took a seat by the fire, her face as stormy as I felt. "Karen invited me to come to a reunion weekend, and the next thing I knew—" She practically growled.

"So you played with us all," Ashley said. "I don't believe this. I thought I could trust you all and you did this!" She stormed upstairs and I heard our door slam.

"So Ashley wasn't involved?" I asked.

"No, she wasn't," Karen said, blankly staring toward the staircase.

I looked at her, then the rest of the group. There was a chance they were lying about that, as this entire weekend was a lie. But if they weren't, if she hadn't been a part of the plot—and would Ashley, sweet little Ashley, have gone so far as to almost seduce me as part of an insane plot?

I didn't think so, and if this weekend had taught me anything, it was that sometimes you didn't get any more chances.

I dashed up the staircase, taking the steps two at a time. Our door was indeed closed. I knocked gently on it.

"Leave me alone!" Ashley yelled. I could hear her tossing things around in the room. She apparently forgot that regardless of everything else, being snowed in was not some trick or hoax, it was for real, and there was probably no way we were gonna be able to get out even yet.

"Ashley, it's me, it's me. It's Irish."

"I said leave me alone, or don't you Gaelics understand English very well?"

I opened the door.

"You bitch!" Ashley yelled. She then grabbed my half-packed bag and threw it at me. Fortunately, it was a fairly soft bag and her aim was really bad.

"Ash!"

"How could you! How could you make me think you meant it?" Her face was red and a few tears trickled down.

"I did!"

"How could you play along with them like that?" Tears were freely streaming down her face now.

"I didn't," I said, walking over to her and holding her just above her elbows. She tilted her head up so our eyes met and then tried to pull away, to turn her head. "Ashley, look at me."

Her gaze met mine in a challenge—but I wasn't sure what sort of a battle it was. Was it of wills, love or something more like a cat-staring contest? I wasn't sure, I just knew it was important, very, *very* important.

"Don't do this to me, Shawn," Ashley said. She waited, probably for me to back down or say something. I did neither. "Don't do this to me," she repeated, her voice dropping to a whisper, "not unless you mean it."

"Do *you* mean it?" I whispered back, stepping a fraction of a breath closer, "*Mo gra?*"

Ashley paused, I could almost see her processing everything that was going on, everything that had been said and, finally, translating that bit of Gaelic. She had to reach back to our college days, to a conversation we had had one drunken night in a car.

I never used that phrase with any of the women I dated, not even my girlfriends. But I had teased Ashley with it when we were doing a play together, and I had forgotten about it, until now.

It had taken Ashley a while to get the translation from me, and I suspected she had already discovered it, but still I wouldn't tell. Till one night after class when I was giving her a lift back to her apartment—her and her alone. We stopped by a liquor store and picked up a fifth of cheap whiskey before we pulled into Ashley's apartment parking lot.

And there Ashley and I had stayed, puffing and sipping away while talking, and that was when I finally admitted that *mo gra* meant, "my love."

The night was silent outside. I looked into Ashley's eyes and knew I wanted to be one with this incredible woman. I wanted to taste her, smell her, be with her and know her. I wanted to experience her.

She whispered, "*Mo gra*," and began to unbutton her sweater.

I helped her with the sweater, tossing it onto the floor, so I could kiss farther down her neck, enjoying the salty sweet taste of her and the musky scent of her perfume. I trailed my hand down over her full breasts and to the top of her jeans, undoing the snap and zipper. I could feel my own arousal increasing when I slipped my hands under Ash's jeans and realized she wasn't wearing any underwear.

Ashley raised her head to stretch her neck and entice me to continue kissing her there. I moved up to her ear, gently teasing it with my tongue before nibbling on the lobe.

"Oh, God, Shawn, please."

I grinned and brought my hands up to cup her breasts, feeling the nipples harden and extend under my palms. My tongue tangoed with Ashley's as I deftly unbuttoned her blouse, exposing the satiny white of her bra to the moonlight. I reached behind her and undid it, slowly kissing down her chest as I lowered the lacy bra over nicely toned arms until I took the ripe nipples into my mouth, first teasing them with my tongue, running it back and forth over the hardened buds, then gently biting them, drawing them deeper into my mouth.

I dropped down to my knees, licking my way down Ashley's stomach. I pulled her jeans down, revealing more and more of her beautifully sculpted body in my wake. I helped Ashley step out of them and gently blew on the triangle of blond hair nestled between her luscious thighs, causing Ashley's moans to increase.

Ashley's hands were again in my hair, directing me back to my feet.

"Oh, Irish, I need to feel you," Ashley said, her breathing hoarse while she fumbled with the buttons on my shirt. I pressed my own thigh between Ashley's legs, pushing into her, while she struggled with my clothes and I struggled to feel as much of her as possible. "Help me," Ashley finally said.

Always one to help a lady in distress, I quickly peeled off my shirt, jeans, socks and underwear, then led Ashley to the bed, laying her down before stretching out on top of her, molding our bodies together, breasts to breasts, thighs to thighs, stomach to stomach.

I could feel how wet she was, and knew how wet I was, but I still wanted to get closer. I needed to feel as one with Ashley and it seemed as if Ashley needed it too, for she urged me closer with her hands in my hair, pulling me nearer.

I could feel the sweat on our bodies lubricating our movements as Ashley arched against me. I wanted to be all over Ashley all at once. I moved down her body, kissing, licking and teasing my way over the smooth curves and the warmly toned muscles until I was right between her thighs.

I moved my hands down her thighs, spreading them wider, then lifted them up across my shoulders and tasted her, losing myself in the musky scent, the warm flowing, the sweet taste of her. I loved feeling her soft skin under my fingers as I ran my hands over the sinuous body while I dove deeper into her, lapping her up, making her moan and thrust and writhe across the bed, taking her closer and closer to the top, until finally in a frenzy she crested, her legs tight around my head, her hands entwined in my hair, her muscles tight as she rode my mouth.

I nestled Ashley in my arms. Her hair under my fingers was as incredibly silky as I had remembered and dreamed about.

I couldn't stay too angry with my friends about the trick they had played on me when it ended up like this. I could understand how they thought it wouldn't piss us off like it did. I was pissed, and I didn't know what to do with it. It was easier to just . . . forget about it. To just let it go.

Even if I already knew that Shawn Donnelly always gets even.

Now, I *could* worry about what they had in mind next. But I'd worry about that tomorrow.

"A long time ago," the old woman said on that night many years ago, *"upon this very land, there were many wars, and after the wars the people decided on a king, but another felt entitled to that ranking, so the king gave unto Lir, his first-born daughter—"*

"Ma!" Frances yelled from the kitchen. *"Do you have any real biscuits?"*

"Don't eat 'em if you don't like 'em," Eileen yelled back. She pulled a flask out from under her chair's cushion and took a swig of the water of life (a.k.a. whiskey) to ease her throat for the tale to tell. *"Oh, well,"* she said to the baby. *"The past isn't really that interesting and you don't really need to know it all. You can read about it when you're older if you're really interested. Anyway, you're related to those children of Lir, and it's a maternal linkage that passes from mother to daughter, from mother to daughter, from . . . Well, you get the point. So I'm guessing you'll be needing to know a bit about those children of Lir, to understand what is to become of you, in your life . . ."*

Part Two:

Another One Bites the Dust

1

Just Another Day to Die

"Excuse me—are you Shawn?" the woman asked from right behind me, lightly rapping on the metal frame of my cubicle.

It was too little, too late. I shot up out of my seat, practically hitting the ceiling before I landed facing her. She started to smile, obviously trying not to laugh. Didn't work. She all but fell over.

"For feck's sake, what sort of gobshite are you?" I asked. "Sneaking up on poor unsuspecting folk like some kind of malicious leprechaun!"

"I wasn't sneaking. I knocked and everything."

"As you snuck! It was kinda late to knock, since you'd already scared the bejesus outta me, don't you think?"

"You're just going to town on all this, aren't you? You're at work—people are going to come up to you with questions. Deal with it already." She had her hands on her hips as she squared off

111

to stand against me. She really was quite attractive.

"I'm cutting you a break. This time," I said. "So what the devil's got you roaming about like some sort of nefarious character anyway?"

"I'm not *roaming* around like anything. The copy machine's jammed, and I was told you were the one who could fix it."

"Oh, yeah, sure," I said, walking out of my little cube arena and over to that dread machine. I glanced at the display, then started yanking it apart, carefully pulling out bits and pieces of paper that were trapped between rollers and in other places. "What the bloody hell did you do to this thing?" There were scraps and pieces lodged throughout it. I kept telling everyone to let me know at the *first* sign of trouble, instead of making it more difficult by ripping the hell out of all the jammed pieces, leaving me with only scraps to try to pry out.

"I didn't do anything to it. I just came over here to copy this and it was already all jammed up. I remembered what Dawn said when I started—about you being able to fix any of the office machines and being a lot closer, nicer and better than any of the IT personnel—so I came to get you."

I yanked out one last shred of paper, then blithely divested the woman of the manila folder she held.

"Hey!" she said, grabbing for it.

I whipped around so she faced my back. "Is this some new ad campaign? I'm gonna end up seeing it some time, you know."

"No, it's not—it's personal and I shouldn't have been copying it at work so give it back!" She tried to reach over my shoulder, but I danced away, keeping it from her.

I ran down the hall, just ahead of her, looking through the folder, which was filled with newspaper clippings—*Missing Man Found in Dumpster, Dean Foster Still Missing after 28 Days, Missing Clerk Suspected Dead*. I stopped in my tracks. "You're a bit obsessive, aren't you? You got a thing for missing guys or something?"

"It's just an interest," she said, reclaiming the folder and holding it protectively in her arms. "Research. Now do you mind? I need to get to work."

"Hey, who are you anyway?" She wasn't bad looking with her long, dark hair, slightly dark, exotic-looking skin, slender frame and long legs—but she wasn't my Ashley, either. Though sometimes I wasn't so sure about Ashley wanting to be all mine all the time quite yet. I wasn't sure if I wanted to still be looking, or couldn't believe I was so lucky.

She sighed. "Kelly Everson. Copywriter. I started here last week."

I grabbed her hand and bowed. "Shawn Donnelly. Media buyer/planner. Pleasure's all mine." I smiled.

She pulled away. "Um, yeah, I know. Nice to meet you. But I really do have a deadline to meet. Gotta get some copy done for that new fruit juice we just picked up. See ya around!"

I stared after her. I worked with some rather odd folk.

"Stop brooding and come have a paczki." Brenda, my boss and a bit of a pal, appeared from out of nowhere as usual, easily dropped a case of paper next to the printer and dragged me toward the kitchen. She can drag me somewhat successfully as she's eight inches taller and a good sixty pounds more than I.

"Bren, you know they're suck paczkis—we get 'em free, after all."

"Only you would question one of our clients giving us free eats." She grabbed the newspaper from the table.

"C'mon, would it ever cross the non-existent mind of anyone who works here to actually get the good ones from Hamtramck?" I glanced over the box looking for a custard one. "Y'know, it takes *eastern* Europeans to *feck* up something good like pastry. I mean, who but a buncha Polacks would make prune doughnuts, spell it with a zee and say it punch-key?"

Brenda gave me a withering glance. "Like Gaelic makes any spelling sense at all."

"Oh, God, please don't tell me that's the last custard," Courtney said from behind me as I snatched what very well might have been the object of her interest. I wondered if I could simply flee right now. Courtney Van Dyke was even shorter than me, with short blond hair and obvious dark roots. Her M.O. was to corner folks and go on and on about how screwed up something was.

"The raspberry are quite nice, too," Brenda said while trying to nonchalantly inch away from her. It was really quite funny seeing a woman as big as Brenda practically cowering from the teeny, tiny Evil Courtney.

"Well, I guess if there's no more custard left, I'll have to try one of those." Courtney took a raspberry paczki, but was still eyeing my custard, even as I bit into it. "I just don't see why every year they send us so many of the other types when everybody's favorite is custard. It just doesn't make any sense!" Courtney was a number cruncher in accounting, and I sometimes thought the numbers got to her one day and made her the way she was: as thick as two short planks. As far as she was concerned, there was no horse too dead to flog. There wasn't a law against it, so dammit, she was gonna go right ahead and keep on with the flogging!

Regardless if she was saying something interesting or not, the best plan was to escape from Evil Courtney's clutches ASAP.

"Omigod!" Courtney said, around a mouthful of substandard pastry, hitting Brenda's newspaper-holding arm with her powdered-sugar-coated hand. "Did you hear? They found *another* body—right near here! The police are checking all the Dumpsters in the area for more!"

"*Another* body?" I said, walking directly into her trap. "I didn't know they'd found a first!" I scratched the back of my neck. I hoped it was just itchy and not that it was hinting about anything regarding these dead bodies.

"Don't you even read the newspapers? Hello? Dean Foster?

The missing cashier? I'm willing to bet it's all connected," Courtney said.

"Oh, c'mon, there's no reason to believe today's body is related to any other. They didn't say it in the paper or on the news," Brenda said, pulling her newspaper away from Courtney as she apparently searched for the article Courtney was talking about.

"Did you see that big orange X on the Dumpster out back this morning?" Courtney said. "That means the cops have already checked it out." She looked over Brenda's shoulder. "C'mon, it's on the front page!"

"Couldn't the killer mark the Dumpster he left bodies in himself? So the cops would think they'd already checked it out and pass it over in their search?" Damn—I'd fallen into her clutches!

"Body parts," Brenda said.

I looked up at her.

"Body parts, not bodies, they found body parts in the Dumpster," Brenda said, flipping through the pages.

"Well, I hope they're keeping a written track of where they've checked," Courtney said. "But the cops don't seem to be paying enough attention to detail—there's been no mention that whoever dumped this body might've dumped a few others as well."

"What do you mean?"

"A big part of my job is to pay attention to details—cost centers and all that—and there's no way a lot of different people would keep dumping bodies in Dumpsters in the same place at the same time—"

"It's not the same time!" Brenda said. "Nobody's been killed in this area in a while—"

"Not killed *and* found, that is," Courtney said. "I don't bet, but I'd be willing to gamble that clerk and Dean Foster and that guy who was found in the McDonald's Dumpster and that other one—well, you know. They're all related! C'mon, it's all gone down in like two months!"

115

"They probably deserved it," Brenda said, reading. When she realized we were both looking at her she quickly continued. "I mean, we're always assuming that when people get killed north of Eight Mile that there's no reason. For all we know, all these guys beat up prostitutes or something. I just don't like that everyone's always assuming all these white males who get killed are totally innocent."

"That's an interesting take," Courtney said, pausing as if considering it all.

"Get away with ya!" I said, looking at my watch. "Tiffany needs me to do a proposal analysis, Becky—Becky something needs me to cost out a fifty-market radio buy, and I still have to finish costing out that twenty-three-market newspaper buy for Ortega. Or was that Wonderbra?" I was edging toward the door. I knew I should try to save Brenda, but when Courtney got going on her conspiracy theories, it definitely became every woman for herself.

"Good luck on all that," Brenda said, trying to escape on my coattails, as if finally realizing what she'd said was a guaranteed sentence to spending an awfully long time with Courtney. "The last person in your position woulda taken two weeks to do all that. At least. I'm so thankful we have you now—but I need to explain—"

"I just never understood why they kept her around," Courtney said as she put a hand on Brenda's arm. "Media seems to stick with some real losers, you know?"

That was the last I heard as I fled the scene.

Back at my desk I opened up several Excel workbooks, spread the relevant papers across my desk, and put it all in order. The newspaper buy was in the West, so it didn't make sense to start calling again for prices this early, since they were three hours behind us.

But I could do everything but call them, so I analyzed the proposal for Tiff, wrote up the responding memo, glanced at my newspaper and finished my custard paczki while finding online the articles to which the others had referred.

I'd read there were always serial killers active in the U.S. that we didn't know about. I'd heard it—serial killing—was a lot more prevalent than we—the general public—thought or knew. But this article—part of a series—made it a lot more real. Like it was here and now and . . . A real threat. The Motor City Murderer was working a little too close to all of us.

No wonder Kelly'd been so interested—and Courtney—and Brenda, even. People getting killed randomly all around you really could make you a little paranoid and a wee bit interested. Kinda like most folks on a freeway near a car accident.

Jesus! There was a picture. It really wasn't pleasant.

Okay, now, since we washed up on these shores when I was thirteen, my mum had refused to read the papers for fear of bad news about the troubles at home in Belfast. I'd taken after her for the last decade for the most part, but for another reason entirely. I tried not to read the papers because the truth was I could get, well . . . *Obsessive* is such an unpleasant word. Now, I *had* heard folks mention killers—on the radio, TV, at work, and the grocery store and my Ma and Pa and . . .

I called the West Coast, trying to convince them to let my clients run on others' rate cards. It was one of my best moves in newspaper negotiations, since newspapers didn't negotiate.

They'd get back to me.

I was in.

And then I realized there were a lot of articles online, plus more unpleasant photographs. Click a link here, sift through search results there and I was able to read all about the Dumpster murders. It was clear to even me that he—the rote and addicted killer—had been active at least four to eight weeks, killing seemingly innocent men throughout the suburbs of Detroit.

I was totally gobsmacked about it all. How had I not known

about all of this?

The latest body'd been found in the Dumpster of the gas station I always filled up at! If Ma knew, she'd croak. Or go into one of her rants about how I should dress more femininely.

Another had been found at a Mickey D's right near Ashley's!

No wonder my inner voice had been buggin' me to look into this.

Using search strings incorporating the headlines I'd seen the new girl copying, I got a lot of hits that tied into what was apparently one killer. Now, even I knew the cops often withheld info so they could try to track and apprehend the homicidal lunatic—that same info would let reporters know whether or not they had a serial on their hands. But because I didn't have that info either, I couldn't know for sure.

Even though I couldn't convince Ma otherwise, Detroit wasn't the Murder Capital anymore. Still, there were way more folks getting wasted around here than other places, so what was unrelated, what was coincidence, and what was related?

I tapped my pencil on my pad and realized I had work to do. I used basic info to do overall costing for general market buys. No need to go making a bunch of phone calls or such when the advertisers were just considering making a buy. I'd give 'em an estimate, and if they went with the buy I'd get them the best deal possible, saving them a boatload of money and coming across the right hero as well.

I also went about analyzing the recent murders like I went about my media work—I started trying to rule out those that were obviously unrelated, and then plot out the others on a map.

Of course, my media stuff didn't usually entail dead bodies—but it did usually involve methodical consideration from all aspects. I did like a good puzzle, and I was really bored with media buys right now.

It was right about then that I realized the most suspicious thing of all: First I ran across that new girl—Kelly Everson.

Everson, Everyman—Everywoman—whatever, photocopying articles about serial killers, then Courtney made sure I knew *all* about the serial killer in the area (who might not even be a serial killer), and Brenda reinforced it all. I couldn't stop thinking about that horrible weekend not too long ago and how my own intuition had let me down. I didn't care if I had the weirdest-assed tickle of foreboding right now about all this shite about serial killers. This time I would not be caught.

"Hey stranger." A hand clutched my shoulder.

I spun about and smashed back against my desk all in one move—so quickly I fell out of my chair.

"God, Shawn, I am *so* sorry," Ashley said, pushing my chair out of the way and holding a hand out to me. "I thought you might like to have lunch? With me? I really didn't mean to . . . Scare you? Frighten you?"

I jumped to my feet. "I'm not afraid. Startled. Scared. Frightened. Nope. Not me." She stepped back, crossed her arms and smiled. I could tell she was holding in a laugh, so I decided to go for broke on the laugh-o-meter. I reached back, grabbed my arse and said, "Yuppers, still dry."

"You really are crazy." She wanted to put her arms around me, but held herself back out of shyness. At least I hoped that was why she didn't hug me. I'd have liked a hug. Sometimes I knew just what she was thinking and other times I was bog-bound.

"You get I said that just to be funny—it's not like I'm Fecky the Ninth or anything."

She smiled. "*Fecky the Ninth?* Irish, sometimes I don't under-stand a word you say." She grabbed me by my shirt and came right up to me to whisper in my ear, "It should be a turnoff, but for some reason, it's just another reason for me to love you."

"It means *complete idiot*." I put my hands on her hips. I was totally out at work. But I reckoned we ought to leave soon, since having all my coworkers *know* something and having them *see* something were two entirely different things. I grabbed my coat. "So what do you fancy for lunch?" I guided her out with an arm around her waist.

"Shawn! Are you going to introduce me to your . . . friend?" Ed, Brenda's new boss, joined us in the hall. He was a brash, bold man, and he didn't hide for a moment that he was checking out Ashley. Brenda had not been pleased when upper management had brought Ed in two months before instead of promoting her. Fortunately, she'd seemed to have gotten over it, though she did still occasionally mumble about how it really took a woman to get a job done right. She also seemed to have a thing about male entitlement, especially white male entitlement.

"Uh, yeah. Ashley, this is Ed Steele, V.P. of Media here. Ed, this is Ashley."

"Pleased to meet you." Ashley shook his outstretched hand with that polite but distant air that meant "never in a million years." Yet another thing for me to lo . . . like about her. I'd bet she was a right pro in giving the cool brush-off to overeager Y-chromosome types.

"And you two are just slipping out for a quick *lunch*?" he asked. He obviously approved. And if he weren't recently married for the third time, he would've been trying to change Ashley's mind about which team she batted for.

"Yeah, so don't wait up," I said. I *really* didn't like the way he was ogling her. I already knew the lads back home would refer to her as "a right stiffener and all."

"I'd watch out for her around Ed," Brenda said, walking by us on the staircase.

"Oh, Ash, I'd like you to meet Brenda, my immediate boss," I said.

"Nice to meet you. Don't worry, we're not all like Ed," Brenda said, shaking Ashley's hand. Maybe she wasn't as over Ed as I'd thought. And with the way she was looking at Ash, I had to rethink which team she was batting for—after all, she wasn't married, and never seemed to seriously date anyone.

It was all rather questionable.

"Nice to meet you," Ashley said. "And I never pay guys like Ed any attention at all, so don't worry about me."

Brenda gave Ash and me the look, then said, "No, I wouldn't expect you to look twice at Ed, or any guy, at all. But that doesn't mean you should trust him. He's just like the rest of his sex—untrustworthy."

"We have to get going," Ash said. "Lunch and all."

"I'm with her," I said, following Ash down the stairs and out the door. Brenda watched us all the way.

"I'll drive," Ashley said once we were outside. "My car will still be warm, since I just got here and all."

"Yeah, yeah. Let me guess—you're just scared of my driving."

"Well, that, too. I remember when you were driving us all to that party at end of term, but Karen was sitting on Jamie's lap in the front seat of your rather small car, so she kept hitting the shift and putting you into neutral when you turned."

"It was hell in the turnabouts."

"I imagine it was." As we climbed into her dark green Lexus, she looked over at me, then reached out to run her hand down my arm. "I really like this coat. Especially on you."

It was brown suede that came to just below my hips, with a nice snuggly sheepskin lining that was quite warm. "I'm glad I was wearing a parka at the lake, though. It was much better with all the quick-drying and such."

Ashley pulled me in for a nice, long, slow kiss. It was only when we heard some catcalls from people outside that she let me go. "So any good drive-thrus between here and your place?" she said.

My knees went weak as soon as I realized what she was planning. I was having no trouble at all reading her mind now. "I've got the makings for turkey sandwiches at home. And, I, uh . . . I might even have a selection of chips and macaroni salad and other stuff. Maybe even pickles. Yes, I think I have pickles, too." Pickles. Pickles weren't funny. But with my mind in the gutter and all, pickles came across as wicked hysterical.

Ashley tossed me a smile as she guided the vehicle out of the lot. Once she was safely on the street, she stuck her cute little pink tongue out of her full and perfect lips while she tried not to laugh out loud at me.

"And just what are you laughing at, missy?" I asked.

"It's funny when you get thrown off track and yet still blither on."

I didn't know what to do, so I pouted.

"You know, I haven't been to your place yet."

"Yeah, I know. But somehow you're heading in the right direction."

"Well, I MapQuested it."

"You are such the car top!"

"*Car top*? What do you mean by that?"

"Well, kinda like an S/M top, y'know? They top the scene —are in charge and all that. You get in a car and become a top— have to be in charge of everything—driving and all else. And thus, you are a car top."

"You're all right with that?"

"No problems here." I slipped my hand through the slit in her long skirt and caressed her knee. I ran my hand up her shapely thigh, fondling it and working my way inward and upward. "All the better to enjoy you."

I'd pointed the house out to her and told her where to park. Ever courtly, I helped her from the car and escorted her to the front door. I opened it for her with a bow, but as soon as she cleared the threshold, I grabbed her from behind and pushed her up against a wall as I closed the door with my foot. I couldn't believe I was being so bold with her.

And then we both leaned forward for a kiss and bumped heads and noses instead.

We laughed and fell onto each other's shoulders.

Then I tried to be big with the butch and pick her up, to carry her to my bedroom, but as soon as I reached down to pick her up, my feet slid on the wet linoleum and we went flying. The best I could do was break Ashley's fall with my own body.

"Well, that was an invigorating and surprising trip," Ashley said, once she got her breath, even as she obviously tried to hold in her laughter. She rolled over to straddle me.

"Easy for you to say," I gasped out, still trying to regain my breath.

She held my arms down against the floor, above my head. She leaned down to whisper in my ear. "God, Shawn, I've been wanting—needing—to feel you inside me ever since I woke up this morning."

I practically soaked my underwear at that statement, and so I struggled upward to nibble on her neck as I pushed her coat off her shoulders and to the floor so I could run my hands over her nubile figure. "Oh, Ash, tell me again why we didn't spend last night together?"

"I had to work late, and we don't want to move too quickly," Ashley said, arching against me. She groaned then said, "I had things to do."

I pushed her up so I could kneel in front of her, lifting her left leg onto my shoulder as I ran my hands all the way up her legs. She was wearing thigh-highs. And no underwear. Which I'd already discovered in the car. She knew it turned me on. What can I say? We'd had a few interesting phone convos of late. It's ever so much easier to lose inhibitions over the line than in person, after all.

And yet, I wanted to *show* her how it turned me on. Now, I

already knew what she'd done this morning when she awoke without me and thought about me during her morning shower. She'd told me *all* about it in the car on the drive over. And thinking about *that* turned me on as well. Especially knowing she was thinking that much, that naughtily, about me, when I wasn't there.

I burrowed under her skirt, putting my hands on her bare ass and pulling her up against my face. I pulled her cunt against my forehead, then gradually started raising my face, until my closed lips were against her lips. Were against her now-shaven pussy.

I guess she got a little frisky without me there to help her wash up. I'd just have to tell her it was hot, but not mandatory. After all, nicks would be a major detriment against me getting nookie.

I breathed her in, still unable to believe I could be here, on my knees, worshipping the woman I'd fantasized about for oh-so-many years.

"Shawn, please," she said, so low I could barely hear her.

I looked up at her, keeping my fingers on her, running them lightly over her, under her skirt. "Tell me."

"I've wanted you for so long . . . God. Take me to bed, please."

I stood, took her hand and led her to the bedroom. I laid her down on the bed, and lay down on top of her, molding our bodies together as we kissed, slowly running our lips over each other's until I let my tongue follow the sweet curve of her lips and dip inside her.

"What do you want, Ashley?"

"You. Inside me. Please." She took my hand in hers and guided it down, under her skirt, between her thighs, into her wetness.

She felt amazing. She was dripping.

I couldn't help myself. I kissed her again, then moved down her body to raise her skirt and look at her.

Okay. It was frickin' hot. She was hot. And her utter defenselessness of her privates made me even hotter.

I breathed her in, and allowed my breath to caress her wet flesh, to make her writhe even more.

I'd wanted this so much, I still couldn't believe it was happening, that I was with Ashley.

I couldn't hold myself back anymore. I lapped her up, running my tongue along her clit, pushing it up to separate her lips and feel and taste her even deeper and greater.

Ashley twined her fingers in my hair, burying my face between her thighs. "Shawn, please, inside."

I continued licking her, eating her, as I brought my right hand to the front of her thigh and buried two fingers inside her. She quivered and groaned.

"God, Shawn . . ." She writhed slowly against me, her insides tightening around me. As she raised and lowered her hips, grinding against me, fucking my face, she pulled my hair so hard it hurt.

"Shawn, please, yes . . ." Her muscles clamped down on my fingers, even as she squished my shoulders between her really strong legs. "YES!"

Her legs were tight around me, her insides contracted against my fingers, and as it all almost hurt, I loved that she was coming for me.

"Shawn!"

And, yeah, it made me hot and bothered and turned me on wicked to hear her cry my name like that.

I rode out her contractions, gentling her down, then cleaning her up.

"Oh, Shawn, we don't have time," she said, trying to bring me up to face her. " 'Specially not if you want something." She ran her hands down my body, then tugged at my belt.

"Whoa, no time, baby. Not if we want to eat—"

"I know what I'd like to eat," she said, running her hand

down to cup my crotch.

"Hypoglycemic here, babe. I need my turkey sandwich." I pulled her hand away from me and pressed it down to the ground. "If you want to make my day, then eat lunch topless. I love your breasts." I looked up at her. "Please?"

"You don't want me to go down on you—fuck you? You just want me to . . ." She turned bright red.

"Ash . . . I . . ." How could I say this? How could I tell her all I was feeling? "I love . . . your body. I love seeing you naked. I love pleasing you—giving you pleasure and making you come. That's what does it for me. That and your utter and complete sexiness." I touched her face. I dropped my hand down to cup a breast. "I . . . I still can't believe I can touch you like this."

She unbuttoned her blouse. It was a ruby-red satin one. Very beautiful, but nothing to compare with her. She pushed the top open, revealing her lacy black bra. It had a front clasp.

I looked into her eyes. "You really did plot this from this morning," I said, unclasping her bra and pushing it open, show-ing off her soft, suckable breasts.

"I have, like, four years of celibacy to make up for," she said, even as my neck started to itch.

I tried to keep looking into her eyes, but I really couldn't. Especially not once she looked into my eyes and pushed off her bra and top.

"You are so unbelievably gorgeous," I said.

"I'm never like this. This . . . wanton."

"I like you wantin'." I licked and sucked her gorgeous breasts. They weren't too big, not too small—it was like they were . . . mine.

I teased a nipple with my tongue, caressing the other breast and nipple with a hand.

"Oh, God, Shawn . . . If you wanna eat, you really shouldn't be doing *that*!"

2

Do You Want Fries with That?

When I was walking back to my desk after lunch, I happened to pass by Kelly's desk—after all, it was in the same building as mine. Granted, it was along the scenic route to my area—but really, I was en route to my own zone so it made total sense.

No matter how many times I said I wouldn't be hoodwinked again, that wouldn't shut up the annoying voice in my head that kept saying something wasn't quite right here. You could take the girl out of Ireland, but couldn't get the Irish outta the girl, after all.

Plus, well, the obnoxious and colorful paper bag puppets on her desk could grab an eye better'n any catcher's mitt. There was a vampire with pipe cleaner fangs dripping blood, a youth with a blue-and-yellow propeller hat, an obvious married couple. Like I said, I work with interesting people.

Anyway, it was so totally not my fault when my hand dropped

and hit her mouse. The computer woke up and . . . lookie there, she didn't have it password-protected on the awakening, so I could see quite clearly that she had just been surfing a Web site about physical reactions to pain just before she went on lunch. And looking through her history, I could tell she'd also recently been at some other rather interesting-looking sites, including Smith & Wesson online, one with really evil looking knives, and one about various types of drugs, including Rohypnol, GHB and various narcotics and other wicked painkillers.

Now, if she really was guilty of some sort of wrongdoing, you'd think she'd have the sense to close these incriminating windows. Unless, of course, she was really stupid, which was a possibility. Regardless, I probably shouldn't be caught snooping in her cube—even though I wasn't snooping—I was just en route back to my desk after lunch.

But that wasn't something I wanted to try to convince a serial killer of. Besides, I knew she really *wasn't* a serial killer, since my so-called friends had actually set all this up. I didn't know why they'd want to convince me someone I worked with was a killer—but then again, why had they wanted to convince me one of them was a killer? And that an ex-lover was dead?

Anyway, they weren't going to catch me twice in a row, no sirree Bob, I wasn't buying that yet again. I don't care how much the back of my neck itched and how I couldn't stop thinking there was something only I could figure out.

I was just gonna go back to my desk and do my job. Going now.

"Can I help you with something?"

Oh, shit, I was snared rapid. "Um, yeah. Carol wasn't in, and she's the one I usually go to for help with language. English."

"Okay, so what exactly do you need?" Kelly asked, glaring at me with her arms crossed in front of her. As far as body language went, hers was telling me to move to another country. Or continent.

"I'm proofing a presentation Media's put together for a new-client pitch and I always get *affect* and *effect* mixed up—which is which again?"

"*Affect* is usually the proper form for verb usage, whereas *effect* is usually the noun." She pulled out a usage guide. She flipped through it to the appropriate passages and handed it to me.

"Ah, yes," I said, reading. "I think I get it now. Do you mind if I look something else up?" I flipped to *farther*, to read up on its usage versus *further*. "This is a great book! When you weren't here, I was hoping you'd have a usage guide somewhere." I grabbed a Post-it and wrote down the name of the book. "I need to get one of these myself." I might as well play my ruse to the max.

"Is there anything else I can do for you?" The glare apparently wasn't leaving anytime soon.

"What?" I asked. "Oh, no. This is good. That's all I was looking for. Thanks!" I put the book down and turned to go.

"Wait a minute," she said, reaching out for my arm. "You came into my cube, searching for me or a usage guide, in your rather nice and soft coat?"

Was she coming onto me? "I went out for lunch. While eating, I remembered that I needed to finish proofing this presentation, and that's when I realized I'd never answered my question from yesterday about whether *effect* was being properly used. It wasn't, as it turns out. Since I'm rather attention deprived, I figured I ought to come and check it out while it was on my mind—hence, still being in the coat and all."

She was smiling softly at me now.

"I tend to ramble."

"I noticed."

"I'm going now."

"Tell me one thing, Shawn Donnelly."

"What?"

"Does your hair always do that?" she said, pointing.

"Only when it's excited." I brushed my fingertips over the spikey bits Ashley had dubbed my baby-bird hair, and thought I ought to trademark the phrase.

She smiled at that, and I was able to flee for my own cube.

She hadn't noticed—or at least hadn't mentioned—that I'd messed with her computer. Now, I did have a cover ready for that as well (it was a really clever one, all about how I thought maybe her dictionary might give me the info I needed, and I hit her mouse by accident when I was reaching for it). If she were guilty, she'd likely have noticed it, and then confronted me.

That is, unless she didn't want to draw attention to the fact she'd noticed I'd been playing with her computer because she wanted me to think she hadn't noticed, when really she had, and was already plotting my most untimely demise.

As I hung up my coat in my cubicle I told myself maybe there was a perfectly rational and reasonable reason she'd been surfing gun and knife sites. Too bad I couldn't think of any. It's not like we represented any of those companies or their competitors. We weren't in those categories and she was obviously not doing work-related research or anything. That meant guns and knives were personal, somehow, just like having a folder full of articles about a serial killer was personal. It was disquieting even if it wasn't any of my business.

Or then again, it could all be some sort of a setup. Scratching the back of my neck, I settled down to work. The lingering scent of Ashley on my fingers was a welcome distraction.

I was ping-ponging faster than believable on whether it was a setup or there was something truly evil afoot. I just couldn't seem to make up my mind and stick with it.

"How are you coming on that buy, Shawn?" Brenda said, walking up behind me.

I shot out of my seat but didn't cover my screen. Brenda was cool. I wished she'd been promoted to VP because, well, besides

130

the fact that she wasn't at all creepy, she wouldn't turn me in for doing some private stuff on company time.

She knew I did my job, did it well, and got it all done on time. That was what mattered, after all, wasn't it?

I spent the afternoon working on a ten-state newspaper buy in the South. I had to call each newspaper individually to negotiate us piggybacking on a larger client's rate sheet, which made sense, since we were saying the product was available at those national retailers. Cooperative ad buys gave us much better prices. I spent less than half what Brenda had estimated. Someday I hoped to be rewarded for my genius.

Of course, I pulled my socks up on that when anyone was listening or watching. When nobody was, I was looking into all the recently deceased by unnatural means in the Detroit Metro area.

I did my job in half the time of my feckless predecessor, and took on more work, but only to a point. It was easier to look like the miracle worker I was if no one knew exactly how quickly I could finish something.

Anyway, it didn't take long for me to start an Excel spreadsheet laying out the murders, places, outcomes and any other pertinent data. I was trying to determine which murders were related, or possibly related, and what the common threads were between incidents and all other possibly related things. A spreadsheet let me clearly see all related elements at once.

"Well, that looks interesting and not at all related to Wonderbra. Or Lean Cuisine even," Brenda said from behind me.

Again, I almost hit the ceiling. One of these days I was going to string cowbells across the cube opening.

"You know, Shawn, someone as tightly wound as you ought to develop better senses. You should realize when someone is coming up behind you."

"I normally do. But not everyone's as sneaky as you."

"I'm not sneaky at all. Damn, Shawn, you're lucky you're so good at what you do, because you're so crazy I'd let you go otherwise."

"I'm not touched at all." But I was sure acting like it, going on and all about the serial killer who, coincidentally, kept coming up of late. And that was just the opening I needed. "I told you what happened when Karen had that little get together a week and a half ago, right?"

"Yeah. They set you up and got you good. As I recall, you came back mighty pissed at all of 'em. Except Ashley, of course."

I smiled at her. "Well, they're trying to do it again, but 'Fool me once, shame on you. Fool me twice, shame on me.' I don't know why, but they are—it makes no sense, but that's not stopping them from trying." I did a little happy dance inside my own head. Someone else was seeing it! It was now all making the sort of sense I could live with. I could deal with this, because now I knew for sure.

"I'm really not tracking here, Shawn. What are you on about this time?"

"My so-called friends are setting me up again!" It was all suddenly making total and complete sense. That was a good thing. "That's the only reasonable explanation. There's no such thing as coincidence, so there's no way that, *coincidentally*, one particular thing could keep coming up in one day. I mean, first thing this morn I run into Kelly Everyperson—"

"Everson."

"Whatever—making copies of all sorts of serial killer-type stuff—"

"Oh, hold on," Brenda said. "I know where this is going. The first time I caught her talking about murder and homicide, I thought she was a stark-raving maniac. For all I know, she really could be, anyway. So how's that newspaper buy going?"

"Oh, I finished that an hour ago." Ash and I were having

dinner that night. Together we'd find out who was behind it, and make 'em 'fess up to it all. She'd help me. I could trust her. Or at least I thought so. "Bren, I don't like folks messing with my head. There's enough going on in here as it is." I pointed at my forehead. "And that's exactly what my so-called friends are doing—I've known these folk longer than anyone else in my life, 'cept Ma and Pa, and they're screwing with me. My friends, not Ma and Pa." I grabbed the papers from the printer, quickly going through them to find the layout of the newspaper buy. "Here's the buy. You estimated it at fifty-five grand. I brought it in at fourteen five. Oh, and here's a memo and supporting docs I need you to sign off on before I deliver."

Brenda ignored the papers I handed her. She knew she didn't really need to look at them. Instead she grabbed the ones I withheld. "And these are your notes on serial killers in America?"

"No, just deaths in Detroit. In and around. But it all makes sense now."

"I'm glad." She traded my papers for hers.

"I'm not completely sack of hammers, you know."

"I know you're brilliant in your own way. And you get your work done quickly and correctly. You do a great job, Shawn. But yeah, you are totally insane as far as I'm concerned."

"Oh, good. I'd hate to be mistaken for some sort of boring sane person."

"You do realize all these murders can't be related, right?" Brenda asked. "I mean, chances are, all these murders have nothing to do with one another. You know this, right?"

"Well, of course. There's too many of them. I'm just trying to find the patterns and such. I know my friends are behind all of this. Now I just need to break them down and get them to admit it."

"Still not tracking here. But I'll just go with it. If you're looking for a serial killer, you should look for common denominators—like the same type of victim."

133

"That was my next step." Using a variety of differently colored highlighters, I began noting the trends and anomalies of my data. "Anything else you can point out? Outside observation is always important in data analysis." I looked up at Brenda to stress my point. "At least, to me it is."

"What are you doing this for again, anyway? Please tell me there's a client involved somewhere in it."

"Brenda, this is all for a client. It's all about the clients, after all."

That night I got home, quickly showered and changed, and went to pick up Ashley. I really didn't need to shower and change, but sometimes it don't hurt to have your girl know you're willing to go the extra for her, y'know?

'Specially when she's a right hot babe.

So I put on a nice-feeling black silk shirt and a pair of black trousers with a black leather belt with a large silver belt buckle. Okay, fine, it was kinda cowboyish with a horse and shite. And I put on a pair of boots. Black leather cowboy-style boots—but they were from Harley Davidson, so they were really biker boots. That's me, Shawn Donnelly, Biker. Not.

Nothing even remotely interesting happened until I knocked on Ashley's front door. She opened it, and my life was interesting again. That was all it took. I saw her and, well, became someone else. I channeled someone who knew who she was, some sure-as-shit butch or such.

I kicked the door shut behind me and scooped her up. She wrapped her legs around my waist and her skirt jacked up—all the way. I shoved her against the wall as she rode my big-ass belt buckle, grinding herself into it. I slipped my hand between our bodies and felt her heat.

I wanted to touch that heat. I wanted to be who I was portraying, but I wasn't.

"God, Shawn," Ashley said, grinding against me. Her face was buried in my neck.

I wanted to touch her and be close to her. We'd been intimate, but I still wasn't sure of myself when I touched her. I wasn't sure about making my fantasies come true (while, hopefully, making some of hers happen as well).

I braced her against the wall, buried my face against her neck, kissing it, and then, finally, after a shiver of anticipation and hope made its way through my body, worked my fingers around her silky thong and into her.

I held her against the wall with the pressure of my body against hers. I pushed her sweater and bra up, baring her breasts to my devouring mouth.

This wasn't me. But whoever was possessing me was doing a wonderful job of making all my dreams come true—not only was I doing stuff I could only do in my wettest dreams, but I was being who I always wanted to be. I was powerful, in control, and topping the scene.

"Do it, Shawn, please do me." A beautiful flush rose on her shoulders and neck.

I fingered her hot and wet cunt while I licked and sucked her ripe tits.

"Baby, don't tease me," she begged. She'd been ready from the moment I touched her.

"You call this teasing?" She was hot and wet and I slid my fingers up into her.

"Shawn, yes, please, God . . . Uh!"

It was hard, fast, sweaty and nasty. It was what I'd always wanted but never dared take.

I was inside her as she convulsed around my fingers. I curled my fingers inside her till I felt her come . . . again . . . soaking my hand and her skirt as she came in that way only a wicked hot g-spot orgasm does.

I'd never experienced one of those before. I'd read about

them, sure, but feeling Ashley's muscles and soft, wet places turn inside out for me, oh that was definitely a first.

Cool.

"God, what was that for?" Ashley asked, leaning limply against me.

Bloody hell, this was all like all those dreams I'd had. Holding her. Loving her. "I missed you."

"You saw me this afternoon."

"I missed you. I miss you when I'm not near you. Is that a criminal offense?" I escorted her to the sofa and she gratefully sank into the cushions as I grinned down at her.

"Shawn, you are imprinted everywhere on my body. You are all over me."

"As I should be. You are mine."

"Are you becoming territorial? Am I gonna have to start watching out for you pissing all over me and my furniture?"

I slammed my closed fist against my chest, Tarzan style. "I have woman. I've had sex. Now I need food. And answers."

Ashley reached over to run her fingers along my wet collar, then down the equally wet tails of my shirt and onto my wet pants. "I'd suggest we go out, but I think we have some laundry to do. So strip."

"Is this your way of getting me naked? Or proving you can cook?"

"I can't. That's why you're cooking. And it all serves you right for doing such wonderful things to me."

"Wonderful, huh?" I was so shit-grinning I didn't even notice as she pulled off my shirt, boots and trousers.

"Okay, so if you don't cook, I don't get why you'd have all this food around the house," I said, standing at the stove and frying up some scallops.

"They came frozen. I keep some simple stuff around here, in

case I get desperate. Plus, we've been dating a week and a half and I was feeling especially optimistic when I hit Trader Joe's this week." She stepped up behind me, pressing her body against mine and cupping my ass.

I jolted forward against the stove. "Ash! I'm cooking here!"

"You sure are."

"You'd better let me pay attention to the food unless you want it all burned!" (She had her hands on my breasts now, and I was sure she'd be pulling off my bra in a moment.)

"We can order out," she whispered into my ear.

I yanked away from her, tossed lemon juice on the scallops, stirred the rice and asparagus, and whipped around to face her. "Behave!"

"I am! You've got a fantastic ass!"

"Get me a robe, woman!"

I can't share all the nasty details, but after we'd eaten, she'd been done again, I'd been done (it was fucking incredible), and my clothes were again clean and fresh—not necessarily in that order . . .

. . . and then there was more sex . . . and Ashley mentioned how difficult it was shaving herself, and I said it was hot, but not necessary, and she suggested that if I liked it, maybe I could do the shaving next time . . . and I had to remind myself that she'd only been with men thus far, since men were the ones who truly thought that was hot.

And I kept away thoughts of how so many lesbian relationships ended: With Lesbian Bed Death. I couldn't deal with any imaginings that the woman I'd loved and lusted after for so long might not be with me on the forever-after bits of my hopes. I'd earned my happily ever after, dammit!

Just as we were getting ready to head out, the phone rang. Ashley glanced at the phone, at me, then at the phone again.

"Why don't you grab our coats, honey?" she said to me. "While I just take care of this quickly?"

"Okay," I said.

She picked up the phone just as the machine was about to kick in.

"Hello?" she said into the phone. "Yes, it's me." She glanced over at me and turned away. "This really isn't a good time. We can talk about it later." There was a pause and I quickly gathered our coats. "Yes. Fine. Tomorrow. At work."

She let me help her into her coat and we walked outside. "So, um, what was that about?" I asked.

"Oh, that was just a coworker who doesn't know the meaning of the phrase *appropriate boundaries*."

"Oh, okay," I said, opening her door for her and helping her in.

"So where are we off to now, so suddenly?" she asked.

"Jamie's. I need some answers," I said.

"What are you on about now, Irish?" Ashley said.

"I'm being set up again. People today kept talking about this serial killer—that the cops aren't identifying as such—active in the area right now. The only thing they didn't do was put up signs with arrows saying 'Clue' and 'Killer.'"

"Were you always this paranoid?" Ashley asked.

"Um, yes? But really, when my neck itches, it's not paranoia—it just means someone really is out to get me. Or cause other trouble. Or some such."

I told Ashley all about my day as she whisked us to Jamie's. I was hoping a surprise visit would get the truth out of her. Jamie, that is. I knew there was badness afoot, but I also knew my friends were setting me up. Or at least I thought so.

Ashley, however, was still stuck on my apparent AD/HDness. "So instead of lazing about in a haze of fulfillment, we're running all over town now because . . . ?"

"I can't focus while something's scratchin' at the inside of my skull. I need to work this all out, y'know?"

"You're one odd duck, Shawn Donnelly."

" 'Odd duck'? You've been hanging with me too long, Greenly."

"Oh, oh, oh!" Jamie said, opening her front door to Ashley's knock. "Just the two I was thinking about! You gotta see what I've got going on!" She reached over and picked up an amazingly realistic bloody head. "Check these props."

"Nice," I said. "So do you have any idea why everyone today keeps talking to me about some serial killer in the area?"

"Uh, no. But check this blood!" Jamie said, pouring some from a bottle onto a trashbag-coated table.

"Isn't that what you used for blood before?" Ashley asked.

"Yeah, but, it wasn't quite this precise mix. I've got it down now. We can *replicate* this. One cup of corn syrup to two tablespoons of red food coloring and one tablespoon of flour— shaken, not stirred."

"So you're telling me you have nothing to do with anything going on with me lately—like since the cabin?" I said.

"Uh. Yeah. We've already given you our sales pitch, so why do anything more? You're either in or not," Jamie said. "But I gotta say, some of my whacked sculptures and props are gonna tip the scales in our favor. If you don't want in on all this, you need your head examined."

"I'm still pretty pissed off at all of you. And if you're involved at all in anything right now, you'd better tell me, or else I'm out of it all," I replied.

Ashley squeezed my hand. "Irish, I can tell you I'm not involved with making you think someone around you is a serial killer. I wasn't involved before, and I'm not now."

"I'm not either," Jamie said, looking directly at me. Suddenly the merry prankster who delighted in re-creating dismembered, severed and mutilated body parts was gone, replaced with the one-time lover and caring friend who was once incredibly important in my life.

"So you're both saying you have nothing to do with anything that's happening right now, correct?" I asked.

"Yeah, that's about what 'No, we're not involved' breaks down to," Jamie said, once again the happy merrymaker.

So maybe it wasn't a setup. Maybe I was just noticing coincidences. Or not-coincidences. "I haven't forgiven you all quite yet, but I will seriously think about it."

"Ooo, goodie!" Ashley cried, jumping up and wrapping her arms and legs around me. Her getting on board with this meant something to me, because I remembered just how hard all that happened at Karen's cottage hit her.

"Crikey!" I said, grabbing Ashley's arse and holding her up like that.

"Listen, baby," Ashley said, "I'm sure whatever you think you've been seeing, or thinking you're seeing, is just your over-active imagination."

By the next morning I'd scratched the back of my neck raw.

3

The Early Bird Gets the Worm

The next morning I awoke extra early, jumped through a shower, put on the clean clothes I'd only worn briefly the night before to Jamie's and gave Ashley a quick kiss before slinking silently from her house and going to work.

As it happened, I was the first one there. I was all alone. Even Kelly Everson wasn't in yet. Golly gee. You might think I got in early just to snoop about her stuff some more, but that wasn't it at all.

Nope. Not at all. I'd gotten my fill the day before.

As if.

Although there was no such thing as coincidence, I now was pretty sure that my friends were not involved with the serial killer—and so I just wanted to ensure that nobody I knew was involved. I needed to *make sure* it was all just coincidence. I couldn't sleep till I knew nothing was afoot.

Plus, along with all the tingling of my Spider senses (well, my faerie-given senses of foreboding and premonition), I didn't like that this dude, or dudette, was working my neighborhoods—mine and, more importantly, Ashley's.

I turned on the light in the Creative Department and went to Kelly's cubicle. Her computer was off, and I knew folks who turned off their computers did so out of habit—so if I were suddenly caught, she'd know even more if the machine were on. It'd be a right fine clue that I was sticking my nose where it ought not be. I knew I had to be dog wide with this little adventure.

Plus, it might be password protected. So I'd just have to see if there was anything to be found in hard copy elsewheres about the cube. For instance, there was a file folder on some new fruit juice product. And one on Wonderbra. And some handwritten notes outlining the focal points and objectives of various pieces that were in development, as well as some catchy phrases and lines of copy for various products.

Some of it was even pretty good—better than a lot of the shite we'd put out before. It would be a bloody shame if she turned out to be some sort of psychopathic killer or homicidal maniac or anything bad like that. Awful thing actually, since she really seemed to have some talent.

She hadn't been with us long, but she did have a number of folders in her drawers already—and one drawer in particular drew my interest when I found the photocopies and originals of the newspaper clippings she'd been running around with the day before. I grabbed a pad of paper and jotted the dates, publications, names and headlines of the articles she had decided to archive to look up later. I wanted to know which incidences had her attention.

As for this second in time, there were all sorts of other incriminating items for me to study—such as drawings that looked like crime scene sketches with labels like "Body" and arrows pointing to body outlines. I didn't need to be Albert

Einstein or some sort of brainiac to reckon Kelly likely also subscribed to *True Crime* magazine or was doing what every other copywriter in town did—writing a novel on the side. (My first-ever advertising boss was an art director who'd become a character in an Elmore "Dutch" Leonard book who was later played by Clint Eastwood because of a copywriter who wrote novels on the side.)

'Course, she could really be a serial killer.

At the back of the drawer was a worn manila envelope, awkwardly folded closed. After a peek inside, I slithered the contents onto the desk: a cross on a thick silver chain; a set of dog tags with the name *Dean Foster* and his info on them; a single dagger earring; a University of Michigan class ring, gold, with the name *X. Davis Channing* engraved inside the band.

There was red on some of these items. A deep, dark red, too deep and dark to be blood. Unless it was. It wasn't like I knew a lot about blood and how it looked when it dried and all. I was only expert in Jamie's fake theatrical blood.

I jotted a quick inventory on my pad, and realized that if she was a serial killer, I *so* did not want to be caught digging through her drawers. I put everything away as close to their original positions as possible and left, posthaste.

Then I realized she might notice her notepad missing, but if I just took the sheets I'd written on, she might be able to shade the page below with a pencil and see what I'd been writing on it. Or she could count the pages left and realize someone had stolen three pages from it and, bloody hell, I was being overly worried and paranoid. The back of my neck was itching like crazy.

I tore off my sheets and put the notepad back in exactly the same position I'd found it. I put out the lights and went to my desk to brood about all this new info.

I booted my computer and started searching for details on the articles I'd found in Kelly's stuff. My stomach growled and I realized there might be paczki left from the day before.

"Oh my God," Courtney said, charging up from behind me as I scoped the paczki situation in the kitchen. "Did you read that there's a serial killer loose *right now*? It was all over the papers this morning! I was *so* right!"

"Statistically speaking, there are always serial killers active in a lot of different places." Huh, there was only prune left.

"But not always right *here*, right *now*."

"Courtney, is there something you're not telling me?"

"What? I'm telling you"—she paused, and I could practically see her doing the math to figure out what I was intimating—"oh, ha ha. No. I'm not a killer or anything like that. Besides, it's obviously some guy, because how many women are even able to move those sorts of big, heavy bodies? Plus, it's always men."

She had a point. Kelly was no Amazon, so obviously she either had an accomplice or was covering or helping someone else. Or maybe had been bitten by a radioactive spider sometime in her past.

Anyway, beyond all that, based on overwhelming statistics, men were more likely to kill than women. Women usually only killed to protect themselves or those they loved. The Wournoses of the world were rare.

Which led me to think that maybe Kelly *was* in with the gang on making me look like some sorta loon by convincing me she was the killer, when she really wasn't.

I scratched the back of my neck and wondered if even clueless Courtney was in on it.

"—hello? Shawn?" Courtney was saying, waving a hand in front of my face, apparently trying to get my attention back to her pratless ramble—"Aren't you paying attention? Aren't you even the least bit worried there's a killer in our midst?"

That was it. I shoved her hand away from my face. "Hello? Courtney love, Detroit was the murder capital of the entire bloody country for how long? There's always a murderer in our midst. Always has been." I released her hand. I was frustrated with her and with my own inability to decide whether or not this was another put-on or if it was someone I knew. "Anyway, do you realize how vastly huge this area is? Michigan itself is larger than the entire country of Ireland, and the Detroit metro area has a population greater than *all* of Ireland. So it's a pretty darn big vast we're talking about here. And don't ever put your bleedin' hand in my bloody face again." I was rather annoyed, especially since I had apparently taken on her annoying habit of stressing various words in each sentence I spoke.

"Whoa! I don't know who took a dump in *your* Cheerios this morning, but I was just being friendly. I thought you—*especially you of all people*—might be interested to hear the latest news. You seemed interested when I told you about it *yesterday*."

"What do you mean, *especially me*?"

"You're *always* up on the latest news, and are *always* into your research and all. I thought *you'd* like the information." She turned like she was about to stalk off.

"Courtney, I'm sorry. I'm just not myself this morn. I'm in here pretty bloody early, I haven't eaten, and am just irritable as all hell. That's it. Really. That's all."

"Oh, God. I should've noticed. You're never here this early! Of course you're here for some reason, and I bet you need to get into whatever work it is you're here early to do so you don't need the news update since you're about to read all about it in the newspaper and all and—"

"Yeah, so off I go—to work! Heigh ho!" I sometimes wondered if she even needed to breathe. Maybe she was a creature of the dark, not needing oxygen, food, drink or anything else. She was perchance some sort of evil daemon sent to torture those of us intent on *accomplishing something.*

Annoyed, hungry and frustrated, I fled to my cubicle. It was as if Courtney had appeared out of nowhere to talk to me about the killer just to draw attention toward the murders and murderer. Kelly couldn't be the killer. It just wasn't physically possible. Courtney's daft assertions had forced me to face reality, too, and consider that there were millions of other possible suspects all over the area. Why was I so fixated that it was someone I knew? It was illogical and made no sense.

Everything wasn't always about me, after all.

I'd just gotten to my desk when my phone rang. "Shawn Donnelly," I said, answering it.

"Okay, so you snuck out while it was still dark, without waking me. Should I take that as a hint?" Ashley asked.

"Oh, for feck's sake—Ash, please, *please*, please don't be like that. This. I just needed to get into work early. I had things—stuff—to do."

"Shawn, I'm just yanking your chain. Now, I do wish you'd left me a note or something, but—"

"I would have, honey, sweetheart, my heart's desire—I would have, but I'm not real literate first thing in the morning, you know? You think my handwriting's bad usually? You haven't seen it before I'm well and truly awake."

I'm guessing she heard me typing and clicking my mouse, because she said, "Yeah, well, I'll let you off this time. Now you want to tell me exactly why you had to go sneaking out?"

"Oy, it don't matter no more, since I've realized I was insane."

And with that, I went back to my life as usual, flirting lightly with Ash before hanging up and returning to work.

Except then I picked up a paper and saw a picture of my brand-spanking new coworker at the finding of a body.

4

Suspectors Anonymous, May I Help You?

I didn't call the police, but, because of the photo in the paper, whenever I had a spare moment, I worked on the spreadsheet-of-proof I was putting together. It was rather sparse right now, but I couldn't resist looking at everything going on with this case—after all, if I was to be involved with some sort of mystery-weekend gig, I ought to get my heels wet with some mysterious stuff—or, at least, that seemed a right fine excuse to get involved with whatever was going on here.

Kelly was keeping articles tracking various deaths and disappearances. Okay, not that weird. She had been surfing various sites on serial killers, and ways, methods and means of murder. Kinda weird. She had other stuff relating to these incidents in her cube. That was bona fide weird. She had moved to town about the time the incidents began. That one fact was so absolutely weird I couldn't stop digging.

I wondered how I could get more information. I could go to HR and see what they could tell me about her—check out her résumé, maybe make some calls to her references and past employers, and whatever else I could discover.

I needed to make a list! I *liked* lists. I liked making them and being able to make them. It all made me feel so *organized*.

Let the list making commence!

Discovery:
- Google her and conduct further online research based on that
- Get résumé from HR
- Look at employee file in HR (how to do this? Break into HR? Or obtain her file in another way?)
- Call references
- Call past employers (use ruse of being a potential employer)

But I knew I had to expand my thinking. If she really was a murderer, I *so* needed to . . . good God, dare I say? Think outside the box.

- Follow Kelly
- Find out where she lives and go there. At least look in from outside
- Find out more about her. Like, maybe go out to lunch with her
- Talk with others in her department

This was beginning to look like an actionable plan. I could start to make this work. I *could* make this work. Even if actionable wasn't a real word. I wasn't a writer, so which words were real and which ones weren't really didn't matter.

I scratched the back of my neck as I again told myself that I was doing it only to hone my skills for the mystery-weekend madness.

But at some point even I wasn't buying it any more.

So as I analyzed, wrote and obsessed about work-related matters, I also Googled Kelly Everson, trying to see if I could find out anything about her. Even with the use of qualifiers and quotation marks, I ended up with more hits than I could deal with. I didn't know enough about her to use better qualifiers and whittle the list down much, to my one, specific Kelly Everson.

So, whenever I was on the phone, I worked my way through all the hits, and was so glad for the upgrade from my home dial-up service. Speediness really did make a diff.

I was sighing with the defeat, thinking I would never get any substantial knowledge about my Kelly Everson online when I realized a key point: I could find someone to help me, and I knew just who to ask. Maybe not so much with the online, but real-time was better than online every time.

"Yo, this is Jamie," she answered on the third ring.

"This is Shawn. I've got a favor to ask."

"Hang on a sec." She came back about a minute later. "Sorry, my hands were a mess. I'm tuning up my neighbors' Beemer. You need something?"

"Do you have any free time tonight?"

"Depends on what for."

"I want you to follow a coworker of mine."

"That's extreme. Why?"

"I think she's a serial murderer."

"Ooo, the clot thickens. Tell me more."

I leaned into the receiver, hooding it with my palm, even while I looked around to ensure my privacy. "Okay, so yesterday morning when I got in, she was copying all these articles about serial killers and missing people and dead folks."

"Which proves all of . . . Nothing! Nada! The big zippo! Ya got anything else?"

"She's surfing a lot of evil sites online—"

"How do you know that?"

"I was in her cube looking for a usage guide—I needed to check whether to use *affect* or *effect* in a particular instance—and hit her mouse and happened to notice."

"So you were snooping."

"Of course. And then, this morning, when I got in early . . . God, James, she all but had relics in her desk drawers."

"Zippo-rama."

"You think I'm psychotic."

"Yeah, that's about the size of. You have nothing. But I'm all into helping one of the partners of Adventures Unlimited."

"Adventures Unlimited?"

"It's what we're thinking of calling it. We don't want to give it all away to the unwary and all."

"But then how will folks find you? Know what you're about? Now, okay-fine, maybe you've got a cover name and such going on, but you have to give folks a clue, y'know?"

"Makes sense."

"So maybe something more like Murder, Inc. Murder Express, maybe. Murders 'R' Us?"

"Ain't those a little, well, negative?"

"We probably all need to have a brainstorming session to determine how to best target and name this new enterprise. Anyway, I need you to follow this woman—Kelly Everson. She knows me, and what I look like. I need someone with a lower profile to keep track of her and all. Keep an eye on her and all that." I glanced around, feeling paranoid, like someone was watching me, or listening in on my phone call. Maybe even Kelly! I stood and looked around even more. Just some folks by the copy machine and an impromptu meeting or two several feet from me. I wondered if I should help Brenda with the laser printer, until she closed the cover and gleamed in victory.

"This has got something to do with what you were all on

about last night, doesn't it?"

I picked at my fingernails, trying to dislodge unseen dirt from beneath them. "Yes, it does."

"So 'fess up with the four-one-one and I'll be all over it."

"Jamester, sometimes I don't understand a single bloody word you're saying."

"Huh?"

"Say it again in English."

"Oh, like you do all the time—Shawn, you've been in this country for more'n a decade, what's with all this Gaelic crap?"

I shrugged. "You can take the girl outta Ireland, but can't take the Irish outta the girl."

"C'mon, Irish, everybody knows what four-one-one is."

It was suddenly quite bloody apparent why, if not for all the gazillion other reasons, Jamie and I were exes. At least on the bright side, I might have a bunch of exes, but they were all entirely different, so it wasn't like I kept making the same mistake over and over. I gritted my teeth. "Humor me."

"You call four-one-one for information? Duh, Shawnie, where've you been? Everybody knows this shit!"

"So you want information?"

"Yeah, the sitch. Give me the details."

"I told you—I figure her for a serial killer!" God, she was so beyond frustrating at times!

"For all your denying, I already figured that much out. What I mean is, what does she look like, what kind of car does she drive, where does she live? Bottom line, how will I find her, know her and follow her?"

"She's about five-six, has Angelina Jolie's complexion, long black hair, and could stand to gain a few pounds."

"Sounds like a hottie."

"She is a right beaut. But she may also be crazier than a squirrel in a peanut factory. If I'm right, she's killed at least four times—all men, though."

"So I ain't got nothing to worry 'bout, huh?"

I thought about what I was asking this dear friend to do—keep track of a possible serial killer for me. "I don't know much about this all, James. I'm going to find out more—her address and all of that. But I also know that it looks as if she's keeping track of some folks who aren't dead yet as well. Or at least, their bodies haven't been found yet."

"So what are you going to be doing, while I'm out risking life and limb following this so-called serial killer?"

"Getting more info on her and her crimes. Finding the proof that'll get the police to see her for the serial killer she is or convince me forever that I'm a loon."

"Isn't that kinda what I'll be doing, too?"

"Yes. But if she is a killer, it'd probably be good to keep an eye on her—so if she does look like she's gonna kill again, we maybe might be able to stop her. And get proof. And get the cops involved. And all that."

"Let me get this right—you want me breathing down the neck of a serial killer, and you want me to jump in if it looks like she might kill again?"

"No! Are you completely nutters?" It felt as if little creatures were crawling all over me. I knew my faeries had left me high and dry at Karen's cottage, but they couldn't be this wrong. I knew something was up with all this! "If she does anything suspicious, I want you to call the coppers. Keep watching if you can, but if you can't, then get the bloody hell outta there. Oh, and you can also call me."

"What? So you can go and get yourself all dead, too?"

"Jamie, I'm serious. There's something not right with this girl and I want to get to the bottom of it. We have the chance to save lives here and I think we should take it."

"You're gonna need someone following her for more than one night, then. I'll call Kevin. He might be able to help out."

"Kevin? The flaming fag boy? Are you completely bonkers?"

"One, he's self-employed, so he's got the time and availability. Two, he'll be willing to do it to get an idea of what it's like to do a stakeout—his imagination will go hog wild with this sort of thing. Kinda like having Don dress up as a swashbuckling pirate and all."

"But we're talking about a killer here, Jamie." I wasn't seeing how Kevin would be safe at all in such a situation, or helpful either.

"He'll go running like the sissy boy he is at the first sign of trouble. That makes him perfect for it. He won't go trying to act the hero at all."

"Oh." Was it serious enough to pull in Kevin? Did I believe my own ridiculous notions enough to bring in not one but two people? "I don't think this is some sort of flight o' fancy, Jamie. I really, seriously, think this woman is a killer." I scratched the back of my neck and all up and down my arms. Maybe I shouldn't risk my friends to this and just call the cops, instead? *With what, Irish? Tales of itches and faeries and naught else? But, really, maybe my neck itching at the lake was just trying to tell me that my friends were up to no good—so it was actually spot-on?*

"Just want to make sure," Jamie said. "What with you and your *gobshite* and *leprechauns* and *screaming banshees* and all."

"There's no such thing as leprechauns, any fool knows that." Her accusations made me even more sure of myself, impossibly more certain, in fact. Maybe it was all theory before, but now it was real. "Listen, okay, fine. Meet you in the parking lot here at four forty-five p.m. I'll follow her out, and then, well, you'll know who it is."

"And where exactly is here? You really are with us in the new business, right?"

"Of course. But I can always change my mind, y'know?"

"Yeah. And I'd have to kill you then. And make it look like some serial killer'd done you in."

⤫⤫⤫

I met Jamie in the parking lot and chatted with her casually until Kelly left, saying good-bye to us en route. I put Jamie on her tail, with all appropriate words of caution about taking care and all that rigmarole. Then I looked at my watch: five thirty. The folks in Human Resources—next stop on my list—were probably long gone. They were right nine-to-fivers after all.

I jogged across the lot to the main building, quickly nodding to the receptionist before heading up the stairs to HR.

"Hey, Stace," I said, "how're the kids?"

"Oh, good, good, Shawn," she said, turning off the lamp on her desk and picking up her purse. "We all have to get together sometime soon—Tina was *so* thankful to you for scanning and fixing those photos for her. She'd thought they were totally lost."

"Oh, good," I said. "I don't have the greatest eye, so sometimes I'm a tad worried about my Photoshop work." I followed her to the door, palming a piece of paper to block the door from latching shut behind us.

"Um, Shawn?" Stacy said. "You do realize there's also a deadbolt on this door, right? So whatever you're trying to do there won't work."

"Oh."

She opened the door back up and led me back inside. "What is it you want, Shawn?"

"That new girl over in my building? Kelly Everson? She's a new copywriter?"

"Yeah, she started just a few weeks ago. What about her?"

"Well, it's just that I'm curious about her is all. Nothing in particular, 'cause particulars are how rumors are started, and I don't want to start any rumors—"

"What? You think she's a member of the tribe?"

"Oh, no, not at all. I barely know her."

"Then what?" When I wouldn't meet her gaze, instead looking down while I tried to figure out just how much to let her in on, she continued. "So what is it? Looking to recruit her? But I thought you'd just gotten yourself a girlfriend?"

"No, well, yes, but no. Anyway, could I just, well, maybe you could just let me glance through her employee files for a few minutes?"

"Shawn?"

"Yes?"

"Are you on crack?"

"Uh, no."

"Then how can you convince yourself that I might let you have your hands—and eyes—all over confidential employee files?"

"I seem to remember a certain networking meeting—"

Stacy turned red and also turned away from me. "You can't keep bringing that stuff up, Shawnie." She walked to a wall of filing cabinets. The first time we'd met, I'd saved her from a boy with too many hands.

I'd known Stacy for a great many years. It was kind of nice that our paths kept crossing—all coincidental-like. And coincidence, real, true, pure coincidence, wasn't supposed to actually happen, as I'd been thinking to myself an awful lot of late. But I guess it actually happened all the time—if you tried hard enough you could always make connections between events.

"This is the last time you can use that against me," Stacy finally said, sighing. "Okay, fine, what do you want to know about Kelly?"

"Last time for that one," I agreed, leaning over to pull the file from her hands. I had loads more to pull from.

"Hey! Give it!"

I dodged her, putting the desk between us and keeping my back to her. I glanced through the file, not sure what I was looking for, but noting the primary dates, locations and events of Kelly Everson's life. As well as her address.

And I kept moving all the while.

"Shawn! I'm so gonna tell your mother!"

155

"And I'll tell Tina all about that time I caught you in the restroom at—"

"Just hand over the file and I'll forget this happened."

"Here you go," I said, returning it to her. "Thanks ever so much."

"At least this time it wasn't Brenda," she said, locking up behind us. "She's had a chip on her shoulder ever since we brought in Ed."

"Well, the guy is a right arse."

"But he knows his stuff."

"Whatever you say."

5

Which Way Did She Go?

"Jamie, where the heck are you?" I said into my cell just after I left the building. (I'd broken down and gotten a cell phone so as to better communicate with Ashley. The things we do for love.) I was busily jotting in my notebook everything I remembered about Kelly's employee file.

"Stuck in traffic. Just a few cars behind your girl. Oh, fuck you, you bastard!"

"Excuse me?"

"Sorry, some jackass just cut me off."

"Where exactly are you?"

"On six-ninety-six heading west from Oakland County right into Macomb. Good God, I think we're in . . . Warren. Ew."

"Is that all? How bad is traffic out there?"

"She stopped to fill up and get some smokes. God, I want one. And a shot of Jack to go with. I'll behave now."

God, she really was on the wagon. "Have you talked with Kevin yet?"

"Yeah, he's really excited about it. He was packing some snacks and pops in a cooler so he'd be all set to join me once she settles somewhere long enough for it to be possible."

"Well, if she gets off on Hoover, she's likely going home."

"Someone young and hot lives in Warren?"

"Yeah, she lives near Thirteen and Schoenherr."

"Poor bitch. Okay, I'm gonna let you go so I can call Kevin and give him the four-one-one."

"You talk with too many numbers."

"Catch ya on the flip side," she said, just before hanging up.

I hung up my phone and gazed at the parking lot. I had Kelly's address. I knew where she lived. I knew where Jamie and Kevin were likely heading—as they followed Kelly, who was likely a serial killer. I really didn't want to risk having them go off after a killer all by themselves. I should go with. Meet them there before I went home to do more research.

I took off toward I-696, figuring I could take that across to Hoover, just as Jamie and Kelly had. I pulled out my phone and dialed Ash's cell.

"Ashley Greenly, how can I help you?"

"Hey, honey. We didn't have any really specific plans for tonight, did we?"

"Um, no, we didn't. I was meaning to call you, though. I've got to work late tonight, preparing for an early morning meeting—and then I've got the meeting first thing tomorrow at eight."

"Tired of the fabulous sex and Irish wit already?" I joked with her, but she'd had a lot of things going on lately. I wondered if I should worry.

"Oh, honey, you know I *always* want to see you, Shawn. I went way too long without seeing you to not want to see you now as often as I can—it's just we've been seeing so much of each other there hasn't been time for things like house cleaning. Plus, I don't know when I'll finish tonight and by the time I stop by home—"

"Baby, baby, it's fine. It's all good. I understand completely. I was just checking in because there was something I was . . . thinking . . . about doing tonight—"

"And now you can. So it works out all ways," Ashley said, then, seductively, "but I will see you tomorrow night, right?"

"Yeah. You will, *mo gra*. You will."

"I like it when you say that. Call me that. I like it a lot, Shawn, my love."

Another quick call to Jamie confirmed that Kelly had indeed gone home. Jamie gave me precise directions, which saved me getting lost in one of the more warren-like parts of metro Detroit. It was even named Warren in a rare fit of civic honesty.

By the time I stowed my car around the corner from Kelly's and jogged over to Jamie's van, Kevin had already joined her.

"Where is she?" I asked Jamie, climbing up next to her.

"Why, hello there," Kevin said, opening his cooler. "Can I get you anything? Some goat cheese crostini, perhaps?"

"She got home about fifteen minutes ago," Jamie said.

"Do either of you have a picture of her?" Kevin asked. "I think it'd really help if I knew what she looked like."

"Kevin, dude, did I really just run by your car like two feet away?" I asked. I didn't bother asking just what goat cheese crostini was. It seemed a truly frightening thing.

"Yeah, I saw Jamie's van and parked just behind it."

"Did you not ever see any TV shows or movies about evasive behavior and clandestine operations?" I asked.

"Ooo," Kevin said, "I loved *The Bourne Supremacy!*"

"And yet you learned nothing about being all sneaky-like?" I asked.

"Don't worry, Irish," Jamie said. "I'm sure he'll pick it all up."

"That was really stupid of me, huh?" Kevin said. "You can really tell I write romances and not spy or detective novels.

Hey—but maybe I'll take to writing those next, given everything I'm bound to learn with all you're putting me through lately!"

"Nice to see you're finding the bright about a serial killer," I said. "So she's inside now?"

"Yup," Jamie said, pulling out a pair of binoculars. "She pulled up at six seventeen, used her remote to open the garage, parked, checked her mailbox, went in and closed the garage door."

"And she's been there ever since," Kevin said. "I got here about six thirtyish myself. Pulled up behind Jamie, and she—Jamie—has been filling me in since. While we've been keeping an eye on the house, of course."

"And enjoying this gourmet feast," Jamie said, grabbing something from the cooler.

"Ooo, is that a mini-quiche?" I asked, spying something in a tray on the backseat. "I *love* mini-quiches!"

For the next fifteen minutes, I finished filling Kevin and Jamie in on all the details while we kept an eye on the house, enjoyed gourmet treaties and discussed what we would do if she hit the road.

"One thing's occurring to me, though," Kevin said, looking across the street. "It's been dark for a bit now, and it's just her kitchen light that's still on. I haven't seen any movement anywhere else in the house."

"Are you saying the lights are on but no one's home?" I asked. "And can we just pretend I didn't say that?"

"I've been watching," Jamie said. "She's in there—because she sure as hell ain't left. You two sit tight." With that, she popped out the back door of the van farthest from Kelly's house, and dodged her way cautiously across the street.

Kevin and I watched in rapt fascination as she used trees, cars and anything else available to conceal her movements. "See, now that's sneaky," I said.

"I need to learn me some of that," Kevin said, watching how Jamie carefully peered in one window after another, completely checking out Kelly's house before she sneaked back to the van.

"The lights really are on but nobody's home," Jamie said. "I didn't see jack."

"Well, I just don't see how that's possible," Kevin said. "We've been watching."

"Except when we've been talking and not paying that much attention," I said. "Which you likely did before I showed up as well."

"No, no," Jamie said. "Even when we were talking I was keeping an eye on the house. If she got out, she snuck out. As in, she must have known we were here, or been really lucky. She could be in the basement, or in the attic. If she *did* leave, I'm guessing she went out the back door. There's a gate in the fence back there into her neighbor's yard."

"That's the way I would've gone, then," I said. "If I were a serial killer wanting to kill and knowing I was followed—I'd be big with the sneaking around bits of life like that."

"But how would she have known we were here?" Kevin asked.

"Hello?" I said. "You parked right behind Jamie and snuck up into her van. Or else boldly strode up here in plain sight. It was probably wicked obvious." I looked at my watch. Eight forty-nine. I went toward the van's back passenger-side door, just like Jamie had.

"Where are you going?" Jamie asked.

"I want to scope the house myself. I might see something you two wouldn't," I said.

"God, top much?" Kevin flamed as I slid out the door and worked my way carefully across the street. "You know it's all about trust!" he loudly stage-whispered at me.

Her house was a small, two-bedroom, one-story structure that likely had some sort of name, but one I didn't know. I wasn't up on all the latest, or even earlier, architectural styles, after all. But I could tell, even from my quick look-see around the neighborhood, that it was a cookie-cutter house, just like all the others nearby. Out here in the suburbs, neighborhoods were all developed with one or two, maybe up to three, styles of homes. Underneath all the crime, killing and drug dealing, Detroit and its suburbs really weren't that interesting.

This style made it easy for me to ascertain that no one was home. Unless she was sitting alone in a dark room, which I highly doubted. As I made my way around the house again, I tried all the doors, to no avail. It was locked up tight.

As I rounded the corner to the front, I saw a bubble gum machine pull up. I quickly assessed the chances of me escaping unscathed: slim to none. They, the cops inside the black-and-white with flashing lights, *so* wouldn't believe me if I told them what was going on, why I was there, and what I was doing.

So I headed for the back gate, which was exactly where and like Jamie said it was, even as I hoped they'd followed the car that'd just pulled out of the drive of a nearby house. I slipped into the next yard before the cops spotted me. Fortunately, I don't think they heard me tripping over the junk in the yard, since they likely would have come chasing after if they had. Instead, after tripping, bruising, and all that stuff, I finally navigated the yard full of desolate auto parts and regained the street.

I ran around to my car and called Jamie.

"So you got away okay?" Jamie answered.

"Yeah, I snuck out the back gate, went through the neighbors' yard, and am now back at my car. Which isn't across the street from her house."

"Point taken," Kevin said.

"Oh, Kevin's still here, too," Jamie said. "We're lying on our backs in my van, sharing the cell."

"What're the cops doing?" I asked.

"Looking around," Jamie said.

"I'm guessing somebody saw either you or Jamie lurking about and called the Neighborhood Watch," Kevin added.

"Let's just hope she doesn't get home soon and get tipped off by the cops," I said. "If she didn't already know we were onto her, that'd sure as fuck do it."

"Shawn, why don't you just go home?" Jamie said. "You have to be to work in the morning. Kevin and I don't. Besides, if you're going to do this, what do you need us for?"

"But still, this is my coworker," I said.

"We've lost her tonight," Jamie said. "Better for you to be fresh tomorrow. We'll follow her into work in the morning, and I'll get you up-to-date on everything that's going on."

By the time I got home, I was wicked tired. Being all suspicious really took a lot out of one. I really just wanted to crash for a good long night's rest, but first I checked my messages (one from Ashley, saying she'd love to have lunch on the morrow, but couldn't, so recommended dinner instead. Well, perhaps dinner *and* dessert), and then checked my e-mail (I *so* needed to get DSL or cable, as opposed to my old-fashioned dial-up service) while I threw together a bag lunch for tomorrow. Ashley'd left me two schmoopy mails, and Ma and Da each left me one from their work addresses, two people wanted to sell me penile enlargement devices, a very rich woman from Nigeria wanted to pay me a lot of money to help her transfer money from one place to another, and some Broward County business association was really sure I needed information about their meetings.

I wanted to call Ashley back, but she'd said she had an early meeting in the morning, after a late night tonight, and now it was after midnight, so I reckoned I ought to just catch a few Zzzzs myself, since tomorrow was likely to be another amusement-park/roller-coaster fun day.

Regardless, I spent the next few hours finishing Googling Kelly Everson, to no avail. Given all I now knew about her, her past, and her past employers, I still couldn't pin her down too much online. Didn't everyone have a blog nowadays? Why didn't she? Like maybe something at serialkillersrus.com?

6

The Day After

As soon as I got into work the next morning, I walked the floor, assessing who was in and who wasn't. Kelly wasn't yet in. I got some go-go juice from the kitchen and made my way to my desk, from which I called Jamie.

"Yo, Irish, looks like your girl's heading into the office," Jamie answered.

"You're not big with the hellos, are you?"

"Not so much. Kevin and I slept in shifts last night, but I think we both are in serious need of some hard Z time."

"Since you're following her into work, is it safe to assume she came back home last night?" I got up and stretched the phone cord so as to ensure no one was lurking nearby. I was alone. Still, I cupped the mouthpiece with my hand and spoke in guarded tones.

"Yeah, she did. Like around two. She pulled up on a bike and went in. I can only guess that she went out the back way to get her bike last night, and, since we weren't looking for a bike, that's also why we didn't see her take off earlier."

"Ten-speed? Mountain bike?"

"Triumph," Jamie said. I could just about imagine her shit-eating grin. I liked Triumphs as well.

"Any idea where she'd gone?" I asked.

"Not a clue. But Kevin and I talked about it, and we're okay with keeping an eye on your girl for a couple of days," Jamie said. "When she's not at work."

"I'll let you guys know if I anticipate any variation in her working hours."

"Just remember your promise about Murder, Inc. We're having a meeting this weekend to vote on the name, and decide on a few other things as well."

"Got it. Count Ash and me in."

"You are one lucky dawg hooking it up with that hot thing. And we're here. I'm handing your package over to you for safe-keeping, honey. Catch ya later, alligator." With that, Jamie hung up the phone.

"Okay, so either you're cheating on your brand-spanking-new girlfriend"—Brenda said from behind me. I nearly leapt to the ceiling she startled me so badly—"or you're participating in insider trading, you bad girl."

"Brenda! You scared me half to death!"

"So what is it, Donnelly? I know you're up to something. I can see it."

"Well, as a matter of fact, I'm really hoping to get the cell Martha Stewart so kindly remodeled a few years ago. And Ashley and I aren't up to spanking yet."

"TMI! TMI!" Brenda yelled, her hands over her ears.

"Coffee time." I brushed past her to the kitchen. Brenda wasn't far behind. As soon as I refilled my mug and turned around she was there, arms crossed in front of her.

Then she reached out a hand and ran her fingers across the tops of my well-gelled hairs. "Wow. You've *really* got baby bird hair today. I just gotta touch it. And I think it adds at least another inch or two to your height. So what exactly are you up to?"

"About five-four—without the hair lift. And I'm not about to say more right now, since I don't really need any more of a rep as the office loony."

"So what do you guys think about the latest developments?" Courtney said, walking in and pouring herself a cup of coffee.

"What're you talking about?" I stopped so suddenly Brenda bumped into me and we both lost some joe over the matter as it sloshed out of our mugs.

"Don't you two ever read the newspapers? Listen to the radio? Watch the morning news, for chrissakes? They found another one!"

"Another what?" I asked.

"Another body. It was that guy who worked at BB&D—I can't believe you haven't heard about it. C'mon, he worked for the competition. Are you insane? You haven't heard about it?"

I glanced around the kitchen, looking for a newspaper, to no avail. I remembered hearing that in the good ole days, you couldn't walk through an office without tripping over one. Now we were expected to get our news fixes online. Or by word of mouth. Was this some sort of devolution or what?

"So where was he found? What happened to him? What was his name?" At least Brenda was quick with the rapid-fire questions.

"It looks *just* like at least two of the others—he was held, tortured and killed. They found his body—totally toasted—buried in some field out by Tiger Stadium. It was some kid and his dog that found him."

"Sounds like maybe BB&D is short, what? A mid-level AE?" I said.

"I'm not sure what he did there exactly," Courtney said. "But I did hear Preston Alexander was one big asshole."

"Where'd you hear that?" I asked.

"The guy was a jerk," Brenda said. I turned to look at her and she stepped back, apparently on the same boat as me—wanting to leave the train wreck that was Courtney. "I . . . I heard stuff. We're all in the same biz and all. After all." She literally backed herself into a corner.

"So he was an asshole," I said.

"Yeah, from what I read, he was like one of those smooth-talking types," Courtney said. "You know—if you say no, then you must . . . like women. Or be a bitch. Or frigid."

"So it's always something about the woman," Brenda said.

"God, I hate guys like that!" I said. "Makes me glad he got his, finally." I said it before I could stop the words from flying out like shrapnel.

"From what I've read," Brenda said, "all these guys were kinda misogynistic."

"So you're in support of the serial killer then," Courtney said, staring at us wide-eyed.

"Well, no, not exactly, I mean, it's not like I support killing or anything—except maybe animals," I said, and continued when Courtney and Brenda stared at me like I'd grown a third head or something. "For eating. So long as they're raised and killed in a humane way and all. You know?"

"You people are crazy," Courtney said. "Sometimes I don't even know why I bother trying to be nice to you." She shook her head and left.

"Wow," Brenda said, watching Courtney's retreating figure. "I never would've believed it."

"That she ever left a conversation first?"

"No. That she'd use words like *bitch* and *frigid*."

"Oh. Right-o. Yeah, wouldn't have expected that myself. You know, I need to get to work now," I said, turning to go back to my cube.

"Yeah. Right. You're off to find out more about that murder. I see that light in your eyes. What's up, Shawnie? Why so interested in it all?"

Brenda was my closest at-work friend, even though she was my boss. I talked to her quite a bit, about a lot of different important things, and she knew me rather well. Could even reckon the way I thought occasionally, which was truly an astounding feat.

I glanced around and saw folks scurrying to their offices, cubes and work areas. I took Brenda by the elbow and led her to the media closet, where we kept all our reference materials. But the door wouldn't open. The handle turned, but the door wouldn't budge.

That sort of thing seemed to be happening a lot to me of late.

"Step back, Donnelly," Brenda said, putting her shoulder to the door and pushing in with all her substantial might, slowly but surely shoving it open. "Good lord, there's a file cabinet against the door!"

"Um, Bren? Correct me if I'm wrong here, but this room was closed with no other entrance. How could that filing cabinet have moved over to block the door by a few inches?"

"I'll leave you to ponder that imponderable," Brenda said. "So what's with all the need for hush hush?"

"What do you think about that new copywriter?" I asked, all quiet-like, once the door was closed behind us.

"Which one? That Kelly girl?"

I had a feeling she was deliberately punning me, but decided to let it slide nonetheless. "Kelly Everson, and yes, her."

"Nothing, really. She seems nice enough."

"I think she's behind all these killings."

Brenda broke out laughing. "Omigod—Donnelly, that's just too funny!"

"She's acting all suspicious-like, keeping close track of all these murders, has a veritable file of murder keepsakes—and just listen to her talk!"

"Um, Shawn?"

"Jamie and Kevin—those old college classmates I told you about—have agreed to follow her outside of work for a while. But we just started it last night, and they lost her for several hours. Way I figure it, they lost her just long enough for her to go out and kill this guy!"

"Shawn—this is wrong on so many levels, I practically don't know where to begin."

"Yeah, I know. Working with a serial killer? Who'd have thought it?"

"Shawn, dear, I think you need to speak with Alex about buying a clue. For starters, the guy the police found last night was killed several days ago. Next up, he's been missing for nearly two whole weeks."

"She did something last night, Brenda. I know it. She slipped out of our sights long enough to do something and she did it. She must have caught onto us, and that's what happened—someone died. We're not going to slip up again, though."

"Your friends pulling that stunt with you at the lake has you looking for crimes in all the wrong places. You're trying to solve these murders because you're still frustrated from all of that."

"Don't go trying to psychoanalyze me and shite, Bren. Yes, that thing with my friends bugged me, but this isn't about that. This is about Kelly being a murderer. I know you don't want to hear about a coworker being something like that, because we never want it to be so close to home. We never want it to be someone we know hurting, harming and killing folks, but, Bren, you've got to believe me. I know this."

"Shawn, this isn't about Kelly being a serial killer. I think I understand it all now."

"No, you don't—"

"It's about her being a writer."

"You're just . . . She's a writer? Copywriter, you mean?" Oh, no. Not again. Not another alternate reality.

"No. Yes. I mean. She's both."

"And what does that have to do with the price of rice in Uruguay?" This just wasn't possible. This sort of shite could not possibly keep happening to one person.

"Nothing. But I was in the kitchen last week, listening to her talking with some other copywriters, and I heard her talking about her next novel—yes, *next*, as in further beyond the past ones that have already been published—which is about a, *hello*, serial killer."

"What?"

"If she's said anything, done anything, looked suspicious about anything—she's just trying to work out the details of her next book. Work out the details and get into the mindset of the killer."

"No. She's a killer. She's *the* killer, in fact. I just know it." I just couldn't believe I was wrong yet again. Wouldn't people ever stop playing with my head? I felt such a fool. Brenda wouldn't ever trust my judgment again.

"Shawn, you need to start looking for the normal in everyday life, because that's usually what's going on. I need to get to work—hot new presentation to put together. And you need to get to that fifty-state radio estimate, if I'm not mistaken." With that, she turned her back on me and left, leaving the door open behind her.

I sometimes forgot she was my boss, which was probably the worst thing I could do for my career.

I knew she knew a lot about media. She also knew how to play office politics. I could learn a lot from her. And I had to make sure I kept her happy, I thought as I scratched the back of my neck.

❧

"So, you know, I've got to thank you," Kelly said, sneaking up behind me.

"Yii!" I screamed, leaping up, turning about and spilling my coffee.

"Omigod, let me help you with that," Kelly said, grabbing a handful of tissue from the box on my desk and mopping up the spilled liquid while righting the mug.

I tried to block my monitor enough to turn it off before she could see what I had been doing—looking at—when she so unceremoniously scared the crap outta me.

"God, I hope there wasn't anything important here," she said, picking up my sopping legal pad.

I wrenched it from her, so she couldn't even try to figure out that the scrawls on it were all about her. "No, no big, just a few notes. Nothing critical or crucial or anything."

"Oh, hey," she said, leaning around me to see my monitor. "You've heard I'm a writer, huh?"

"Oh, yeah, someone said something about it and what can I say? I'm a curious sort—research director and all."

"I thought you were a media buyer and planner?"

"That, too. I wear a few different hats around here."

"I guess so—fix the copier, make the buys, do the research— tell me, do you also bring home the tofu and fry it up in a pan?"

"Huh?"

"I'm sorry—I saw you with that girl yesterday and thought you two were, well, that you two were . . ."

"Jamie?"

"It was like five thirty? I was leaving and saw you on my way out. We spoke? Remember? Yesterday?"

"My ex, Jamie? I mean, we're barely exes since we were barely together in the first place, but she was who I was with last night before we went home. To our separate houses. Homes. Where we live. Separately."

"I knew it! I knew it—that you two were together!"

171

"In the past tense."

"So I thought you two were—had been—involved, and figured that with being, uh, *Lebanese* and all, you wouldn't be bringing home the *bacon* and frying it up in a pan—you'd be bringing home the *tofu* and frying it up in a pan. Get it? Aren't all lesbians vegetarians, after all?"

She really had to have a serious mental ailment to think that was funny. She *really* could be a serial killer. "That wasn't funny."

"I'm sorry. I said hi to you two on my way out last night, and then, later on, I saw a van just like the one I noticed in the lot, when I said hello to you two. Big ole blue panel job. You know the type."

"Yeah, Jamie drives a Ford van. Cheapest model. What are you saying, exactly?"

She laughed. "I saw your friend's van and then saw one just like it later—in fact, I kept seeing similar-looking vans throughout the night."

"Oh really? How . . . interesting."

"Yeah—I was driving home, and *there* it was. I was at home, and there was *another* one—parked right across the street from me. *The entire night.*"

"Interesting. So what did you do?"

"Well, it got my imagination going. I pictured it being the same people in that van, across the street from me, as I saw earlier, and then I wondered how it all came together . . . It got me through my writer's block! I saw that van across the street from my house and I suddenly realized it was a major point in the story I'm trying to work out right now! It was fabulous! Amazing, even!"

"So all good then, eh?"

"Yeah, all good."

"So you stayed home all night, by yourself, writing, huh?"

"Yes, that's what I just said."

She was lying to me. I knew this. And with the way she was

looking at me she knew that I knew she was lying. So was she telling me all this in order to get me to call her on her lie, thus admitting that it was me and mine that were following her the night before? That way she'd know for certain it was, and be able to directly confront me on it—and also wonder why we'd been doing such?

Or maybe she was telling me this because she didn't yet know that we knew she'd slipped out the night before—and she had something to hide about it all. Or else she knew it was me and wanted to know exactly which of my friends helped me and who knew about it because she needed to clean up any loose ends! Just when I thought the world made sense again, Kelly was shredding all reality. I wanted to find Brenda and tell her that just because someone was a writer didn't mean they weren't also a serial killer. Why did I think of the perfect retort too late?

"Hello? Shawn?" Kelly said, waving a hand in front of me. "Are you with me?"

"Oh, uh, yeah—I was just thinking about . . . this buy I need to put together for Wonderbra. That's all." I was a loose end. She was going to do me in, too. I couldn't admit anything to her. "So, uh, was there anything else you wanted?"

"No, no, not at all. Just trying to make nice with the coworkers and all, and figured you and your *friend*—*ex*-friend—would like to know how you helped me out and all—with the writer's block. And that I'm fine with, well, all that."

"She's still my friend," I said without thinking. Being protective of her would make her all the more important as a leveraging tool against me. Stupid, stupid, stupid!

"I suppose she is. I'll let you get back to that buy now. I shouldn't have kept you so long as it is."

I needed to call the Jamester yesterday to let her know about this latest development.

7

Writers Are Liars by Definition

I stared at my watch. It was just north of noon. If Jamie had been up all night, I couldn't rightly call her yet—she hadn't had eight hours, and I reckoned that, like me, as she got older, she required more sleep.

So I called Ashley instead. I dragged my phone into the media library (aka the closet, as in *also known as*, I was gettin' all up on my criminal vocabulary) and called her. "Ash, you wouldn't believe this. She's claiming to be a writer now!" I whispered urgently when she picked up on the fourth ring.

"Shawn, is that you?"

"Yes, yes it is. I just spoke to Kelly. She came snooping around my cube, just as I was Googling her!"

"You Googled her?"

"Yeah, and she came over to make sure I knew she was—get this, a writer."

"Well, Shawn, didn't you say she was a copy*writer*?"

"Yes, but she *says* she's working on a mystery."

"As in, like a detective working a case, or as a writer creating one?"

"As in a writer," I said. Hadn't she been paying attention? "She's trying to explain all her weirdness away by putting it down to, well, what she's doing to construct this so-called mystery she's writing."

"So she's not really a writer?"

"No, well, yes, she's a copywriter. And she's on Amazon and all, but I'm not buying this at all for a second. Not even a nano-second."

"Hold on, she's on Amazon?"

"Yeah. Of course. Everyone and their second cousin twice removed is these days."

"Are you?"

"No. I'm not a writer."

"Shawn, I understand, you're all paranoid crazy because of what the gang did to you. That's over. You have to regain reality now."

"I'm in reality. I'm in the now, even. I'm telling you what's what, and we just need to figure out what to do next." She wasn't getting that this was all real. Weren't girlfriends supposed to understand you? Be the ones to be right with you on the edge of your thoughts? "You might be in danger, you know." I couldn't believe she wasn't believing me.

"Shawn, dear, where are you? You sound all echoey."

"I'm in the closet." She was changing the subject?

"Since when?"

"No, I mean I'm literally in the closet. I needed a private place to call you from, so I brought the phone into the closet."

"Shawn!" Brenda said, barging in behind me. "Where's the Wonderbra plan? I needed that last year! Oh, sorry, are you on the phone?"

175

I turned to face her. "I'm talking with Ashley right now." I was most exasperated.

"Oh," Brenda said. "Sorry. Hi, Ashley!"

"Brenda says hi," I said to Ashley.

"So where's the Wonderbra stuff?" Brenda asked.

"Hello?" I said, "I'm working on it and I'm talking with my girlfriend here."

"Hi back," Ashley said.

"Ash says hi back,'" I said to Brenda. "And I'm all over Wonderbra."

"Do you even know what's going on with it?" Brenda asked.

"Whose Wonderbra are you all over?" Ashley asked.

To Brenda I said, "I'm all over it like the peanut butter on a PB and J—or, better yet, I'm so over it, I'm like all that chocolate surrounding the peanut butter in a Reese's Peanut Butter Cup."

Brenda crossed her arms in front of her.

"Shawn, please tell me you didn't just say all that to your boss?" Ashley said. "Because that really didn't make sense even to me, and if you like your employment, well, you might want to rethink this strategy."

I couldn't take this Rubik's Cube of a convo any longer. I had to keep carrying it over from one to another, and stuff was complicated enough without this conversational dilemma to confuse me even further. But before I could beg off the call, Ashley cut in.

"Shawn, dear, I hate to do this, but I've got another call I've got to take," she said.

"Yeah, okay," I said. "I'll call you later, babe."

"You better." Somehow, in those two words, she conveyed that I'd both better let her go, in order to deal with matters of my job, and also that I'd better call her later to fill her in on why I'd called her and what had just happened.

Femmes could be so concise sometimes. It was amazing, really. I could practically cry over how tight they were with their language, it was that beautiful.

I lowered the receiver to my side and looked at Brenda. "Look, I know you weren't believing me earlier, but now I'm even more certain Kelly's the killer. She stopped by my cube earlier to try to ensure I realized she was innocent and had all the perfect excuses for all of her mightily suspicious behaviors, which was, itself, the most suspicious thing she could do."

Brenda stared at me. She frowned. She furrowed her brow. She started to speak. She closed her mouth. She raised a hand as if to point a finger at me and make a point, then she dropped it. She sighed. And finally said, "You've finally done it."

"What?"

"Lost it. I always knew you were a little off-kilter, and now you've finally spun totally out of it. What the hell are you thinking, Donnelly?"

"I've told you what I'm thinking. Kelly's a killer, and I want to prove it before she kills anyone else."

"Shawn, it doesn't matter what happened in the past—what matters now is that you do your job. You have that radio buy to put together and I need the Wonderbra info—seriously, as in, I'm waiting on it."

I walked out of the closet—coming out of it even—and slammed my phone on my desk, picked up a folder and handed it to her.

"What's this?"

"The Wonderbra stuff that's so dreadfully important."

"So you had it done."

"Of course." I picked up another folder. "And here's that Stouffer's radio buy. I didn't think they'd like the full buy with the parameters I was given, so I also ran figures for a few other variations I thought would be good."

Brenda opened that folder. "God, I love you."

"Yeah, remember that before you try to ream me again." I turned, sat at my desk, and continued browsing Kelly's books on

Amazon. "Also, remembering it before deciding my next raise would be good as well."

"Duly noted," she snapped. "But, please, Shawn, can you stop stalking your coworkers? Please?"

"Duly noted, and I'll take it under consideration." Again, not the smartest thing to say to one's boss.

"I really hope you get over all of this pretty darned soon," Brenda said. "Before it—or your attitude—affect your employment. You'd just better not even think about stalking me." She stalked off.

I reached over and hit redial on the phone. "Ash, it's me."

"And I'm with a client right now."

"'Kay, talk later." I let her go, even while wondering . . . Well, like thirty seconds before, she was all "You'd better call me back." Was she getting tired of me already? Or had I pissed her off? Was there something seriously wrong with me? That I kept scaring women off? Was I mentally unstable?

I wanted to cry. But I was at work, so couldn't.

I tapped my fingers on my desk. I needed to talk about all this with someone. Jamie and Kevin were sleeping—or should be—and Ashley was busy.

So I picked up the phone and called Karen.

"Shawn, I'm in tax season, okay? I'm a CPA and it's between January one and April fifteen. Are you tracking this?"

"Yo, babe, you opened this entire can of worms with Murder, Inc. and all that."

"Yes. And that's a sideline. Some way to take me away from all this insanity. To top it all off, the firm changed from the software I loved to some piece of crap that doesn't make sense. I have to get back to work, okay? You need to talk, call me at home between ten and eleven tonight, okay?"

"Yeah, got it. Talk to ya later." But I was already talking to a dead line. I steepled my fingers and stared at the phone. Everyone was at work, busy. Or asleep. There was no one I could talk with about it all.

Except, maybe . . .

I got up and went back to Creative.

And for the first time that day, I got lucky. "Hey, Kelly—sorry I was so, well, abrupt, earlier," I said, standing in the entryway of her cubicle.

"So it's not that I smelled funny or anything?" she said, facing forward toward her computer.

"No, not at all, it's that I obsess about things, and this morning I was all about Wonderbras . . . and that sounds really bad."

Kelly spun around in her chair with a smirk on her face. "It *so* did." She stood up and grabbed her parka and purse. "So where you want to go for lunch?"

"I didn't say anything about lunch yet."

"No, but you were going to. It's about that time, and you came back here being nice and all—only makes sense. You're very easy to read, you know."

"So I've been told," I said, following her back to my cube, where I donned my own coat, gloves and hat. "What do you fancy?"

"I barely know anyplace around here, so just take me someplace . . . *different*. And you're driving, because not only do I not know where we're going, but, also, folks around here don't like how I drive in this white stuff very much. I haven't driven much in it at all."

"Where are you from? Mine's the Sundance with manual lockage," I opened her door for her.

"Butt-fuck-nowhere Georgia," she said, climbing in. "Take me someplace *interesting*."

"So not bog standard." It was snowing lightly as I pulled out onto Northwest Highway. "So you're not from around here, eh?"

"Nope. Some folks think Atlanta's the big time, and it might be. But it was still so close to home it was safe, and I was tired of

179

everything being so safe all the time. I wanted something a little more daring."

"I've been to Atlanta. I've been to Georgia. Where exactly are you from?"

"You've never heard of it," she said.

"Try me. I'm in media. I know lots of small towns." I was trying to get a feel for her, understand her motivations, what made her work and how she thought.

"Climax, all right?"

"Excuse me?" Granted, some of my queries weren't drawn from the sole purpose of getting to know her better, but more from pure curiosity.

"I come from Climax, Georgia. It's down near Florida."

"Climax. Why does like every single bloody state have a Climax?"

"I'm just excited to know there's a Hell, Michigan."

"Dear God, everywhere in Michigan is hell. Why'd you come here?" I was just glad she hadn't insisted on driving. Too many non-snow drivers think there's nothing to driving in snow.

"New York and Chicago scared me," she said, glancing around as if memorizing where we were and where we were going.

"Hello? Detroit? Murder capital?" Frankly, it can be a right mess when they step into such assumptions.

"Actually, that's D.C. these days," she corrected me with information I already, actually, knew. "And that's not what I was talking about. I meant the cost of living in New York and Chicago were scary. Detroit's close enough to Climax for safety, it's possible to live within my means, and use it as a step up to a job in the real advertising creative centers."

"For someone who's creative you're surprising with the forethought."

"I write murder mysteries as well, so I really know how to plot and plan and consider all ramifications of any particular move."

"Well, I certainly hope you really knew what you were getting yourself into when you moved to Detroit," I said, pulling into a parking space and shutting off the ignition.

"Why? What do you mean?"

"We've got a couple blocks to walk. In this cold. This is downtown Royal Oak, honey, so there's never parking where you want to be. It's kinda like those bigger metros that way." I opened my door. "Make sure to lock your door behind you. I don't have any nifty gadgets to do it for you."

"Well, this is a *Buy American* town and all," she said, zipping and snapping her parka, then pulling on her hat and gloves.

"I hate my car. I just couldn't afford better." I pulled on my own hat and gloves, as it really was rather brisk.

"Where are you taking me?"

"Pronto's 608."

"What's the 608 mean?"

"It's their address. Creative wasn't on the agenda when they named the joint, I guess." I smiled at the hostess. On a previous visit I'd finally realized she used to work for me at a Burger King I'd managed years before. She was straight, but cute. Most importantly, she always got me seated fairly quickly.

"Wow, they've got a really great vegetarian selection," Kelly said, studying the menu once we were seated.

"Yeah, they do. It seems to have become a really hip and with-it sort of joint." At some places I had favorites, but at Pronto's I'd just go through trends—always eating the same thing for several visits in a row, till moving along to another menu item. "Everything's really tasty."

"I've been thinking of becoming vegetarian," Kelly said. "There's a lot of health reasons for it, and, plus, I really don't like the way most food animals are treated. I'd like to not help make corporations, ranchers and . . . *everyone else* . . . rich by shoving as many living, breathing animals into as little space as possible.

Giving them short, horrible lives just so the owners can make as much money as possible."

"I've got a lot of veggie friends. They love this place." Sure, she's against killing—and eating—varmints. But what about people, for feck's sake?

She looked around. Yet again. I was wondering if she'd bought a vowel from Vanna. She leaned toward me and whispered, "Is this a *gay* place?"

"Uh, yeah."

"Wow. *Cool.*"

The waiter came and we placed our orders. Kelly'd been perceptive in seeing its gaiety this quickly. Most of the lunchtime clientele didn't have a clue as to the restaurant's true origins—or that the loafer-light fags frequented the connected bar at night.

"So how long have you been, er, writing?" I asked.

"All my life. I got my first novel accepted for publication when I was twenty-five, though. That's what most people really want to know. Or mean, when they ask the question you just did."

"So I guess all the murder and mayhem in Detroit really helps your writing, eh?"

"God yes. All I have to do is pick up the paper in the morning to get another great plot. I just wish I could write them so fast!"

"But you said earlier today something about block?"

"Well, yeah, you get an idea and start to run with it, but then it becomes actual work, and it becomes hard and block can set in. This is the first time I'm working without an outline, so I don't have backup if I get blocked. I guess it means I didn't do my pre-work well enough. I didn't see my end from my beginning, so I didn't know what went in between." She looked at me as she rolled the wrapper from the straw that came with her water. "I got into writing it, without outlining, and just ran with it. Then I hit a dead end." She folded the wrapper along its creased border. "So last night, seeing that van, and, well, when I stopped

182

at a gas station, I was sure I saw your friend behind the wheel of that van. It was just too weird."

Our food got dropped off.

We tucked in. At least Kelly wasn't one of those annoying straight girls who never ate.

"So you write mysteries," I finally said. "How does one research what it feels like to kill someone?"

Kelly giggled. "I have no idea. Everything I write is first-person from the POV of the detective."

"Really? So you don't have to know what the killer goes through in his—or her—mind?"

"Not at all. I don't go in for all that, let's tease the reader with a paragraph here and there from the killer's POV thing. I focus on the crime and the puzzle of solving it."

"But then what do you need to research, besides police procedural and such?"

"I've got to come up with interesting plotlines. Good characters. Hard-to-figure-out crimes. I have to create the puzzle the detective must decipher. So all these people dying around here right now—it might be everyday stuff to y'all, but to me, it's fodder for many books. I thought I came to Detroit to move up in advertising, but—" She stopped.

"Oh no. You can't talk about all this sort of stuff and then stop. 'Fess up, Kelly."

"I hate saying that all these people dying is helping my writing, but they are, and it is, and . . ." She shrugged.

"C'mon, admit it, wouldn't you like to be there when this *dude's* killing folks? See what it's like? See what it feels like to do so? Wouldn't you?" I was leaning across the table, barely in my seat, whispering heatedly to her. It was practically a hiss by the end.

She shivered. "It'd be interesting, intellectually. Just like the academic part of my mind would like to visit the Detroit Morgue and watch an autopsy. I just . . . I get queasy at the sight of blood.

And I hate seeing things in pain. It's part of why I'd like to become a vegetarian. Should become one, in fact."

She was either playing her part quite well, or else not playing at all.

I missed a lot of what she was saying, because I was so busy and distracted trying to work out just how evil she was, but I did find reality in time to catch, "So, really, bottom line, I figure we're all going to die someday, so it doesn't really matter where I live."

"Do you ever run red lights?" The words were out of my mouth before I could stop them. She was just playing this innocent act up too much.

"Sometimes, yes. But if I do, I tend to stop before pink after that for a while, because I figure getting through a red without a crash or ticket means I've taxed that particular karma for a while, so I owe it back. There's a balance in the world. I try to put out what I take in." She shrugged and looked back toward her veggie sandwich.

It was all too sincere. Which meant she was either telling one worthy of Paul Bunyan, or else it was all lies worthy of a Shrub—lies that could tear apart reality.

"You've got," I said, "what, three books out now? How did you come up with all those ideas? I mean, you're so young."

She smiled, blushed and looked down at her sandwich. "Five books. And I read. I read the papers, books, stories—watch TV and movies. I'm sure even you've heard that there are like ten plots in all of lit—and everything outside of those are reworkings, replacements, remixes of all those. I read something and just so long as I know it's my own idea I'm coming up with—nothing regurgitated from something else—I can use it. I can find a death and wonder how it happened. I can find a scene in a movie and work out what came before and how it might end in death and then it's mine. I might turn off the movie to ensure I don't steal, but I'm willing to let it inspire me."

"A lot of people I know are writers. They do poetry, or online fanfic, or other things without real deadlines or commitments. Regardless, everyone I know has a fabulous idea for a movie or book and wants me to hook them up with some writer I know to help them with it."

"They want a writer to write it. Many fear the blank page. And, also, don't have the sheer bullheadedness to write an entire book. It takes time and the ability to not do a lot of other things so you can write instead."

"So you don't run around stealing ideas, then?"

"I have too many ideas."

"So, um, what do you worry about?"

She took a bite of her sandwich and carefully found the smallest chip to eat with it, before finally answering, "Not finding anything motivational enough to really impel me into the next book. I fear obscurity."

I looked across the table at her. She feared nobody knowing her. I heard her say that and thought it was her condemnation, but then I realized she was still twisting it all. She could fear obscurity and so write her best and make the most of her life, but then she could also let fear drive her to grasp immortality as a serial killer.

Granted, she'd have to be caught for the latter to occur, but maybe that was part of her plot as well.

8

Don't Ask Me, I'm Clueless—as in, Without a Clue

"Okay, so you say she's a writer," Trisha said, pacing Karen and Don's living room later that night.

"Yeah," I replied. "I checked her out and everything. Amazon. Google. The whole box o' Cheerios."

"She's a writer, a *mystery* writer, so it would make sense for her to research murders and mysteries," Trisha said.

"Makes sense," Robert said, tossing back another Scotch. "Why don't we focus on the work? All this talk about Shawn's crazy coworker really isn't getting us anywhere or doing anything for us."

"No, it isn't," I said. "But thinking that I'm working with a mass-murdering lunatic is somewhat distracting from, well, thoughts of murder, mayhem and marketing."

"But, Shawn," Karen said, bringing a plate of appetizers in and putting it on the coffee table. "She's not a mass-murdering lunatic. She's a writer. Yes, maybe she talks about weird things, but c'mon, it wasn't too long ago you thought one of us was a killer."

"Because you all went way far out to convince me of such," I said, leaning forward to snag a stuffed mushroom. "She's not trying." I really hoped it was stuffed with something mighty tasty, which I really suspected it was.

"You said she's a creative sort," Denise said. "They're nuts that way."

I didn't like that I had to stop enjoying the stuffed 'shroom to speak, but 'twas the life of a busy crime-fighter I'd gotten myself into, after all. "Later on, even Brenda said, 'The first time I walked in and heard her going on, I thought she was a stark-raving maniac.'"

"Yeah," Ashley said, hanging up her cell as she came in from another room. "But you told me, 'If you just heard her talking, you'd think she was a homicidal maniac. Especially with the puppets and all.'"

"Which just adds to my entire point," I said. It seemed that, ever since the cell phone knockout of our first weekend together, Ashley was always on the phone, either calling someone or being called. If I was giving out awards for shifty behavior, she'd sure be topping the list with all her cell-phonage. Except for her being such a busy businesswoman and all.

"So you apparently didn't get the memo on the subtext of, 'If you *just* heard her talking,'" Ashley replied. "It means that there's something beyond the talking that might convince one otherwise."

"Puppets?" Don grabbed a wedge of pita bread and dipped half of it in spinach dip while liberally coating the other half with hummus. "What's this about puppets?"

"C'mon, the entire 'I'm a writer so I'm innocent and all' routine is *so* old and overused," I said, snagging some pita and dip of my own. Give me a break, I lived by myself. "What a lame-o excuse it is—and it's pretty much, well, embarrassing that everyone else is buying it. All the folks who hear her go on? All the people who see her with her puppets and they're thinking she's simply creative."

"Um, well," Robert said. "Isn't that kinda in her job description? Her title even?" He grazed all across the table, like, well, for feck's sake, we all were doing.

"It isn't in her job title, but it is in her job description." I rounded on my heel to face him. "Which makes it the perfect cover. No matter what, she can hide behind her title, her book writing, her creativity. Meanwhile, she's out killing her little heart out. She's nabbing folks, holding them—probably torturing them even—then killing them. You ask her, she'll likely go on about—"

"What, Shawn?" Karen asked.

"She'd tell you all about how it's all research." Nobody here was taking me seriously. Not even my girlfriend—not even Ashley was getting how serious this was. My tic was going crazy, and they weren't—*she* wasn't—believing me. And the mad, runaway freight that was my mind came to a grinding halt. That was it. My tic. That irritating itch at the back of my neck. "My tic!" I said. I whipped about and pointed at Karen. "Remember when you told me I was fey 'cause I wanted to take the long way home that night after class? When someone was mugged and killed by those three guys when and where we woulda been if we hadn't followed the itch on the back of my neck?"

"Oh, God, here we go again," Robert said. "Irish going all *fey* with her *sixth sense*. Her *second sight*." He openly mocked me.

I immediately turned to face him. "You think it was just coincidence that I woke your sorry arse up and forced you to class the day you had that pop quiz in the engineering class you almost failed? What woulda happened if you'd missed it?"

"I would've failed," Robert said.

"What's she talking about?" Denise asked.

I faced off with Kevin. "Car accident. Avoided. Need I say more?"

"Shawn's got this eerie sense—" Karen started.

"Her neck itches to let her know something's wrong," Ashley whispered.

"I didn't let any of you know about it for quite the while," I said. " 'Cause I knew you'd think I was fey or such."

"Well, what about at the cottage?" Don said into the now silent room.

I looked about at all those who now surrounded me. No one said a word. "Oh, for feck's sake," I said. "It's not like it sends me a memo. It just goes off when something's wrong. At the cottage, I knew something was wrong. I just didn't get that the something that was wrong was that my friends were all lying to me."

"So how do we know it's not just that this Kelly is acting all weird is why your Spider sense is tingling?" Robert said.

"Because that—her acting all wonky—is obvious. My itch itches for the unseen," I said. "You know, I came here for help—both to give and receive such. You all went way far wicked to try to recruit me into your entire scheme, for *me* to help you. You took me to the brink and made me doubt and mistrust everything and everyone, and, well, that really sucked. And now you all ain't believing a word I say. And I ain't seeing a single"—I looked right at Ashley—"a single hand raised to help me. Doesn't seem fair at all. I hadn't mentioned my tic before, 'cause, well, yes, it did seem to let me down of late."

Ashley shook her head as she stood. "Shawn, honey, you know I'll do anything I can to help you. I just don't think you're onto anything, but I'll do whatever you need me to, regardless." Just then her phone rang. "Just let me take care of this!" She answered the phone, whispering harshly into it, "Not *now*!" She clicked it shut and, to my questioning glance, said, "Annoying coworker who can't take no for an answer."

"Is this something you need help with?" I asked.

"No. He'll get the hint."

"I guess we're at least partly responsible for this," Karen said, sitting next to where I'd sat next to Ashley. "So I'm in with helping you out. I don't believe we'll find anything, but it's the least we owe you."

"Okay, yeah, fine," Robert said, "Karen's right."

"And c'mon." Ashley knelt at my feet and slipped her hands into mine. "Jamie and Kevin jumped right in from the start."

"No. They agreed to help when I twisted their arms." I hated that I was pouting, but it seemed called for.

Everyone reluctantly joined in. *Reluctant* being the key point of it all. It was like I forced them or something.

"That's not what I need." I scrambled to my feet. "I don't need people appeasing me with the 'Yeah, all right, fine, what do we do when we can do something?' I need folks who are in with the catching of a mass murderer. I need someone to stop that, and be all proactive with it. You know."

I walked to the closet to grab my coat, wishing it was something long, dark and billowy, instead of short, fuzzy and snug, and then realized it was in the room I'd just been in. So I had to backtrack to it.

Or I could face the cold, dark Michigan night coatless. But going back to get it meant losing face as well as the impact of my hasty exit.

"Irish," Ashley's voice was soft and sultry in my ear. Her hands were warm and inviting on my shoulders. Her breath crossed my ear. I liked it. "Don't go. Don't leave like this. Don't leave *me* like this."

I didn't look at her. I knew if I looked, if I saw her beautiful face and long hair and cute upturned nose, I'd lose it. I wouldn't be able to control myself. "Ashley, I'm really serious about this, and everyone's thinking I'm completely bonkers. Lives are at stake here, and you're all focused on telling me I'm wrong."

"But we're still willing to back you up, aren't we? We're in this with you—even if it's just to ease your mind."

"But it isn't."

"Does it matter? We're *helping* you. Duh."

"Ash—" I leaned face first against the wall.

"Stop being such a stubborn-headed woolly, Shawn! And will you just look at me already?"

" '*Woolly*'? Did you just say *woolly*?"

"You're rubbing off on me, what can I say?"

"Nothing. Because I know what's going to happen. You're all just gonna do a half-ass job and do whatever you can to prove me wrong." I finally turned to look at her. She had my coat with her.

"We won't do that, Shawn. After all, if, on the extremely off chance you ended up being right, we'd never hear the end of it from you. We're *so* gonna go all the way on this, Shawn, if even just to avoid that!"

"That makes sense of the *not*." I replied, grabbing my coat. "Did you all happen to do a lot of crack this afternoon or some-thing?" I suddenly realized she was helping me, or trying to, and I was being a right fucker.

"This is *not* happening," Trisha said, coming up to top the scene in that way she had. "Karen spent half the afternoon on that damned beef bourguignon." She stared at me with her hands on her hips. "You are both staying for dinner."

Ashley looked at her, looked at me, then turned her back on me and stalked off toward the dining room.

"Uh, okay," I said, following. There was no other option. Especially since I'd just realized I was in right hot water with my woman.

After dinner we worked out a plan. We all sat down with pads of paper, pencils, pens, grids and a big white board Karen pulled out of nowhere and wrote all over to coordinate our schedules and plans.

Then, once we were done with an outline of the marketing plan, we worked out our plan for My Evil Coworker, aka the Evil Copywriter (EC for short).

I was glad, though, that we'd now have more people on the case. From everything I'd ever read or seen, we'd need more folks to really tail EC right and fully. This was also good because it made it even more likely that we'd catch her before she killed too many more people.

I'd just gotten home, put the doggie bag Karen had forced on me in my fridge ("Irish, I swear, if you don't start eating more real food, you're gonna die of malnutrition!"), and was taking off my coat and hanging it in the closet when there was a knock-knock-knocking at the front door.

I knew who it was. I'd left without kissing Ash good night. We'd been cordial enough during dinner and after, but we hadn't been, well, us. I'd tried to get back on her good side, to no avail. I'd finally given up.

I opened the door.

"You need to go see her," Denise said. She pushed me aside and walked into my abode. "She was really upset this evening, and I'm not sure it was all about you, and even though I'm new to all this, even I got it. Can you really be as slow as you keep saying you are?"

"Uh, Denise, if it's really all that, why are you here, and not any of my long-time friends instead?"

"I was the one who first stood up—after you and Ash left—and said it. I might be straight, but I saw you two hook up at the cottage, and I've seen how much you love each other. But then, tonight, you two were parting ways. And it wasn't right. You wanted to hold each other and I've watched you two together and it's pretty fucking hot. So don't blow it, Donnelly. Go get the girl. Don't lose her over some stupid caper or such crap. We're all with you and doing what you need us to do, and she's backing you up, too. So give it up and go to her."

"Lock up when you leave," I said, putting on my coat and going to Ash.

All the lights were out, but there was a trellis leading up to her bedroom window. Ashley was either asleep or pretending to be when I arrived, so I decided to do the romantic and climb to her bedroom window.

I did not, however, expect prickly viney bits to poke me as I ascended. Nor did I anticipate splinters. I got both, however, as well as a cracking trellis just as I reached her window.

"Fuck!" I yelled, grabbing her windowsill as my footing disappeared.

"Oh my God," Ashley said, opening the window moments later. "Shawn, is that you?"

"Uh, yeah, last time I checked it was," I gasped, my right leg sprawled off to find some purchase on the now very unstable trellis, which was toppled to my right. Most of my weight was supported by my none-too-firm handhold on the windowsill.

Ashley pulled at the screen. "I can't get it out. Watch out and hold on." She punched, then kicked it, till it went flying. Fortunately, only the springy, wiry screen part glanced off my head. Then her hands were warm on my wrists. "You've got to help me here, you nit. I'm not big with the butch, after all."

"Just give me a moment here, 'kay? And step back." I pulled my chin up to her windowsill, then inched till I was at the far left end of it. I swung my right leg up to hook into the window. Once I was in her room, I tried to joke. "Remind me to never try that again."

"Yeah, next time I'll just call the cops. What the fuck are you doing here, Irish?"

"Apologizing, okay?"

"Really? Then why haven't I heard it yet?" She stood back, crossed her arms over her chest, and tapped her toe. I'd never seen anyone actually do that before.

"I'm sorry, I was a right nit earlier and I'll never do it again," I said, looking down. She continued with her foot tapping. "Ash, this is all beyond the real. I freaked out earlier and took it out on you. Should I get down on my knees now?"

"That might be a good thing."

I dropped to my knees. "Cute slippers," I said. I pouted and turned my gaze up toward her.

"You're too cute to stay angry at," she said, pulling me up by my lapels. "And that whole trellis stunt—"

"So that was a good?"

"Very."

"Does this mean we're okay?"

"Just so long as you stop being an obnoxious, thick-skulled idiot," she said.

"It's part of me. I can be a right eejit at times, but I don't want to lose you."

She wrapped her arms around my neck, bringing our bodies together. "I need to feel you inside me."

I led her to the bed, took off my coat and kicked off my tennis shoes. I lay on her, spreading her legs open for me, so our bodies could mold together. I loved feeling—being—so close to her.

Yes, it was hot. Yes, I wanted to rip her clothes off so I could . . .

As I'd driven over, I'd realized by Denise's seriousness, that this was serious. I might lose Ashley. "I really am sorry," I said.

"Shawn," she said. "Make love to me."

I pushed back her robe and used my feet to push her slippers off her feet. I kissed her, my tongue sliding against hers, even as my leg slid between hers, to rub against her. I kissed her shoulders, her neck, down her collarbone to her breastbone.

Her nightie was slippery against my skin, slick, soft and silky. I cupped one breast through it, then kissed that nipple, again through it, before lowering the neckline so I could lick and nibble on the actual flesh of her breast.

"Oh, God, yes, Shawn, please, Shawn," she said, holding my head against her bosom.

I let my fingers trail down to her hemline, then up her shapely thigh . . . Feeling that she wasn't wearing any underwear . . . even as she pushed me back so she could sit up and pull the robe off her shoulders, push the straps of her nightie off them, too.

I played with one nipple, then the other, with my lips, my tongue, my teeth.

My fingers followed her leg up to her wetness, closely examining her, feeling her, exploring her, sliding into and out of her.

"Shawn, yes, please, God, Shawn, yessssss!"

When the phone rang, I was confused. It was late. Very, very late. I reached over to grab it, and couldn't find it, so I searched around in the darkness for it and then reached too far and fell out of bed, banging my head on the bedside table.

"Huh? What happened?" Ash said, sitting up in bed.

"Answer the phone. It's ringing," I said from the floor next to her bed.

The light came on. I assumed she turned it on as I stood. She looked at me strangely as she answered it. "Hello?—What?—Are you sure?—So what do you think happened?—What do you want us—me—to do?—Okay. Fine. We're on our way. Soon. Now. Once we get ready—"

"What's going on?" She had spoken with such urgency and disbelief—plus, well, any call that comes in the middle of the night carries no good.

She got up and began hurriedly dressing. "What were you doing sleeping on the floor?"

9

Which Way Did S/he Go Now?

We met at the Denny's across from Oakland Mall on 12 just west of John R.

Ashley and I drove separately, but she'd been able to get me roughly up to speed on the little bit she knew while we dressed for the rendezvous. Pretty much, nothing had been happening, it was all quiet, so Jamie went out to get her and Kevin some munchies. When she returned, Kevin was gone.

He wasn't answering his cell. He wasn't in his car around the corner. His car wasn't even there. He wasn't to be found.

"We need to call the police," Denise said, staring down at the table.

"What are we going to tell them?" Karen said.

"The truth," Trisha said. "After all, what could be better?"

"We thought somebody was a mass-murdering machine and so sent a friend to watch her kill some more?" Jamie said, nervously rolling and folding—and unfolding and unrolling—a straw wrapper.

"Where's George?" I asked. "Shouldn't he be here?"

"He's out of town," Jamie said. "He never would've let Kevin out on such a mission without him if he was around."

"We haven't told him yet," Karen said. "We don't even know how to get in touch with him."

"The police won't do anything about it," I said. "He hasn't been gone very long. Folks need to be gone some number of days in order for them to really care."

"Even if he disappeared while staking out a possible/probable serial killer's place?" Jamie asked. I could practically see the smoke pluming out of her ears. She was about to get really pissed and make a right big scene. All that would accomplish would be to get us kicked out of Denny's if we were lucky, and if we weren't, we'd end up wasting a lot of time being questioned by the cops. Which, actually, might not be altogether too bad an idea.

But I really had to avert this somehow, and since everyone, including Jamie and Kevin, had gotten involved in this because of me, it was also my job to come up with our next moves.

"Jamie, calm down," Karen said. "If we get in trouble for causing a scene it'll cost us time we don't have."

I leaned forward and, in an urgent whisper so no one at any of the other tables could overhear me, said, "Okay. Fine. We've got enough people to pretty much cover all the bases. We're gonna stay in teams—for safety. Ashley, you go to the cops, pretend to be Kevin's distraught girlfriend, see if you can get anywhere with them on it. You can pull it off, and they're a lot more likely to listen to a straight-seeming white girl than anyone else. Denise, you be her bestest friend and support provider. You can pull it off."

"No," Ashley said.

"What?" I asked.

197

"You're just trying to keep me safe, and I'd rather we keep someone else safe, because I want to be with you," she said, her eyes flashing.

"You, Karen and Denise are the only white girls we've got who can pull off the straight-girl routine," I said, then turned to Trisha, "Sorry, it's just—"

"Shawn, baby, I know." Trisha ran one hand over her dreads. "The cops just wouldn't like me so much. It's no big. This city is just a racist, sexist, homophobic Roman Catholic conclave. You don't hurt me, just society does."

"So Karen and Denise really are friends," Ashley said.

"And every time you argue," Jamie said, pounding the table, "it's keeping us from finding Kevin. I called you all for help, and if you're not gonna help me find my friend—" She started to stand.

"Sit down, shut up and listen," Trisha said, again topping the scene. "We can all switch roles and parts after we hear the plan. We can discuss it then. But right now it seems Shawn's the girl with the plan, and I'm thinking we'd best listen to her, then argue our britches right off. Got it? Get it. Good."

"Two of the Ashley/Denise/Karen trio are with the cops," I said. "Two others will canvass around Kelly's house—seeing if anyone saw anything. Door-to-door knocking sort of thing."

"Boy, they'll be pissing some folks off—waking 'em up in the middle of the night and all," Trish said. "Sounds like my kinda party."

"And me," Robert said.

Trisha looked at Robert. "Good cop, bad cop?"

"Ooo, I've always wanted to play the bad cop!" Robert flamed.

"Baby, you couldn't be the bad cop in the land of the Smurfs, whereas I'm so Jackie Brown I can blow 'em away with just one look."

"It's all that top energy," Robert said.

"So what else ya got?" Jamie asked.

"I know I want to get into her house. At least look around. I got us all into this—I got *Kevin* into this—so I need to be the one most likely to get arrested. I just need someone to watch my back and let everyone else know when I get my ass arrested."

"That'd be me," Jamie said. "I got your back."

"I don't know what the last pair'll do, though," I admitted. "The city's too big to try to start searching and—"

"I'll be calling one of the investigators the law firm uses," Don said. "She can hack anything and find everything. We need to find out if this woman has any other properties she might hold someone at. We need to discover everything possible about her and where she might hide hostages, corpses or anything else."

"Ashley," Karen said, looking across the table at her, "I'm thinking this leaves you to talk to the cops with Denise—since I've seen this woman Don's talking about."

"A right hot babe, eh?" I said.

"Yes. Plus, she won't think anything of me being with Don, and I might be able to track down some other information using the firm's subscriptions."

"Huh?" Jamie said.

"They pay to have access to tons of info on the Internet," Karen said.

"Then let's do this thing," Jamie said, not giving Ash another chance to object.

Fortunately, Meijer's, which was ALWAYS open, had some good-ass walkie-talkies in stock. It put me back a lot more than I liked, but at least we could try to keep in better contact with each other through them.

I wondered if the cops would pay for them if I was right about Kelly. I wondered if there was a way to recoup the money. Or maybe I could return them tomorrow?

Well, no matter, we could use them in our horror trips, so they'd ultimately be a tax write-off.

Regardless, Jamie and I drove to Kelly Everson's. We each parked about a block away, then rendezvoused across the street from her house.

"Wait here," I told Jamie. "Channel thirteen."

"Got it," she said. "I'll be keeping a close eye on you, though."

I nodded at her, then worked my way across the street to Kelly's house. When I looked back to check on Jamie, she was already hidden so well even I couldn't see her. I slipped the radio into my pocket (thank God I liked my jeans loose), then slithered up to Kelly's house.

The slight glares from various electronics (clocks, VCRs and such) gave me some view into her place. When they didn't, I used the pocket Maglite I'd also acquired at Meijer's to peer through the windows. I was glad it was a one-story house, since I wanted to check out all the rooms before doing anything drastic—like breaking in—and I really wasn't too fond of the idea of further trellis or second-story work these days.

As I peered through windows, I looked for anything I could see—like blinking red lights that might identify an alarm system. Or dead bodies, hatchets, sleeping people, guns, knives . . . Well, feck, anything.

I had to triple check when I realized I was likely looking in Kelly's bedroom window and . . . there was someone in her bed and *it was her*.

I turned off my light and stared into the room.

I'd already passed the point of no return. I'd been suspicious of this woman, and that suspicion had led to one of my friends disappearing. That was a direct connection.

The cops couldn't barge into her home, but if I could find something tangible to connect her to the murders, then it might all be fair game. If I could come up with something solid so they could get a warrant, it'd be good. Or else, well, if I was in there and happened to save someone, his testimony could put her away.

So pretty much I had to break into her home to see what I could find. But whilst I did so, I had to realize she had returned home and could catch me at any moment.

My skin was jitterbugging all over my body. I felt as if all my nerves were on end. I'd been pushing the law, but I was about to cross the line of no return. I could get caught doing this—breaking into Kelly's house—and, for feck's sake, I didn't even know how to really break into someone's house, so, actually, it was really likely. That I would be. Caught, that is.

So chances were right handy I'd end this night on the wrong side of some solid prison bars.

But what the jones, I was a right gowl now, weren't I?

I couldn't kick in a door, or loudly shatter a window. Any noisy thing would likely wake Kelly.

"You've got to turn on your radio to use it, you know," Jamie whispered into my ear.

"Don't do that!" I whispered. Loudly. Right after a noise I'd never made before. Of course it was combined with a jump. Or maybe vertical leap was a more adequate description.

"What's going on?" Jamie asked.

"I need to break in."

"Okay."

"But Kelly's home and I just realized I haven't a clue how to break into somebody's house."

"And thus the reason we're a team," Jamie said. Sometimes I forgot she was also a college grad, but then she'd come up with proper sentence structure. That, or she was imitating some English librarian from a TV show.

Anyway, we walked around the house, me behind her. She checked every door, carefully examining the locking mechanisms, then grabbing my Mag to peer through windows.

Finally, in the backyard, she looked at me. "Let me show you how it's done. Go to Kelly's bedroom and keep an eye on her. Hiss loudly if she wakes up—and then run. Back to your car. I'll meet you there."

"What are you going to do?" I asked.

"Go, window, watch her," she said, blowing me off.

I skedaddled, but kept an eye on Jamie nonetheless. She quickly punched her shirt-covered elbow through a basement window, then looked back at me.

Kelly tossed a bit, as if almost noticing the noise, but then settled back to sleep. I nodded at Jamie.

Jamie slithered through the window. I dropped down to the dew-covered lawn and peered through it after her.

"If you're coming, come," Jamie whispered, grabbing me.

I held back. "Turn on the flashlight," I said, getting a visual on Kelly's basement. Then I followed Jamie's lead down into the basement. It's a lot better dropping into the unknown if it's not so much unknown.

The basement was empty. Well, except for a washer/dryer/ laundry-room setup and spare bathroom without accoutrement.

Once we clearly determined there were no corpses or people being tortured here, I nodded at Jamie and started to lead us upstairs.

Then the door at the top of the stairs, the one leading to the kitchen, creaked open.

"Helloooo?" Kelly whispered down, flipping on the light switch. She saw us, flipped off the light, and slammed the door shut. A moment later I heard the front door slam open, then slam shut.

"Fuck," I whispered.

"Let's do this." Jamie shot past me, up the stairs. I could barely keep up as she rushed through the rooms, searching for incriminating evidence.

I didn't know what to do. I was following her, looking for evidence, and trying to work out what Kelly might be doing. I figured she'd rush to a neighbor's and call the cops. And it'd take the cops a few to get here so Jamie had the right idea.

"Get her computer," Jamie told me. "Just the main part. Forget the monitor and shit."

I quickly ripped the cords from Kelly's computer and picked up the CPU. "You see anything?" I asked Jamie.

"Not really," she said, grabbing a Dayrunner and stack of papers from Kelly's desk.

"Then let's go."

We raced out the back door, through the back gate and across the neighbor's lawn. We had to be careful of all the parts lying about since it appeared he was a mechanic, or at least redneck variety of such, and then we were on the street again, racing to Jamie's van. I held on to the computer, she tossed the papers into the backseat and burned rubber as she ripped away.

"If she doesn't have the victims and evidence in her house, where are they? Where is Kevin?" I asked Jamie.

"That's what that's for," she said, indicating the computer. "To tell us what we need to know."

We went to Don's law firm. Sandra, his assistant, cracked this machine as well. It was helpful that Kelly didn't password protect anything.

And we found the big Nada. Zippo.

As Sandra had previously during her investigations of Kelly.

"She moved up here from Climax, Georgia, just a few months ago," Sandra said, just before going through everything I'd seen on her résumé—proving to me, without knowing she was doing so, that Kelly had told the truth on her résumé and when I'd talked with her.

Which all left us leadless as to where Kelly'd hide her victims—or about any guilt at all with regard to her. Also, she'd acted like a real person when she found Jamie and me in her basement—not like someone guilty of, and hiding, something.

But her seeming innocence didn't make Kevin appear out of thin air. And I could only figure he was gone because of me. And all my suspicions.

And we had no leads toward finding him.

Except his disappearance. If he was only gone because of me and my suspicions, then there was an interconnectedness.

"Hey, whaddya know," Sandra said. "Looks like our gal is a writer. And her latest book—well, she got as far as to write to where her main character looks out her front window and sees a big, blue Ford economy van parked outside. She suddenly realizes how much she's been seeing that exact same van a lot lately." She looked at Jamie. "Isn't that the kind of van you drive?"

I looked at Jamie. "You *do* get around!"

She shrugged and said, with a sly grin, "It's not all hearsay."

"I've occasionally used Jamie as an independent contractor," Don said.

"Hold on, Sandra," I said. "When did Kelly write that? Can you tell?"

"The last time she altered the file was just after midnight. As in, just a few hours ago when I was hitting the hay, planning on a good night's sleep."

I looked up at Jamie. "When did Kevin disappear?"

"Right about then."

"But still, we have no idea where he could be—where she might've taken him, or anything."

"It looked like she was home when I got back and found him gone."

"You *found him gone*?" Sandra asked, popping her chewing gum.

We all ignored her. "Was she or wasn't she?" Don asked.

"If she was, then she couldn't have taken him far, if anywhere," I said. "We need to get back there, pronto."

204

"Or else have someone else take up the stake out—and see what happens with the cops and all," Karen said. "Let's see what Trisha and Robert have found out." She picked up the phone and dialed. "What's the good word?" She listened, holding the phone a little bit from her ear, as if whomever she was talking with was talking really loudly. "Yeah-huh—I understand—I know—hold on—really?—No, go back to the descrip—Really? And at what time was this?" She hung up and looked at us. "We're in luck. Apparently among Kelly's neighbors are an insomniac, a practicing alcoholic and a rabid gossip."

"Oh, yes, that's always good," I said.

"What that means is that they all were still awake when Robert and Trisha got to them. All three have, apparently, been keeping tabs on Kevin and Jamie and everything else. It seems that when Jamie went out for snacks, our girl Kelly had a visitor. A tall, Amazonian, dark-haired woman who drove a dark Nissan Pathfinder. The alcoholic, an unemployed autoworker, had a few choice words to say about that. Anyway, she popped in and out of Kelly's, then drove off."

"Do we have any idea who she is?" I asked.

"Only Kelly could give us that info," Jamie said.

I turned to look at Jamie. "To the Batmobile!"

"Shawnie!" Karen exclaimed, grabbing my arm and stopping me from running off. "The woman almost caught you breaking into her house earlier. What's she gonna do with you waking her up in the middle of the night now?"

"She didn't almost catch us breaking in," Jamie said. "She almost caught us inside her house—as in, we'd already broken in."

"Besides," I added, "we left, she called the cops, she's still awake. We'll just go and beat her up till she confesses. Or at least tells us who the hell came a-calling in the middle of the night."

Sandra raised her hand and waved it about slightly. "Um, 'scuse me, but the longer we chit-chat, the better the chances your girl's gonna go to sleep. And that something bad's gonna happen to your homey."

"Sandra," Jamie said, looking at her. "You're upper-middle-class white. Embrace it."

"Besides, you're not coming with me," I said.

"You woke me in the middle of the night for my expertise. The hell I'm not coming!"

There were five of us and we decided to take two vehicles. Strangely enough, Sandra ended up with us.

"Shotgun!" she yelled, pretty much leaping toward Jamie's van. "Hey, what's this?" she said, picking up the papers from the floor of the passenger's front seat.

"Shit, James," I said, "we forgot about those." Then, to Sandra, "Jamie grabbed those from Kelly's place."

"There's nothing much here," Sandra said as Jamie drove us back to Kelly's. "Hello. Except for this. Maybe." She held up a small bit of metal in a little plastic container. She grabbed her laptop case from the ground and slipped the disk into the camera she had secreted in a side pocket of her case.

I leaned forward, looking over her shoulder.

The disk contained pictures of people beaten and tied up. Kevin gagged and unconscious in the van . . .

I looked at Jamie. "We've got it now."

10

Dig Till You Reach Bottom

"Her lights are on," I said. "She's obviously home. But still, we need think through this."

"Not so much, no," Jamie said. "Every moment we spend shitting around out here is another moment she can spend torturing, mutilating or killing Kevin. We need to get on this."

"We need to come up with a plan, so we all know the four-one-one," I said. I was getting the hang of Jamie's lingo, little by little. "Get it?"

"Donnelly, it's my partner they grabbed, so don't fuck with me on this."

"How about this—we go in, and have Karen and Don keep an eye on us from outside. Her lights are on so we know she's awake and will likely answer the door—especially if I'm the one knocking, since she knows me."

Jamie climbed out of the van. "Fine."

"Just keep an eye out and your phone ready to call the cops!" I whispered urgently to Don and Karen, who had pulled up behind us in their own car, just before I chased after Jamie.

"Sandra? What's going on?" I heard Don say behind me.

I reckoned he could keep her in line. We really didn't need all three of us in the line of fire.

"Shawn? Shawn Donnelly?" Kelly said, opening the door when Jamie knocked (I quickly stepped in front of her so Kelly'd see me first). "What are you doing here—at my home—in the middle of the night?"

"I was—we were just in the neighborhood and saw your lights on and all—do you mind if we come in from the cold? Brrr. Rather a nippy night, doncha think?" I said, sidling my way through the door. "So what are you doing up this late? After all, it *is* like the middle of the night and all."

"It's been the craziest damn-ass night ever," Kelly said, shaking her head. "You weren't kidding when you said it was different here from Climax. I mean, at least there, it's only folks you know—and are on, like, say, actual speaking terms with—who stop by to say hello in the middle of the night."

"Who else stopped by?" I said, before Jamie could say anything.

"Are you going to introduce me to your friend? Or—hold on—didn't we meet the other day in the parking lot?"

"Yeah," Jamie said. "I'm Jamie. Jamie Reed. So who else stopped by?"

"What is it with you people?" Kelly said. "I just had some creeps break into my house! This has been a *very stressful* night!"

"And it'll become a helluva lot more stressful unless you start talking," Jamie said, stalking up to her menacingly.

"Easy, Killer," I said, holding up a hand. Kelly was practically cowering in a corner. I eased up to her. "So who else *did* stop by?'

"Brenda." Then, to my clueless look, "Your boss, Brenda Malzewski. She stopped by earlier," Kelly said, staring at Jamie.

"She came in, we visited, she left. It was all rather short. And didn't make a lot of sense."

"Looks like Xena and drives a Pathfinder," I mused. "That really *is* Brenda."

"So your boss came to visit her suddenly in the middle of the night?" Jamie said.

"What's going on?" Kelly asked. "What's with all the interest suddenly?"

"Kelly, this is really important," I said. "Jamie's really cranky 'cause we've just misplaced a really good friend tonight, and we're thinking maybe you've got him. You know, holding him to torture, maim, kill—just like you've done with all the others?"

"What the hell are you talking about?" Kelly asked. I was about ready to believe her.

"Don't fuckin' play with us," Jamie said, right into her face. "You've got him, and we want him back."

"I don't know who you're talking about," Kelly said. "I don't know *what* you're talking about."

Jamie grabbed her by the lapels of her pajamas and thrust her against the wall so hard her head bounced off it. "We can do this the easy way or the not-so-easy way. You've been killing people—probably a bunch of bastards who deserved to die anyway—and I wasn't giving a rat's ass about any of it. We came here for Shawnie. But you went just a bit too far when you grabbed Kevin."

"Hold on—you really *were* watching me?" Kelly choked out. "When I saw that van out there the other night, I thought I was just being paranoid."

"Let her breathe," I told Jamie. Kelly's face was getting wicked red—so red it couldn't be healthy. And if she died, we'd lose any chance at regaining Kevin whole and alive.

Kelly kicked Jamie across the backs of her knees, causing her to drop her. "I wrote . . . I saw you and I wrote . . . and it was all real? What the fuck are you all playing at? Are you on drugs, or are you just crazy?"

"You talked about killing people," I said. "You went to Web sites about killing people. You kept souvenirs—"

"And I told you that I'm a writer! I need to research and get into their minds and make it all happen inside my head."

"So you're saying you didn't kill those men—you're *not* the Motor City Murderer?" Jamie said, using the latest title the media had come up with for the killer. "You didn't grab Kevin—you have no idea where he's at?"

"I don't even know who the fuck Kevin is!"

"Don't keep giving us this shit," Jamie yelled, grabbing her under the arms and knocking her against the wall. Repeatedly.

I remembered Courtney and I talking about how she couldn't possibly be the killer, 'cause she simply couldn't handle the physical requirements of what was being done. Kelly was on the edge of it, but Brenda definitely could do it all. "Don't," I said. "Jamie, stop. She's not the one. Brenda came knocking to plant the disk with the pics on it. Brenda recognized Kevin—and you—and Kevin recognized her as well. She had to grab him. Probably used chloroform or something—whatever she keeps on hand for when she realizes she needs to grab someone."

"Hold on," Jamie said, turning to face me and dropping Kelly to the ground. "You're saying you were . . . wrong?"

"Yeah. She's innocent. But my boss is guilty. Really, what are the odds?"

I pulled out my walkie. "We need Sandra, and her computer," I said to Don and Karen.

"Okay," Kelly said shakily. "Let me see if I've got this right. You're telling me that you thought I was some serial-killing lunatic because all of my work on my mystery novels made me look suspicious."

"Yeah, that's about right," I said. Jamie opened the door for Karen, Don and Sandra. "Really, what would Scooby Doo?"

"So she's not our girl then?" Don said, entering and pointing at Kelly, who was obviously unrestrained.

"Irish don't think so," Jamie said, staring at Kelly. "I'm still liking her myself."

Kelly backed right into a corner under the weight of Jamie's stare. She looked at all of us. "You know, if I wrote this—down to the fact that it's not me, but someone else you know—your boss in fact—nobody would ever believe it. This is so far beyond insane there's just no DSM entry for it."

"So what the hell am I looking for?" Sandra said, setting up her laptop.

"If you're so innocent," Jamie said to Kelly, "you won't mind me taking a look around then, huh?"

"Have at it," Kelly said. "I'm kinda thinking you would regardless of what I think or say."

"Brenda Malzewski," I said to Sandra. "She's my boss, unmarried, I don't know where she lives, but it can't be too far, since, well, she works with me."

"How do you spell that?" Sandra asked. "Is there a *C* in it?"

"Sans *C*," I said.

"Should we like," Kelly said, "maybe call the cops or something? If you think she's a killer and has your friend—"

"Nope, we're gonna find the bitch and take her down ourselves," Jamie said.

"Okay, so there's three Brenda Malzewskis around here," Sandra said. "I need a little more to go on."

"She works with me at BB&B Advertising," I said.

"Got it." She tapped a few more keys. "Got her, too."

"I'm just gonna use the little girls' room before we go avenging," Karen said.

By the time we got to Brenda's, it was awash with police. They were everywhere. It was almost a letdown, actually. I was looking forward to some big-time action to finish the night off with—maybe some good fisticuffs or something—not this *nothing*.

And then I saw Kevin sitting at the back end of an ambulance.

I flew out of Jamie's van and rushed over to him. "Kevin!"

He looked up at me and, well, he didn't really look too good. His eyes were puffy, where I could see them around the bruising and bleeding. "I'll live," he said to me.

"What's all this about?" Jamie asked, waving her hand around.

"I called the cops when I went to the john," Karen said. "Gave them an anonymous tip. Enough that they'd get a warrant on a case this hot. After all, up till Kevin it was all straight, white men. Just what they like tracking down."

I never saw Brenda again. All I knew was what I read in the papers, and what Kevin told me. It made me realize that my friends just playing with me about death before really was the easy way. Yes, this was all fun and exciting and a mad chase and a massive rush, but real people had really died, and it really wasn't so much fun anymore. Brenda had been a pal, but I obviously hadn't known her at all. I scratched the back of my neck raw thinking about that. I looked back at all I had overlooked—her hauling about cases of paper while we discussed that it had to be a man or a large and strong woman . . . and all the other clues she'd left lying about.

I felt really and truly stupid. As in dimmer than a two-watt lightbulb.

I just really hoped my friends hadn't started some sort of a bizarre trend in my life wherein people all around me would keep inexplicably dying or getting into trouble à la *Murder, She Wrote*.

After all, this was real life.

"Lir's children came to no good end. Long story short, their evil stepmother turned them into swans, and they live a long, long *time as such—more than nine hundred years—and through that time they suffered a great many pains and sufferings, like having their lil' swanny feet frozen into the ocean—"*

"Aw, Ma, are you telling that same old story again?" Frances said, coming into the room with the tea tray. "And to little Shawnie! You're gonna frighten the life out of her with all that nonsense!"

"Sure and biggory? And all that," Brian said, setting a plate of biscuit and a small cake on the coffee table. He poured her a cup of tea and handed it to her. "I need you to help me check on something in the oven," he said, walking his wife out of the room.

Just outside the room she said, "But there's nothing in the oven yet."

"Yeah, well, your ma needs to slip a shot into her tea, don't she?" He had been over in Ireland for his job for several years now, and would likely be there for many more years to come.

And so Eileen took a sip of tea and slipped some whiskey into it before she commenced her tale. "So Lir's children lived long and hard, and only just before they died did they return to their human form, so they could die Catholic when they had been born pagan. Eh, their end was good indeed, as they were baptized just before they died."

Part Three:

Get

a

Clue

1

The Real *Puppetmaster*

"So why can't you come over tonight?" I asked Ashley. Over the phone. From work. "I know what you said already. But this is the third time this week you haven't wanted to see me. Are we breaking up?" I took a sip from my sippy mug.

"Shawn, it's a busy week for me. I've already told you this. I'm sorry, and no, we're not breaking up. Not unless you want to."

"No! I don't want to! What would make you think that?"

"You're being all weird this week. Shawn, you know my job's demanding and important, and I cut you slack when you want to go off hunting serial killers and all."

"Hey, it's not like I wanted to go off after serial killers. She just kinda landed in my lap." I was pacing inside my cube, feeling all too much like a prairie dog in the tight tunnels of its home.

"And it was *your* friends who pulled us into that entire serial-killer weekend."

"They're your friends too, and you came of your own volition!" Heh, heh. I said *came*. Heh.

"You really don't want to go there right now, Donnelly. Or there, either. In fact, I'm really gonna save your ass right now and let you get back to work."

"What if I'm not ready to go back to work?" I realized my internal subtext was wholly and totally inappropriate for the seriousness of what was going on, but really, things could only go so far in one direction before they popped out the other side. Things had gone to such shite with Ash that I couldn't help but lighten things up. In my own head, at least. I mean, she was always gone, always answering her phone and talking on her phone and it just wasn't right. I didn't like it one bit. It was like she was hiding something, something even more than herself.

"I am," she said, bringing me back into the convo yet again.

"Right, Fine. Be like that. I'll let you go now, then."

"Yes, fine. Talk to you later."

"Later." I hung up. Ash had learned last week that hanging up on me was not a good idea. It really pissed me off. Probably more than most, which I thought was at least slightly irrational, but I'm that kinda gal.

"I got you now," Jamie said into my ear, practically growling as she wrapped an arm around my neck, stranglehold style, all but dragging me back and up from my chair.

Then she gave me a noogie, quickly rubbing her knuckles over the top of my head.

She really never could get a hold of the notion of "appropriate behavior."

But I didn't have time to think about that. Instead I yelled, "Yar!" and threw my fist up over my head and into her face while I headbutted her chest.

"Goddamnit, Irish!" Jamie yelled, pulling away and cupping her nose. "I need that nose!"

"Then give me a bit of a warning the next time, okay? How'd

you get in here anyway?"

"Front door. And you're at work. Do you always attack people at work?" Jamie said.

"Only if they attack me first!" I said, whipping around in my chair and standing to face her. I liked it when we saw eye to eye. Or almost eye to eye, since she was, after all, a wee bit taller than me.

"So you frequently get attacked at work?"

"No, course not." Now I knew she was being silly and really trying to catch me in the bog.

"Especially not now that we've gotten rid of the serial killer," Kelly said, walking up with two cups of coffee. She handed one to Jamie. "So what's the what? We got another mass-murdering maniac, or something more homey, like bank robbers? Muggers? Vigilantes?"

"None of the above," Jamie said, taking one of the cups. "I'm just here to enlist Shawn's aid in some *other* matters."

I wasn't sure what to pay more attention to—Jamie and Kelly's casual togetherness, or Jamie's pronunciation of *other*. I decided the easy one would be to confront her on the *other* thing while leaving her and Kelly on the back burner. For now. So I leaned back against my desk and said, "And just how afraid should I be of what you want this time, Reed?"

"Very. I'm short on crew for our upcoming show, get a clue." She answered my lean with one of her own, but hers was even more casual as she sipped her coffee.

"What can I say?" I said. "I'm clueless. So fill me in."

"No, silly," Kelly said to me, then, to Jamie, "That's the name of the show—*Get a Clue*. It's a mystery, right? Tell me it's a mystery, and can I help?"

"Yes and yes," Jamie said. "But it's Shawn I was really after. C'mon, Irish, you want to help out with this."

"You've got Kelly, so why do you still need me?" I said. "You've got your set of helping hands."

"But you have particular talents we would like to *employ* for this situation."

"Does that mean you'll pay?"

"Hell no. But we need you, Irish!"

"I'm a copywriter, in advertising," Kelly said. "I can do whatever *Irish* can do. Probably better."

"She's right, you know," I said.

"But you're the one who's all depressed about your girl being a little less than fond of you of late," Jamie said. "Your new girl, that is. So you're the one who needs help. C'mon, come play with us and we'll help keep your mind off such things!"

"So you're enlisting me to get my mind off my girlfriend because she's breaking up with me?"

"No! I don't know jack about what Ash is thinking or feeling. All I know is that you need help because things ain't going so well with you and your girl. Think of this as a chance to be busy yourself and get your mind off things."

"So you know things aren't right between me and Ash?"

"Oh, hell, Irish, we all know. You've been—let's see, how would you put it? *Whinging our ears off* about it for some time now."

"I don't need your help!"

"But we need yours. Come on, you'll be helping us, you'll have fun, you'll stop obsessing over Ashley, you'll spend some quality time with me—it'll all be good."

"Look, you just got Kelly to volunteer, so you don't still need me."

"The truth is we need more than one set of hands. Yours is one, Kelly's another, and we can use a few more. C'mon, babe, it'll all be good and fun. It's murder mystery theater, and it's based a bit on Clue, the board game, so you know it'll be a blast! C'mon. You know you want to!" Jamie was downright bouncing.

"Donnelly, are you off on another crime-fighting spree?" Ed Steele asked, walking up with a cup of coffee—emblazoned with the words "World's Worst Boss"—in his hand. "Do we need to buy you a cape and tights?"

"Just make sure they're not in red," Kelly said. "That'd wicked clash with her hair."

I ignored her. For the moment. "Ed, this is Jamie, my ex. And you already know Kelly."

"Yes, of course, what with her working here and all," Ed said. His charm was nowhere near where it'd been at with Ashley. Jamie really was a butch. And, of course, he already knew Kelly. Plus, I wasn't sure he was entirely convinced she wasn't a serial killer, even though she was apparently claiming to be straight still. He turned to me. "So what is this? A social occasion? We're a business here. There's work to be done!"

"Uh," I said. "No, there's not. I finished everything already." I held my hands out in the universally accepted motion for *ain't nothing here.*

"Wow, you're fast. We need more of you here." With that, Ed turned and walked away. I kinda liked having such a hands-off boss.

"I'll see *you* tonight," Kelly said to Jamie with a wink. "And you," she said to me, "remember, no red tights!"

"Shawnie, babe," Jamie said. "I'll catch you at the theater tonight. Seven p.m. sharp."

Instead of going to the theater at seven, I showed up at Jamie's at five thirty.

"Um, Irish?" she said, answering her door and looking at her watch. "It's only five thirty and this isn't the theater."

"Um, Jamie, I rather noticed that, but I didn't know where the theater was, and I wanted to talk more to you about this before I agreed to help out."

"And that would be the purpose of you stopping by at rehearsal tonight—to see what it's all about and decide if you want to help out."

"Oh no, you don't, James," I said, pushing past her and into her house. "I know how you work. As soon as I show up down there, I'm recruited. I'm a part of the team and there's no escape. So don't try that gobshite on me. I'm onto you. I'd have to be a right arse to not be by now." I sat on her couch, picked up what I presumed was a copy of the script from the coffee table and started reading.

"I shoulda known you'd be like this, Irish. Why can't you just go along with something sometime just for the helluva it—or because it's the smart or right or fun thing to do?"

"I'm really not seeing how this is any of those."

"We need you, so it's the right thing to do," Jamie said, going to the kitchen and returning with two bottles of water. She handed one to me. "It's theater, and you'll be playing with me, so it's the fun thing to do, and it's the smart thing to do because I've seen how you've been of late, and Kelly's been telling me all about how you're all with the bitching and moaning because your girl just ain't spending enough quality time with you. This'll keep you busy, and keep you from worrying that she's found somebody else or anything else unfortunate like that."

"I don't think she's running around with someone else." I began reading the script. "I'm just afraid she's just not interested in me anymore."

And that's how the slow, stinging poison of theater began to take hold in me. And that was also how Jamie . . . Well. We won't go there now. Yet.

But the script really did pull me in, wondering who done it and how they were going to do all of this onstage.

2

The Woman Behind the Curtain

Somehow, even after being recruited into theater utterly and totally against my will—as well as discovering that my ex was hitting on my coworker, whom I'd previously suspected of serial killing, with the hitting-on being returned—I was still surprised that night, and it was such a surprise I almost immediately turned tail and walked out of the somewhat derelicty building to flee from the area much as a, well, much as a fleeing person would do, because, of course, when I showed up all unnattily attired to build, paint and construct, the last person I expected to see was—

"Ashley?" I stopped. Dead in my tracks. Flabbergasted. Startled, even. And very worried that I'd walked into yet another setup I didn't want gob all to do with.

"Shawn?" Ashley said, stopping and looking over at me.

"What're you doing here?" we said simultaneously, as if it was like, well, choreographed and all.

Because I'm not the greenest clover in the field—let alone a four-leaf clover—Ashley was the first to recover, saying, "You weren't supposed to know about this—Jamie talked me into it and all . . . I didn't want to end up massively embarrassed if . . . if . . . if I really sucked and all. Y'know?"

"So *this* is the reason you haven't had time for me lately? You've been too busy prancing about on stage like . . . like . . . like . . . well, some sort o' prancing thing?" I said, all indignant-like. As I had every right to be.

"No!" Ashley flew across the stage—though not literally, 'cause that would be impossible, 'cause she wasn't a harpy or any other sort of winged beast. She just ran really, really fast-like—and threw her arms around me. "Jamie just talked me into trying it out like a week ago, maybe two or three, and there were—and are—other things taking up my time."

"But all of that, and this, this nonsense, is more important than you and me and"—I pulled her close to whisper this last part into her ear—"sex?"

"Oh good God no!"

"Then, especially when you have so little spare time, why the feck are you wasting it on this . . . this . . . bloody place when you could be spending it with me? Having fun."

"Oh, c'mon now. This is fun!" someone I didn't know said, far too exuberantly, as she bounced up to the two of us. "I'm Buffy, and you are?"

"Very sorry for you. Did your parents do that to you on purpose?" I said. I didn't really think anybody'd be silly enough to stick their kid with a moniker like that in real life.

"This is my girlfriend, Shawn," Ashley said, wrapping an arm around me even as she jabbed me with an elbow, likely to stop my ruminations on the relative idiocy of American parents.

"Oh wow! So this is the infamous Irish!" Buffy exclaimed.

And that was when I caught Ashley giving Jamie the evil eye, like she really didn't want or expect me to be there, and it made me realize it wasn't all another setup—unless it was one of an entirely different sort, like if Jamie'd realized we were having problems and was maybe trying to help us out, forcing us together to spend time with each other and maybe work out whatever prob—hold on. Ash really didn't seem to want me to be there.

This was *so* not good.

Why didn't she want me to be there?

Was she trying to avoid me? Break up with me? What was going on that she was devising such elaborate schemes to avoid me? Hold on, for such deceptions, maybe it was something even worse—maybe she'd killed someone, or was going to kill someone or—

"Donnelly, *be*have," Ashley said, accenting and elongating the *be* and slugging my arm. "Stop trying to figure out what's going on and just understand that I'm not up to anything—no one's up to anything—and that there's nothing I, or anyone else, is hiding from you."

"So you're not planning on breaking up with me or killing anyone?" I said.

"Wow, you *are* just like they said!" Buffy said.

"I don't understand what you mean," I said to her.

"You Shawn?" another woman said, walking up to me.

"Uh, yeah, who's asking?" I said.

"Nat, I'm having real issues with the third act," a man said, walking up to us and speaking to the last woman whose name I didn't know.

"I'm Natalie," the woman said to me. "I'm the director. Here's your very own script. Jamie will put you to work." She turned to the man. "Misha, you have a different problem with every other beat every single rehearsal. What is it today?" With that, she and Misha walked away together.

"Ooo! I think I better be in on this!" Ashley said, rushing off after Misha and Natalie.

I was feeling more than a wee bit overwhelmed.

"Calm down and come with me," Jamie said, throwing an arm around my shoulders and dragging me to the back of the theater where she had a worktable set up. "Okay, so here we have a diagram of the stage and various drawings and details of the set. You'll see what we have to build, paint and arrange." She flipped through all of the sheets and diagrams she had, showing me colors, dimensions and arrangements.

"Who all is in charge of all this?" I asked.

"Us," Jamie said.

"Us as in . . . ?"

"Us as in you and I."

"Just the two of us for all of this? What about Kelly?"

"What about me?" Kelly said, walking up to us, eating a Taco Bell burrito.

"We three be in charge of the set," Jamie said. She looked at me. "We *might* be able to get some help from the cast and the crew."

"Is it too late for me to walk out?" I asked.

"C'mon, Donnelly," Kelly said. "You've breathed the theatrical air. It's gotten into you. You can't back out now. It's a part of you."

"And how do you know this so well?" I said.

Kelly toed the ground in front of her with her boot. "I did theater in high school," she mumbled. "But I'm really excited about this because I've never done murder mystery theater. I've only worked on shows with set scripts."

"Hold on," I said. "I've seen the script. I have a copy of it now, even. It seems pretty set to me."

"You didn't really read it," Jamie said. "Did you, Irish? If you did, you'd've seen that it's a highly flexible script. There's the potential for quite a lot of improvisation in this show."

" 'Potential'?" Kelly said. "There's no *potential* or *probably* about it. There *will* be improvisation in it. That's why I want to work on it."

"Hold on," I said. "Can somebody explain this to me?" I thought I'd seen some indications of such potential in my brief glancing over of the script, but now I was learning much, much more in a really quick time frame.

Jamie shrugged. "It's murder mystery theater. It changes given the audience and other things."

"Okay, Shawn," Kelly said. "Picture this: The cast and crew set the scene and the story, while involving the audience. The audience is part of the cast. They are really there. It's like, well, you know on *CSI* how the evidence is a character?"

I nodded. I'd watched some of the extras on the DVDs, after all.

"Okay, so in this play, the audience is a character. Or characters. And as such, since each audience is different and comprises different people, it changes from night to night." It was obvious that Kelly was really, *really* excited by all this.

Jamie cocked an eyebrow and smirked. "What makes this type of show even more exciting is that people sometimes try to fuck with us. People will come back to see the show more than once, just to try to fuck with us. And we have to make sure all the actors are up to whatever challenges they, the audience, might come up with. If you know what I mean."

"No, really I have no clue," I said.

"They can try to be funny, or try to screw you up, or maybe do what they think is totally unexpected—especially if they're drunk—and like hit on the actors or something," Kelly said. She really was into it.

"It's a play without a script?" I said.

"Yes!" they said in unison.

"But I read a script for it!" I insisted.

"It's improv within given parameters," Ashley said, coming up and wrapping her arms around me.

227

"Ashley is totally amazing," Jamie said. "No matter how things change and metamorph and all, she's on top of it."

"Totally!" Kelly said.

"It's like she's a born actress, able to improv any sitch," Jamie said. "And she can really sell it, making you believe every word of it—"

"There's a set story," Ashley broke in. "But there's a lot of improv involved as well. So Nat might want you to play a bit of audience at some time while you're working."

"And I'm not getting paid for any of this?" I said.

"Nope. Nada," Jamie said. "But it's fun!"

"If you say so," I said, turning into Ash's arms. "I don't like this, *mo gra*," I whispered into her ear before noticing how delicious her neck looked. I couldn't resist a taste.

"Okay," Kelly said. "There are given constructs: Setup, suspects, background stories, et cetera. The audience Habitrails it, falling into the maze from which the actors help them work out of, leading them along to the correct solution."

"But what's really cool about this one," Ashley said, "is that there isn't just one crime with one villain. It varies so people can come back on different nights and be confused because of subtle changes. That's what really got me interested in this. I figured working on a project like this will help me with my public speaking abilities, as well as with thinking on my feet while talking and acting, all of which will really help me with my job and career." She had mentioned maybe adding more public speaking and presentations onto her work schedule.

"Doesn't that make it all confusing?" I asked.

"That's the point!" Kelly said, clearly frustrated with me.

"We want to confuse the audience to keep them excited and interested," Ashley said. "It's all really rather ingenious."

"Okay, just tell me what to do," I said.

"I can tell you what to do," Ashley whispered into my ear.

Maybe we—me and Ash—still had a chance after all.

I had to admit it, Jamie was very organized about it all, and I never would've believed it, based on what I'd known before. She'd always been the wisecracking piss-arse back at university, now she was the cool, calm and efficient stage manager goddess.

Her diagrams detailed how we needed to cut, construct and paint various set pieces, and how they were to be placed on the stage. What at first seemed to be an overwhelming task turned out to be perhaps manageable, with time, patience and sweat.

Of course, at first Jamie delegated painting duties to me, reserving the power tools for herself. We'd see how things played out over the upcoming weeks, though. After all, she couldn't possibly stay so far ahead of me in her chores so as to ensure that I'd always have things to paint—

"Yo, Irish, come over here and hold this for me, will ya?" Jamie said. And I do mean *said*, since it really wasn't a question.

"Jamie, if I've asked you once, I've asked you a hundred thousand times," Natalie yelled from her spot just in front of the stage, "try to only use the really noisy power tools when we're *not* rehearsing!"

I'd been focused entirely on what we were doing while totally ignoring all the onstage happenings, but now I glanced up, about to deliver a sharp retort to Nat about her ignorance of really butch tools, and got distracted by Ashley looking really cute, if totally annoyed with interruptions, before I could say anything too embarrassing.

Well, actually, it was Jamie who stopped me from being labeled a bit of a nutter when she said, "Don't say it, Irish. Nat might look like a femme, and she is a feminine het woman, but due to her background in theater, she knows more about power tools than you do."

"So you'd rather let her lay hands on your circ saws and drills than me?" I said.

"Yeah-huh. And she really does know all the names for all my tools, and how to use them all."

"*All* of them?"

"Well, not quite *all* all," Jamie said with a wink.

"Fair enough." Natalie might've been straight, but . . . well, she did seem way butcher than me. Plus, hello? Experience. I had to give it up to her.

My sudden, inexplicable curiosity with Natalie, combined with my awareness of Ashley's proximity and wonderment about how the play seemed to work, and that Jamie was totally directing me in my tasks, thus ensuring my safety and ability to not have to pay much attention to what I was doing, all meant that the night passed amazingly quickly.

"So, um, I'm glad you're helping out," Ashley said at the end of the rehearsal, while Jamie and I were packing away all of her equipment and supplies. Well, not *all* her equipment. If you understand what I mean.

"Yeah, well, you know lesbians and their exes. We're tight, we're close, and we help each other move and do construction work and painting after we break up," I said with a shrug.

"You're weird," she said, practically falling into my arms. "You being here made me more self-conscious and more confident, sillily enough," she said while I hugged her tightly. "I'm glad you're here," she whispered into my ear.

"I wish you'd told me about this, though," I said, holding her tightly.

"I was . . . well . . . embarrassed."

"Next time, don't be. You'll be fabulous, you know."

"I'm glad you know now, though. Do you want to run out and grab a late dinner?"

"Yes, please."

An hour later, over Greek food in downtown Detroit's . . . well, Greek Town, Ashley told me more about what was going on.

"I didn't want to embarrass myself in front of you," Ashley said, digging into her spanakoteropeta. "I really haven't done much acting in my time, and, well, I know it was straining things between us—me being gone and unavailable so much of the time—but . . . I had to try this, and I was too worried about you being there if I really, really sucked."

"So you got involved with this just to, what? Get more experience talking in public?"

"That's about it. Plus, well, I had some really great times with the theater we did in college, and, well, I'm suddenly up to exploring all these new possibilities because of all that's happening between you and me. It's really new and exciting." She reached forward to cup my hands between hers. "I hated what they did to us up in Lexington, but it did excite and interest me as well. I was afraid you'd look down on all of that—that I got off on all that adrenaline and all."

"Why would I do that?"

"Because you were really upset with your friends when they pulled that prank on you."

"Well, it wasn't really a prank. They were setting me up to see if their setup and props worked and to get me involved in it all."

Ashley smiled, cupped my chin with her hand, leaned forward and kissed me. "You're really too sweet—always trying to see the bright side of things, and equivocating in favor of your friends."

"Not so much *equivocating* as *understanding*," I said. "And what's gotten into you tonight, *mo gra*? You weren't nearly so understanding of them when it all went down in the first place."

"I'm sorry for everything, Shawn," Ashley said. "I shouldn't have kept you out of all this, but I was afraid you'd make fun or try to talk me out of it or something. I wanted to prove to myself I could do it, then I was going to let you know. Later on in the run. Like, when the show was closed, or was about finished with its run and almost closed. Or such."

"Well, it's all water under the bridge now," I said. "And, hey, this way I can help you practice and learn your lines and all that other good stuff."

"I kinda think Jamie might keep you busy on set-building duty."

"Right now I'm more with the set painting and putting together of parts than any actual set building per se."

Ash had to hold in her chuckle. "Um, well, yeah, I kinda noticed that."

"Smart-aleck."

"You be Jamie's bitch."

"Don't even start with that!"

"Oh, why, what's the big bad Irish gonna do to me? Give me a nasty look?" Ashley took a bite of her moussaka and a sip of wine, followed by a bite of dolmathes and rice.

"Well, there does seem to be something you like me to do that I could . . . *not do* anymore," I said, just before taking a bite of lamb. God, I loved this place. Detroit might not have a Chinatown or anything else that every other major urban area had, but dammit, it had some good Greek food, and some fabulous Polish cuisine in Hamtramck. Well, if you could call Polish food cuisine, which I was pretty sure you couldn't.

"Oh, um, then I won't be doing that again, since I rather like that, er, thing you do."

I leaned over with a smirk and snared a bit of her chicken and rice. It was great, whenever we came to Hellas we always got two very different combo plates and stole grub from each other. We skipped all the preliminary stuff—like appetizers and soups— and just got these two massive meals. We'd developed certain patterns of ordering at various restaurants, so sometimes we'd just eat appetizers, and other places we pigged out on a wonderful variety of flavors and textures.

It'd only been in my life for a short while, but I couldn't see my life continuing without it. Without *her*.

3

A House of Cards Tumbles
When the Table Shakes

About two weeks later, during rehearsal, Nat yelled back to Jamie, Kelly and me, "Yo! Jamester! Looks like you three got things under control!"

"Yo," Jamie said. "We got things so under control, they're like a . . . a substance. A controlled substance!"

"I don't get that," Buffy said from onstage.

"It really wasn't a particularly good analogy," Ashley said.

"It's so controlled, it's like a foreign country," Jamie tried.

"Hello?" I said. "Is that an Iraqian reference? If so, it's totally wrong."

"Yeah, well I know that," Jamie said. She whispered to me, "But I'm cool, so they'll let it all slide."

"Get away with ya. Is that all it takes to be considered cool?"

I asked. "To have a *rep* for being cool?"

"That's about it," Jamie said.

"You know," Nat said, "I don't really care about any of this. Or that. All I need to know is that you all have everything under control and that Jamie's just about ready for the big opening."

Jamie threw an arm about my shoulders. "We be ready. I told you Irish was just what I needed." She threw a smile back over her shoulder at Kelly. "And Kelly did her job as well."

"Good, glad you're all set, then," Nat said, coming to the back of the theater and tossing an arm about my shoulders, to replace the arm Jamie had just barely pulled off. These theater folk were really rather touchy, feely, weren't they? "Because I wanna steal one of your friends. We need somebody to play the audience, now that we're getting into the final stages of pre-show."

"Um," Jamie said, in her always eloquent way. "You already have audience plants in place."

"Just two. But regardless, we know we need regular audience members," Nat said. "Someone to play the regular audience to help us with rehearsals."

"Like, duh," Buffy said.

"You're taking the piss, right?" I said. "Won't that require like, acting?"

"No, you'll just be the audience," Nat said. "No acting. Just be and react."

"But I can't really react right, since I know the show and all," I said. "So it can't be me."

"Kelly knows it just as well," Jamie said. "So you should take Irish."

"No, no, not me, not me. Take her," I said, pointing to Kelly.

"Take me, please," Kelly said, literally jumping up and down and waving her arms about.

"What?" Jamie said. "You don't want to just play with me anymore?"

"Take her!" Kelly said, jumping up and down and pointing at

me. "Take her take her take her!"

"We just need someone to play the part of the audience," Nat said, keeping her arm around my shoulders and leading me up toward the stage. "Just stand in. I mean, everybody just knows anybody can act, right?"

"Oh, hell no!" I yelled, running away in a most dignified manner.

"No, no, it's okay," Ashley said, charging from the stage to pull me into her arms. "It's okay, baby," she whispered in my ear. "You'll be really helping me—and everyone else—by doing this. You'll give us some ideas as to what might happen, so we'll get it down even better that anything can happen. Get it?"

"Ash," Nat said. "Your girl gonna be okay?"

I let Ash hold my head against her breasts. Really, what was wrong with that? It was peaceful and her fingers running through my hair calmed my pounding heart.

"She'll be fine," Ashley said to Nat.

"Good. Then let's get this party started."

I couldn't let my girl down, or make her look bad by backing a losing team, now, could I?

I found it interesting. I didn't like it much when folks focused on me. But I just had to keep running things round in my mind trying to come up with different responses throughout the rehearsals, and there was no telling when they'd use me, or what they'd use me for. Sometimes it was multiple times, sometimes it was practically continuously throughout the rehearsal.

It was all sorts of crazy, but I pulled my socks up on it nonetheless.

It challenged me and it came to be that I didn't feel so exposed and open when I got involved with the show. The cast would talk to me, and I had to reply, and it was all right. It was okay, even.

I got used to it.

Who knew? Maybe all this could help my public-speaking abilities as well.

That'd be all that plus more. Cool.

Or, kewl, as all the ~~cool~~ kewl kids said these days.

Ashley and I spent more time together—during rehearsals, at after-dinner rehearsals, and while discussing the play and . . . rehearsals. But she'd been much too busy for anymore nooners, which was really rather upsetting.

"Whatcha reading?" Ashley said one day, walking up behind me at work.

"Yiiii!" I said, leaping three feet in the air. "God almighty, woman, whatcha at? Trying to kill me?"

"No," she said, pulling the booklet out of my hand. "I had some very different ideas in mind. *Murder at Sea*?" she read from the booklet's cover, just before she reached over to grab the box from my desk.

"Okay, fine," I said, yanking my stuff back. "I eBayed some murder mystery–type games to find out what the feck this play is all about."

"It's a murder mystery. What more do you need to know?"

"I need to understand how it all works—to *grok* it."

"*Grok*?"

"Grok. It's from a Robert Heinlein book, it kinda means to really, fully understand and comprehend something."

"You're really weird, Irish," Ashley said, turning my chair so she could sit astride me and lean down to kiss me.

I wasn't complaining.

But just before her lips met mine, she saw something behind my monitor on my desk. She leaned up and forward, burying my face in her cleavage even as she said, "What's this? Another game?"

I thought about pointing out that I'd already admitted to eBaying the plural of murder mystery games, but quickly got distracted by . . . well, by Ashley's wonderful and ample cleavage. Even though she was wearing a heavy winter coat, it was open and her low-cut blouse was unbuttoned just enough for my face to be buried in the sweet, soft swells of her bosoms.

And Holy Mary mother of God, I'd been reading too much poetry of late.

So I stopped thinking and nuzzled in instead.

"Shawn! We're at work!" Ashley said, throwing the game aside and slapping my hand as I felt her up.

"Hey, you started it!"

She cupped her breasts with my hands and slid up and down against me. "Then why don't we go back to my place and you can finish it?" she whispered into my ear.

Her nipples were hard against my palms, her breasts soft in my hands, and her body, open and straddling me, was driving me over the edge. I loved it when she opened herself like that for me.

"Oh, sorry, am I interrupting something?" Ed said, looking down at us. I was caught red-handed. I had no idea how long the perv had been watching us.

"Yes! My lunch!" I said, standing up with Ashley and grabbing her hand. "We're going now." I yanked Ashley down after me to where she'd parked her car in the fire lane in front of my building. "Pretty sure of yourself, ain't ye?"

"Have I been wrong yet?"

"Don't count your chickens, is all I'm saying." I leaned over, planted a solid one on her lips, and slid my hand between her legs. When she gasped, I slipped my tongue inside her mouth.

After several moments of our tongues tangling, she pushed me back. "Let me get us to our . . . my place," she stuttered out between gasps for air.

I pulled her seat belt in place and strapped her in. "Just protecting precious cargo," I said.

"Don't forget you."

237

We were barely inside her front door before she wrapped a leg around my hips so hard that I slammed her against a wall when I fell off-balance.

"God, yes!" she yelled when I hit her right between the legs with my thigh.

"Couch . . ." I said, between kisses, even as we stripped each other out of our clothes.

"Yes," she said, pushing my coat off and slipping out of her shirt, bra and coat.

"Floor," I said, kissing down her neck and undoing her belt.

"Yes," she said, shoving her pants down even as she slipped out of her shoes and socks. I always wanted to know how she did that!

I gave up. I pulled her up to wrap both her legs around my hips and carried her to the couch. The breezeway was far too cold to get naked in!

"Yes, Shawn, now!" Ash said, yanking my shirt and bra up over my head. "I need to feel you inside." She arched her sweet pussy up against me, looking for resistance . . . or more.

I licked down her neck, over her collarbone, even as I fondled her tummy, then up to her breasts, cupping first one, then the other.

She arched beneath me, pressing up against me.

I slid my fingers up one thigh, then the other. And then I licked one nipple, fondled it with my lips, and sucked it into my mouth, teasing it with my tongue, then with my teeth. And then I moved onto the other breast, the other nipple, while I traced my fingers lightly up and down her thighs until I ran my fingers through her pubic hair, still not touching her directly.

And then I ran my fingers up and down along her, enjoying her slickness as she moaned and squirmed beneath me. I kissed her on the lips again, then slid my fingers up into her, enjoying her warmth, her heat, her wet.

"God, yes, Shawn, please . . ."

I moved down between her thighs, opening them even more with my shoulders, so she was entirely spread for me, like a delicious buffet.

I dove in, tongue first.

I used my fingers, in and out of her, while I slid my tongue up and down her, working her inside and out until she was truly squirming in need against me, writhing on the couch, moaning my name.

Then I focused on her clit, flicking it back and forth with my tongue, ever harder and faster, as I fucked her with my fingers. Ever harder and faster.

"Shawn, please, yes . . ."

I looked up at the beauty of my naked Ash—her full breasts flattened down upon her; her exposed and naked belly, swelling slightly; her beautiful face, with its panting mouth . . . and I lost myself in her. Inside and out. Wholly and totally and truly and completely.

"Oh, God, fuck me! Yes! Shawn! Yes! Oh God!"

"You are so incredible," Ashley said a few minutes later, tucked into my body, my warmth and the blanket I'd tossed over us.

"You're the one who's incredible," I said, feeling along her curves, enjoying her softness and the womanliness of her body. I loved holding her and feeling her against me. Almost as much as I loved touching and feeling her body. But, really, nothing compared with the feeling I got when she let me hold her, especially when she was naked, even more especially after sex—because she was even more vulnerable and exposed then. I knew she truly loved and trusted me.

"So what have you learned from your studies?" Ashley asked a few minutes later, while we were still entwined with each other.

"Huh?"

"The murder mystery games on your desk? What have you learned?"

"I don't know how the games vary from the plays. I couldn't find any other scripts available at a reasonable price online, but I know that the plays seem to have setups, with the various characters having basic descriptions and act-by-act actions." I continued lightly caressing her. "The character names are usually over-the-top, and it's all a bit silly, but makes a lot more sense once you've studied at least three or four. There is a structure, however, and a solution."

"So you've studied that many?"

"You saw two at my work. And I said I'd eBayed *several*." She was so soft, and so curvaceous . . .

"I love you," she said, leaning up and kissing my cheek.

I pulled her in tighter. "This play is different, though," I mused, " 'cause the victim and killer can vary."

Just then, the phone rang, and she got up and hurried to answer it in another room, before the machine could pick up. She'd been getting quite a few strange phone calls of late, and never checked her messages anymore when I was near. I was left again to wonder if I should get curious or jealous.

"Stop brooding, Irish," she said, slipping back down beside me. "It was just a difficult client. Now tell me what else you've learned."

Anyway, of course, Jamie and Kelly didn't totally have all the set and behind-the-scenes work under control, which made me work even harder to ensure that everything was getting done. Also, my obsessive/compulsive side came out, making me start making lists. Oh, the lists that I made! Pre- and post-show checklists; costumes lists; intermission checklists; lighting, sound and music lists; personal and general prop lists; and all manner of other lists to get us totally and completely organized. I even made a list of lists.

And Kelly . . . Kelly went right to town on publicity—taking care of not only press releases, but also creating press lists (with my help, of course), and writing pitches, blurbs and sending out photos. She was all over getting us on calendars and getting some journalist types in for the press opening and doing interviews and other special pieces on us.

I helped her with contact info for appropriate media in our area, letting her determine who might be the best person at each publication, and also letting her know my contacts at the various pubs and radio and TV stations, but pretty much ran and hid when journalists showed up.

And, although I thought I knew the show pretty well from reading the script and paying attention to rehearsals while we put together the set, it turned out I didn't know nearly as much as I thought I did, and I reckoned a lot of that was because the actors were creating their own characters, and Nat had a whole lot of notes and changes she was constantly giving the actors. Plus, there was all the bloody improv going on continuously.

The setup of the play was pretty simple: The basic deceit was that it was the live (with studio audience) taping of Big Dick Peterson's hit prime time comedy, *My Many*, Many *Murders*, and in this episode, the lead, Little Dick Peterson, is throwing a party. The cast of the play portrays the cast and crew of the show, as well as the two detectives who end up working the case. The audience plays, well, the audience. And they help with the investigation.

The *episode* starts with Big Dick Peterson coming out onstage (well, striding out onto it, not coming out/*coming out*) and saying:

You are about to see the very strange case of the *Murder With a Live Studio Audience*. May I warn all viewers that we are about to *Tootsie* it?

Apparently, one of the hooks for this TV series would be that all the murders wouldn't be committed by Little Dick. But some would be. And thus the suspense. 'Course, it was a sit-com, so it was completely twisted. So if it were a real TV show, a lot of the intros would, thus, be the same, but different.

Which made it all much more interesting to me. Well, plus that this particular play had different victims and different killers on different nights, so every night, with the audience participation, it would always be a different play. Never the same twice.

I couldn't wait to see what each actor would say during each run through—how things would differ each time around, and what would happen with each rehearsal.

But little did I know just how much things could differ from one rehearsal to the next until the opening night . . .

You see, just three days before opening, the guy who played Big Dick Peterson stood in the audience and yelled, "Okay, everybody! We're Tootsieing it this time! Let's rock 'n' roll!" and I finally understood what he meant. The line was an homage to the movie *Tootsie*, wherein much truth comes out when they have to act live on TV, because the tape has been destroyed.

I had a feeling this line could mean more, because something was destroyed in the night that they had to *Tootsie* it in the movie, and something new brought to life, but I wasn't someone who analyzed shite that much. It just wasn't in me. I lived and let things be quite as they were and wanted to be.

So that rehearsal, when the woman playing Me'Shell Castaway, immediately ran up the ladder to toss some sparkles on Little Dick's chandelier, and the top rung collapsed under her slight weight, plunging her down toward the stage, where she might have been rather unfortunately impaled upon an upside-down chair if not for someone's swift and courageous move, I didn't think anything untoward was happening.

But when Me'Shell screamed in pain, as did Ash, who had flung her from the upturned chair leg and landed, herself, upon a coffee table, I realized this play was cursed.

I could practically see the banshee upon the roof, wailing in pain. We might as well have been doing that Scottish play.

And I felt a coldness run up and down my spine.

It really wasn't pleasant.

And no sooner did we have Jamie and Kelly hauling Me'Shell off to the ER than Nat was staring at me.

"You're the only person who can possibly learn the lines in time," Nat said to me.

"Jamie could too," I replied.

"Can you run lights and sound for the show?" Nat replied.

I shrugged. "Sure."

She showed me the lighting and sound boards, with their hundreds of buttons, levers, flippy things and components, and I . . .

. . . I guess my look said it all.

"So you'll be taking her part, then?" Nat said.

I stared at the control panels and realized I could feck up the entire show if I was in control of them, whereas if I was onstage, I could only feck up my part. Granted, folks would know who I was if I fecked my part in front of the stage, but it was a lot less responsibility.

"Kelly could run lights and sound, right?" I said.

Nat stared at me, and I realized that Jamie and Nat were now working together, teaming up against me.

"Can't Kelly take the part?" I whined.

"Kelly hasn't been at as many rehearsals as you," Nat said. "What with doing all that press stuff. There's no way she can learn all the lines and stuff in time."

At the next rehearsal, I was Me'Shell Castaway.

Yeah, I'd heard her lines, *all* the lines, enough to have them *all* memorized, but none of that mattered. So much of the show was improvisational, I had to work at thinking on my feet and really understanding the character so I'd know what and how she'd respond to any given situation. The only good about all of it was that Me'Shell didn't have to wear a dress or skirt or any too-girly clothes.

4

Pay No Attention to the Queers In Front of the Curtain

"No, really, Jamie, I got the lines down," I said into the phone, pacing my small kitchen. "And I really mean it this time." I glanced into the fridge.

I was kinda hungry, or maybe a bit more than kinda, and all I had in the fridge was a two-liter of Diet Coke (I preferred Diet Pepsi, but Diet Coke was on sale this week), a couple eggs and some butter. Or maybe it was margarine?

I found some ramen noodles in the cupboard, but those really weren't sounding all that filling. Or appetizing.

"I know that already, Irish," Jamie said. "C'mon, you did great last night!"

"No, I didn't." Ramen noodles it was, then. And no, I don't mean ramen noodles in ramen soup, I mean I drain all the water away and eat them as just noodles. When I want soup, I'll have soup—usually Campbell's Chunky these days, unless I'm sick, wherein I'll just have plain old Campbell's chicken noodle soup, with just a bit less water added, so it's really good and salty, and can cut through any cold-induced taste deadening.

" . . . and I think that'll really help you tonight. Not that last night was all that bad, that is."

Apparently I should've been thinking less about my stomach and concentrating more on what Jamie was saying. Oops. I hoped she hadn't suggested anything truly useful.

"You didn't hear a damned word I said, did you, Irish?" Jamie said.

"Nope."

"Thinking about lunch?"

"Yup."

"I'm not surprised, what with the way you were drinking last night and all."

Oh yeah. That's why I was so hungry and thirsty.

"Have some water and Coke, Shawn," Jamie said. She'd picked me up for last night's show and also dropped me off at home after the cast party, so I could enjoy it to the fullest and not have to worry about drinking and driving. Well, plus, she didn't want me driving to the theater under the influence of way-too-much adrenaline.

Also, I'd been rather upset at the party, since, well, I had blown some bits during the show, and then Ashley'd left the party early, claiming she had to catch up on some paperwork.

I knew I was getting dumped.

So I got good and drunk.

And now I was right hungover. I just wished I could remember maybe just a wee bit more about the night before. I scratched the back of my neck and stared at the water, willing it to boil already.

"I'll be over at four to help you out and run some lines with you," Jamie said. "Then we can go together to the theater. I think maybe it might help if you have a beer or two before. That should also help you tonight."

"Are you completely sack of hammers? You want me drinking *before* the show?"

"It'll calm you down. Trust me. But don't you even think about drinking until I get there, got it?"

"Oh dear Lord in heaven, ain't no way I'm thinking about drinking yet."

"Okay, so I'll see you in a few hours."

"Jamie?"

"Yeah?"

"You think Ashley's gonna dump me?"

"Irish! Will you lay off it already? You were sobbing in your beer for half of last night over that woman. Stop worrying about her. She's completely and totally head over heels for you!"

With that, Jamie hung up on me.

I just had the greatest friends.

I boiled the water, threw in the noodles, drained the water, added the flavoring, and ate 'em all up. Just as I was finishing, the phone rang again.

"Jamie, I'm sitting here going over my script even as we speak," I said, answering it.

"Hey, honey," Ashley replied. "I could come over and run lines with you, if you'd like. Just like we did before."

"And you think you can get out of dumping me last night that easily, eh?"

"No. I *really* am sorry about that! I didn't plan on it, and I hated leaving you, especially since you'd had such a rough night of it and all. How about if I come over, we run lines, we fool around a bit, we go to the show tonight, then we go back to your place after and really fool around?"

"That easily, huh?"

"Um, Shawn?"

"Yes, Ashley?"

"What color underwear should I wear today?"

"What are my choices?" I said, before I even thought.

"Hmm . . . black, red, blue, green . . ." She trailed off.

I was a bit familiar with her lingerie already. "Green." Maybe more than a bit.

"Light or dark?"

"Dark," I said. "You have anything in a nice forest green?"

"Yes . . . so I'll put those on."

"Yes, please. What style, please?" It had become a bit of a ritual where I asked what she was wearing each day and she told me, down to the color and style of her underthings. Unless, of course, she wasn't wearing any. That turned me on, too.

"String bikini and a nice, lacy bra all right?" she said.

"Yes, please. So . . . does this mean you were naked when we started talking?"

"Yeah. Well, actually, when we *started* talking I was wearing a bath towel. So should I plan on driving you to the show and spending the night tonight, then?"

"Yes, please." She really did know how to bend me to her will, didn't she? But I just thought she was so beautiful and smart and talented and I was ass over teakettle for her. I really didn't deserve her, so I was happy that she was mine and that I could have her. 'Specially since I'd mooned over her for so, so long.

I'd been a right gobshite about her, and I wasn't about to let any stupid little thing make me lose her.

And, of course, by the time I got off the phone with her, I'd drank quite a few sodas and a bunch of water, eaten a few packages of ramen noodles, and totally forgotten that Jamie was coming to get me. Ha ha! Ho ho! To the funny farm!

When Jamie showed up, I was pacing back and forth in my living room, repeating my lines over and over to Ashley, even while she threw me different lines, working even more on my

247

improvisational skills.

"Argh!" I yelled. "You really should've just gotten a real actor! Someone who could improv and not shake in her feckin' boots whenever she was in front of a live studio audience!"

"That was funny," Jamie said from the front door. "I think you're really getting the hang of all this. Well, and the over-acting this particular show requires."

"You all are right nutters," I said.

"What are you doing here?" Ashley asked Jamie.

"I came to run lines with Irish," Jamie said. "And then take her to the theater."

"I'm handling all that," Ashley said. "So you can just go."

"No," Jamie said. "I'm someone she can actually rely on. To take her there *and* bring her home. *And* I've got a plan to relax her a bit and help make tonight a bit better than last night."

"And just what sort of plan is that?" Ashley asked.

"Beer," I said. "Beer is good. In fact, I think I'll go have one."

"Nope, not yet," Jamie said, stopping me with a hand on my arm.

"What sort of plan is that?" Ashley asked.

"A good one," Jamie said. "It'll relax her. I think her being too . . . excited . . . last night was part of the problem."

"So I'll go have a beer now," I couldn't believe that beer was starting to sound like a good idea again.

"I want you relaxed, not drunk," Jamie said. "Now let's get back to running lines."

I went to the theater with Ashley, after we'd all run lines for a while. I brought two beers with me, to have in the green room before the show started, so I could relax a bit.

Turned out I needn't have bothered bringing my own beer with me, since some enterprising folks had decided to turn the night's production into a blind pig.

"Hey, what's going on here?" Jamie said, walking out into the theater proper.

The theater was attached to a house in a very bad part of Detroit. The house was owned by an anarchist group, and the theater was converted from an attached stable or some such.

The green room was the room just inside the house from one of the stage exits—the other exit led into the kitchen—and there was a bar setup in the theater, but we hadn't planned on selling any alcohol, since we didn't have a license. But apparently some folks from the anarchist communal/collective that owned the house decided they wanted to make a bit more money and so decided to sell alcohol without a license during our show.

We were already paying them for the rehearsal space and the space for the show, but that didn't really appear to matter to them. They had a keg and they were making use of it.

Or at least, that was what I heard when I was eavesdropping on the yelling happening in the theater from where Ash and I stood in the green room.

"Oh, that doesn't sound good or happy at all," Ashley said, just before she peered out the window, glancing at the driveway and entrance to the theater. She quickly dropped the curtain back in place.

I opened a beer and took a sip, sitting down on a couch and throwing my feet up on a table. "Maybe this means the show won't go on."

"Wishful thinking, Irish," Jamie said, coming back into the green room. "They'll run their blind pig, we'll do our show. No biggy. We just won't do anything special to help them out is all."

Gradually the rest of the cast and crew showed up, the crew setting things up onstage and in the audience, while the cast put on costumes and makeup. Ashley made me up again, just like she had the first night.

"I'm gonna run out front to see what's going on," Ashley said, just as soon as she'd put on the last of my makeup.

"Hold on, we're not supposed to go out there in costume," I said.

"Who's in costume?" Ashley said. "I'm not, yet. I just want to see what's going on out there—see what sort of a crowd and all we've got tonight."

Before I could say a word, she was gone.

"Hey," Kelly said, running up like an overeager Jack Russell terrier begging for someone to throw a ball. "Where's she going? She's not supposed to go out there!"

"Then you'd better go get her," Buffy said, flying on up to us. "How's my hair look? Are my seams straight?" She turned so I could clearly view the shapely backs of her legs. All the way from her short, short hemline—that made her skirt more of a daring questioning of belt versus skirt—to the tops of her come-fuck-me heels. "Shawn? Shawn?" she said, as if trying to catch my attention, which she already had. Entirely. "Shawn?"

"Yeah-huh?" I said.

"Are my seams straight?"

"Uh, yeah."

"Good. Now you'd better go get your girl before she gets in trouble with Nat and Jamie."

Just as I stood, Nat came backstage. "Okay, everybody, gather 'round," she said. "We had an okay opening night. Shawn, I'm sure things will get better, but we need to keep up our energy and really work it tonight."

I really hoped she wouldn't do a head count or anything before Ashley got back.

"So now, let's figure out whodunit tonight!" Nat glanced around—for Jamie I supposed—but held her hand out to me instead. "Pick a paper, any paper," she said. In her hand were three crumpled pieces of white paper. I already knew each had a different murderer/victim combo.

I saw Ashley enter the green room from the stage, so she was behind Nat. I quickly picked a piece of paper from Nat's hand so she wouldn't notice where Ashley'd been.

Kelly was right behind Ashley. "Hey! Donnelly!" Kelly said, bounding into the room. "A whole bunch of folks from work are already here tonight!"

"I'm gonna need more beer," I said, looking dourly into my mostly empty can.

"C'mon, Donnelly, whodunit?" Buffy said, stamping her foot like an impatient thing.

Buffy and Nat both reached for the shred of paper in my palm at the same time, but Ashley yanked it out of their grasp first and, just as she was obviously about to open and read it in a big production number, Jamie came from the other side, took the paper, and read it.

"Katie Did," Jamie said, referring to Ashley by her character name. "You get to kill Big Dick tonight!"

"With a candlestick!" I said, trying to take attention from where Ashley'd been, while also getting into the energy-building spirit. Each set of killer/victims had a different murder weapon—candlestick, revolver and knife being the total of them. During one rehearsal, I brought up the little-known knowledge that in some special editions of Clue, poison is also a murder weapon.

"Yay!" Ashley said. "I get to kill somebody!"

She was being flat-out goofy now. And I told her so. "You're being goofy," I said. It was rather unusual for her. She was, actually, quite giddy, especially for her, since she was never actually giddy.

"Fifteen minutes!" Kelly said, looking at her watch and rushing back out into the theater.

"It'll be okay," Ashley said, wrapping her arms around me and kissing me lightly on the lips. She ran her fingers down my hair, caressing my hair and back lightly and soothingly.

"Did I like suddenly get really pale?" I said.

"God yes," Buffy said. "If not a little green."

"Break a leg," Jamie said, slugging my arm just before she went out into the theater to get started on her lights and sounds. Right now, there was just the pre-show music playing in the theater. Jamie'd put the music together to get the audience into the mood for the show. It was a little bit mysterious, a little bit fun, a little edgy and a bit energetic. It really got the audience going and ready for the show.

I just wished it could also work as some sort of magic balm for me as well. Unfortunately, it did not.

"Just so you know," Ashley whispered into my ear. "Ed Steele's out there, too."

"What the feck?" I said, all but standing and throwing her off my lap.

"Calm down," Ash said. "I just didn't want you to freak if you saw or heard him. I don't want anything to throw you off your performance tonight, okay, hon?" She fed me another sip of beer, then brought her mouth down to mine in a long, deep, open-mouthed kiss. She was still sitting on my lap, as if to either keep me from running out of the theater in fear, or to keep me stable and grounded.

By the time she slipped her legs around so she straddled me, I'd forgotten about . . . all the people rushing around . . . everything going on . . .

Her warmth surrounded me. She opened her body to me, for me. She slid up and down against me and I was lost in her.

Her hands in my hair soothed me, while her parted body on me revved my engines, and somehow, through it all, she took me where she wanted me, just as she always had, always did.

By the time Big Dick Peterson's voice came booming over the loudspeaker, I was ready to run onstage. I hoped tonight wouldn't be as challenging as the night before, but I started bounding around on my toes and building my energy and confidence and I really was thinking that maybe I might be able to do it after all.

"Break a leg, lover," Ashley said, leaping off my lap and running past me and goosing my arse en route to the stage.

Big Dick introduced each of us as we ran out onto the stage, as if he was introducing his cast to the live studio audience. "And now, we have everyone's favorite luscious blonde starlet, the amazing Katie Did! Along with her on-again/off-again boy toy, Little Dick Peterson!" And on it went.

I was the last one mentioned, so I just went right for the ladder and dusted the chandelier covered with sparkly thingies just as Big Dick yelled, "Lights, camera, action!" as if it were the start of filming the episode.

I tossed a handful of sparklies at the chandelier. "This is gonna be quite some party," I said, opening the episode with my first line of the show.

Lightning flashed, thunder roared, and the lights flickered.

"This is turning into quite the storm," Ashley said, coming in from outside.

"Hey, baby," Little Dick said, pulling her into his arms. "Ain't this weather fantastic? It's perfect for what I've got planned for tonight!"

"Back off, big guy," Ashley said, pushing him away. "It's not like your daddy's anywhere near."

"Yeah, no reason to put one on 'cause of little ol' me," I said, indicating my character's knowledge that the two of them were just acting out their affair so Little Dick's Daddy would think he was straight.

I was a tad distracted by someone in the audience breathing quite heavily, as if he was struggling for air.

I felt a tingling at the back of my neck. I knew it'd been too long since I'd had the tingling at the back of my neck. After all, it'd been almost continuous since I'd gotten hooked back up with my old college chums.

I wondered if that in itself should be suspicious or worrying at all.

I was so distracted I almost missed my next line, but I didn't. I was just a tad late with it, a moment shy, just long enough to worry the other actors.

But we went on, with the lights flickering occasionally as the rest of the guests assembled for Little Dick's party. Once Kelly ran by with a sign that said, "Laugh!" and once with a sign that said "Applause!" to goad the audience into action and add to the façade of it being a show that was being taped.

And then, about fifteen minutes into the show, the lights went out, there was a bang, a thud, a scream, the ladder fell over, and when the lights were supposed to come back on, they didn't.

I heard someone retch, and someone else say, "That's disgusting!"

And still the lights didn't come on.

I heard Jamie yell from the lighting and sound booth, "We're experiencing some technical difficulties, so just bear with us a moment and the show will go on!"

There was a thud from the audience.

"What's going on?" Big Dick yelled, apparently forgetting that he was supposed to be all deadlike, but someone else apparently didn't forget, because it wasn't too long before he let out a groan just after what sounded like someone hitting him.

"All the boards just went dead, Little Dick," Jamie yelled back, obviously trying to cover for Big Dick's stupidity. "Just give me a minute to sort it out."

"Hey! Watch what you're doing!" someone in the audience said.

And then the lights came on. The onstage lights.

Big Dick was off his mark, just a foot or so outside of where he ought to have been lying. I saw him and screamed. Just as I was supposed to do. Just as most of the cast and "crew" was supposed to do.

But, instead, there was mayhem. Well, mayhem above and beyond anything that was supposed to happen at this point.

I was confused at first.

I heard people screaming in strange new places, places where screaming people weren't supposed to be, at least not yet. And not so many. And not in voices I didn't recognize.

I felt a tingling at the back of my neck even as I turned toward the audience.

A man was lying facedown on the floor in front of the first row of the audience. He wasn't moving. And it looked like maybe he was lying in his own vomit. That was pretty disgusting.

The tingle at the back of my neck reached electroshock therapy proportions.

5

Dead Man's Party

"Oh, c'mon, quit with the screaming already, lady," a man in the front row said to the woman sitting next to the now-dead man. "It's all part of the show."

"Oh, oh!" she said. "God, do I feel silly now. Of course it is." She sat back down.

In fact, many audience members who had just been riled were now calming and sitting back down with their beers. Some whilst shushing each other loudly.

"Wow, I can't even tell that he's breathing," one guy said, kneeling on the floor to closely examine the corpse. Or what I assumed was a truly dead dude.

By that time, all of us onstage were starting to look back and forth at each other and the dead dude in the audience. We were ready for all sorts of improvisation, but nothing like this. We were all dumbstruck, so the audience was left to its own devices for a few moments while we tried to figure out what to do.

"Somebody do something!" Nat stage-whispered from backstage. She wasn't out there so didn't know what was going on and couldn't see shite. I was pretty sure she was *not* one for giving lines or cues from backstage.

"Look, Big Dick's dead," Ashley finally said, walking up to me and pointing to where Big Dick lay onstage.

The house lights came up slightly and Kelly climbed down from the lighting and sound booth.

Buffy crossed to where Big Dick lay on the stage, kneeling by his side and leaning over so that the audience, and I, got a right nice view down her top. She felt for his pulse (with her thumb on his wrist, so, realistically, it was kinda stupid), then looked up and said, "Oh my God, he's dead!"

Kelly walked over to the guy lying on the floor in the audience and toed him in the ribs. "C'mon, dude, joke's over. Ain't funny no more."

He didn't move.

"Dude, what the fuck is this?" Kelly asked, looking at his sick on the floor.

Onstage, Paul ran over to Big Dick and also checked his pulse. He started to give CPR. Little Dick looked happy, then stricken, as if he was trying to hide how pleased he was. And Jason, who portrayed the assistant director, ran out to front stage center, yelling, "Cut! Cut!"

My brain was ready to burst. I wasn't sure what to do or think or believe, so I just went with what we'd rehearsed. I looked out toward the audience. "Somebody call nine-one-one!" I yelled frantically.

Several people pulled out their cell phones and started dialing. One man hit the woman next to him, slapping her on the arm saying, "Oh, c'mon. It's just a play for chrissakes. Nobody's really dead."

Kelly knelt beside the guy on the floor and checked for his

pulse. Then she rolled him over—with some difficulty—and checked his heart and various pulse points. She even held her hand over his mouth and nose.

"Um," Kelly said, sitting up and waving her hand about slightly. "I don't want to cause a panic or anything, but I think this guy really *is* dead."

Dear God in heaven . . . I . . . I didn't know what to think or feel or . . . it was too much. It was just too fucking much.

By now, the audience appeared quite confused, and I should know, because I'd totally given up on trying to continue the onstage storyline, since what was happening in the audience was far more riveting—mostly because I didn't know what would happen out there, like, whether or not the dude would live or die.

"You've got to be kidding me," Little Dick said onstage. "Who'd want to kill my father? He can't be dead!"

"Who said anything about someone killing him?" Buffy said. "We just said he's dead. But maybe you know something more than we do?"

"Um, really," Kelly said from the audience. "I'm not kidding. I really think this guy is dead and that somebody really ought to call nine-one-one. Really."

Jamie, from up in the lighting and sound booth, turned on the full house lights.

"His head's clearly been bashed in," Little Dick said, kneeling beside Buffy. "I mean, ick." He ran his index finger through the fake blood on Big Dick's head, so it appeared he pulled a blood-covered finger away and held it up for everyone in the audience to see. "Really, ick."

Ashley was looking back and forth, from Big Dick to the guy in the audience.

Jamie ran down the ladder and made her way quickly and discreetly next to where Kelly was. I saw the "ew" look on her face when she realized it was real puke the guy was lying in. She checked the guy's pulse, then lifted one of his arms and let it drop. It did so. Solidly.

Buffy hit my leg with her hand. Once. Then twice. Then again for good measure.

"And I think I see what done him in," I finally said, more out of habit than anything else. I picked up the candlestick holder, which was now covered in fake blood and brain. I attempted to brandish it while actually paying attention to the audience and Jamie and Kelly and the dead guy.

Jamie stood, raised her hands and addressed the audience. "I don't want to upset or distress anybody, but I think we may have a situation here. Could somebody please call nine-one-one?"

Nobody pulled out their cell phone, and I reckoned I knew what the problem was, so I stepped to front stage center and said, "Really, could somebody please call nine-one-one, 'cause I think we really have an emergency here." When no one reacted I continued with, "Really. I'm serious. There's a dead dude here and he's really, really dead. Or at least I think so."

Jamie was performing CPR, and I couldn't see any visible signs of death, besides the rigor, pallor and general not-movey-ness of him.

"Okay, already, I don't know what's going on anymore," Buffy said, huffing up beside me. "You're totally off script now, Shawnie! And they . . . they're not even in the script," she said, indicating Jamie, Kelly and the dead guy.

Ashley ran down to assist Jamie, but I heard her say, "He really is dead."

I heard someone in the audience lean over and say to the person next to her, "They're good. They've really layered in the mysteries with this one. I'm liking it!"

And as that spread about the audience I realized no one was taking this seriously and confusion was the rule of the day, 'cause nobody in the cast or crew knew what to do about it and most of them didn't know what was going on anyway.

So I turned and looked at the cast. "The play is over. Done.

There's a dead guy in the audience and we've got to call the paramedics. The police. Et cetera. And I'm serious." When no one moved I continued with, "C'mon, people, I'm not seeing the cell phones. Somebody start calling already!"

The audience was riveted. As was the cast and crew.

And I realized I hadn't confirmed the dead guy was actually, well, dead. So I hopped down off the stage and knelt next to Jamie and Kelly. I checked the guy's pulse, then felt for his heart, for breathing, for anything—including, I'm ashamed to say, lifting a hand and letting it drop. It did so, quite easily.

"Dude's dead," I said to the audience. "I'm going to go call nine-one-one." I went into the house while murmuring, "Since nobody out here's willing to do so."

Ashley had walked off. I thought I heard her retching in the bathroom.

Behind me I heard things like, "What's going on?" "He's not dead, is he?" "What's real?" "Why isn't my phone working?" "He's not really dead, is he?"

I picked up the house phone and it was dead. Of course. The anarchist collective hadn't paid the bill, so it'd been cut off. I went and tried my cell, and it didn't work either. I knew there was a reason I'd put off getting a cell for so long. Darned things were darned undependable.

I ran back out into the theater to see many people with cells out, all trying, apparently unsuccessfully, to call 911. It seemed as if everyone was starting to realize that there really was a death in the theater that night.

"I'm a doctor," I heard someone say. "No, really, I am. In real life." I had to guess he was replying to someone who was hassling him about being in the show and not really being a doctor.

This probably wasn't helped by the fact that we now had what appeared to be several uniformed Detroit cops in the theater, trying to get close to the body.

They were actors. And now the cast, even Big Dick with his

bloody makeup, were trying to get closer to the dead guy, trying to see what they could, rather like motorists slowing down upon passing an accident, so as to absorb every grisly, gruesome detail.

"He really is dead," the doctor said, kneeling next to the . . . well, corpse. In a very businesslike manner, he stood, pulled out his cell, and tried to call 911. It apparently didn't work too well, though, because he tapped it several times and tried again. He looked around, as if searching for the source of interruption, and then hurried outside, obviously hoping that whatever was blocking his reception would be nonexistent out there.

And that was when I experienced a sudden oh-shit moment. Jamie'd hooked up a cell phone jammer to run during the show so that nobody could call the cops for the false murder. Plus, like it had at the cabin, it added to the suspense and aloneness of the event.

"Everyone," Kelly said. "Back away from the body. Jamie, we need to secure the crime scene."

"What? Are you like a cop or something?" someone said.

"No, but I've studied enough stuff, since I'm a mystery writer, to know a few things," she said.

"But the cops need access!" someone else said.

"They're not real cops!" I said, getting frustrated with the rampant stupidity running wildly all over the place, like a sheep dog who's lost all his woollies. "These people are actors, you shite-brained eejit!"

"Shawn, Shawnie," Ashley said, walking up behind me and rubbing my shoulders. "You need to calm down."

"Jamie," I said. "Can you turn off the cell phone jammer?"

The classic "Oh, fuck-me-with-a-rubber-sheep" look passed across her face. She'd forgotten entirely about the jammer, quite obviously. She ran up to the lighting booth.

The look Kelly gave me told me she'd forgotten about it as well.

And I think that was when I realized I'd have to run this

261

investigation until the real police arrived. I was in charge here now.

Jamie yelled, "It's off now!"

"Can somebody here call the police now?" I said to the audience. At least half of them pulled out their cell phones. About half of those quickly put them away, seeing that the need was now filled. The other half apparently felt so stupid because of everything that had happened, they now had a dying urgency to feel like a hero and make *the* call that would get through.

"The police and EMTs are on their way," the doctor said, coming back into the theater as he put away his cell phone.

"We need to keep everyone here, but clear of the body," Kelly said.

"Yeah, you're right there," I said. "Jamie, this sounds like your territory."

"Yo!" Jamie boomed, in her biggest, situation-controlling voice and persona to all persons and parties present. "Stay in your seats. You must remain here. Stay away from the body—"

"Um, but my seat was right next to him," the woman who had been sitting next to him said.

"Okay, so anybody who was sitting within arm's reach of him, sit on the stage," Jamie said, pointing toward the stage.

"Whose arm length?" someone asked.

"Mine," Jamie replied. She was on top of this, and quickly assuring that the body wasn't messed with any further, but yet ensuring that everyone stayed put.

"How long till the cops show?" one self-important dude asked, looking at his watch.

"I don't know," I said. "A while, and I don't care where you say you need to be or what you should be doing or who you should be seeing. You'd still be here for quite a while watching this play if this dude hadn't dropped dead during it, so stay put."

"And don't talk with anyone!" Kelly ordered.

"But . . . I have to pee!" one woman squealed from the middle of the audience.

"Okay, so go ahead," Jamie said, indicating the restroom at the back of the theater.

"Any idea what it might be?" I asked the doc, pulling him aside. "Heart attack? Stroke? Embolism? Sudden onset cancer?" I was hopeful for a natural death that wouldn't mean anything bad or icky or that someone here was a killer.

"Something this quick and sudden?" he said. "I saw a drink spilled next to him. I'd have to think that it was poisoned. After all, I heard someone say somebody was vomiting early on in the show, and we weren't very far into it at all. Given the pinkish tinge of his skin, the vomiting—if that was him—and the breathing problems I thought I heard—again, if that was him—I'd think poison. Maybe cyanide."

"Cyanide?" I said.

"It's fast acting and all the symptoms fit. Especially the smell."

"What smell?" I asked.

"The bitter almond smell?" he said.

"I didn't smell nothing," I said.

"Oh, well, there's this entire genetic disposition thing," he said. Seeing the blank look on my face, he continued. "It's not important. Not everyone can smell it. I'm fairly certain it's cyanide."

Cyanide was something someone did to somebody. It wasn't a natural death at all. I didn't like it. "So no brain tumor or blood clot suddenly hitting the heart?" I said, hopefully.

He looked at me in all seriousness. "I can't tell for sure without an autopsy, but given everything I've seen, smelled and heard tonight, I would definitely request an autopsy on this one to determine the exact cause of death."

"So you're thinking," I said, then paused, trying to get him to say it, but he wouldn't. So finally I said, "So you're thinking he was murdered?"

"Given what I've seen thus far, I wouldn't rule it out."

That really sucked moldy moose meat.

6

After the Fall

The police arrived. Finally. About an hour and a half after we called them.

It *was* Detroit, after all.

And we had a devil of a time keeping everyone there—they were potential witnesses, after all—and away from the body. Everybody always wants to play detective these days, and we'd already lost his drink cup. People kept saying he'd been drinking from the blind pig . . . and don't get me started. Some folks wanted to dump all the alcohol and get rid of any proof that we'd been running a blind pig, while others wanted to keep all possible proof and evidence exactly as it had been at the time of his unfortunate demise.

Pretty much, it was a right fuck-up all the way around.

So the police and EMTs finally arrived. The paramedics were all like, "He's dead." "Yup, he's dead. Let's try CPR." "How long has he been like this?"

And the police called in for detectives and wanted a place to start talking with people—getting statements, finding out what happened. That sort of thing. The beat cops were just taking quick statements from everyone, and getting names, addresses and phone numbers of everyone present. They couldn't isolate everyone, and it wasn't as if they were going to bring in a paddy wagon to take everyone downtown, but they did use the green room to question people.

My bet was that, since this was Detroit, if the dude who'd gotten killed hadn't been an obviously upper-middle-class white man from the suburbs, the cops wouldn't have been paying nearly this much attention.

But the thing is, well, I kinda kept track of everything. I'd already started asking some questions before the cops showed, but not enough to screw anyone up or make them think what I thought. After all, that was the reason witnesses to a crime weren't supposed to talk with each other or anyone else, they might have an undue effect on each other's opinions and memories of what happened. So I tried to find out just enough to find out maybe something about what maybe might've happened.

What I found out was that he was there with nobody, and nobody knew who he was or what he was doing at the show. He'd come in, gotten a drink, sat down, drank and died.

It was all pretty direct.

I sneaked up on the detectives at the corpse. One was crouched next to the dead body, going through his pockets. He pulled out a wallet and opened it up. "Huh, says here his name's Hardy, Colin Hardy." He went through the rest of the guy's pockets, commenting on the contents and bagging them. "Looks like he just got to town. He's from Massachusetts. Plane ticket here says he just flew in this evening."

"So he came to town and came right to this show?" another detective said.

"So he maybe might've come just for the show?" I said.

"Looks like," the first detective said.

"But y'all have said nobody here knew him, right?" the second detective said.

I nodded. "That's what everyone's saying."

"Mighty interesting," the first detective said. "Mighty."

I guessed that to mean that if no one here knew him, nobody would have a reason to poison him, but someone did, so someone was obviously lying.

"Shawn, I need to talk with you," Jamie said, pulling me aside and away from the coppers.

"What's going on?" I asked.

"I'm not sure," she said, pulling me up into the lighting booth. She pointed to a timer sitting on the floor.

"What's that?" I asked.

"A timer."

"Duh. But, hello? Why are you showing it to me?"

"I don't like cops."

"I'm still not tracking, James. Help me out here."

"I was wondering about when the lights went out and stayed out. Turns out, somebody'd rigged the consoles and everything into this timer, so we'd go black at a pre-established time and stay black for a given length of time."

"So you're saying somebody hooked all your gear into this timer without you knowing it," I said.

"Yes."

"And it was all done purposefully."

"Yes. And I checked the equipment earlier tonight, and it was fine, so this was done just before the show tonight."

"This is fucked and we're fucked."

"Yes."

"Just so we're in agreement," I said.

"Oh, Irish, we so are. I'm pissed somebody came up here and jacked with my shit, and I'm pissed somebody's setting us up like

266

this and I'm fucking pissed off that all this is going down like this. Makes me want a fucking drink. And y'know, none of this fucked-up shit would be happening if those assholes hadn't decided running a blind pig during our fucking show was a fucking good idea."

She was so not a happy camper. "Have you touched that?" I asked about the timer.

"Yes. I had to find it, after all, didn't I?"

"Yeah, but let's not touch it anymore. Maybe it might still have some fingerprints or something on it. Something that'll lead us to the killer."

"Yeah. I been talking with Kelly, y'know?" She was sitting on the floor now, clearly upset and unsure about how to express it.

"Yeah, and . . . ?"

"Well, she said if it *is* cyanide, that person really had to take care not to poison themselves with it. See, cyanide can go through your skin and kill you that way, too. So if you're poisoning somebody, you got to be careful about it all, or else you'll end up dead, too."

Well, that was something I did not know. Interesting. We had a planned murder—after all, who carries cyanide with them on a regular basis?—with a careful killer. A killer who knew this guy was gonna be at the show tonight.

Obviously, someone somewhere was lying.

"Oh, God," Ashley said, coming up to me and wrapping herself in my arms. "I can't stand this. He's so . . . it's scary and making me sick to my stomach."

I held her and gently stroked her hair, trying to calm her. "You'd better give that timer to the police," I said to Jamie.

I thought about the people who had been sitting next to him, wondering if one of them was lying about knowing him. Maybe one of them had come with him, killed him, and was now denying him. Like Judas.

The woman to his right had complained early on about his

267

pallor, vomiting and such. She could have been deliberately throwing us all off her scent.

The guy to his left said he seemed fine. Not at all talkative, he appeared to have come by himself. He bought a drink at the bar, and it was only during the darkness that he started acting funny. The man, Justin Drew, supposed that if someone had poisoned him, they slipped it into his drink during the prolonged period of lights out.

Along about midnight, when the police left, taking the corpse with them, and letting everyone leave, finally, a couple of the officers held back.

"Seeing as you don't have a liquor license," one of them said. "We'll have to be taking that." He pointed to the keg. Two men walked up and picked it up.

David, one of the anarchists who lived at the house, started to complain. "Hey, that's ours."

Natalie grabbed him. "Hey, you want to lose your keg or you want to lose it *and* go to jail *and* have a hefty fine for running a blind pig?"

"Okay, okay, point taken," David said, raising his hands in surrender as he backed up.

There had already been a few reporters nosing around, and I was sure there would soon be more, and that I'd be able to find out even more by reading about it in the morning paper.

"Hey, Kelly," I said, as we walked out to our cars. "If that was cyanide, how long would it take to kill the guy?"

She shrugged. "As little as a minute. And pretty much, with cyanide, there wouldn't be anything anyone could do to help him."

Well, at least it wasn't like someone had poisoned him hours ago and wouldn't have known when he'd have died, so he could've keeled over behind the wheel and taken out various Suburban Assault Vehicles full of soccer moms and golfing children and such.

"Can I spend the night with you?" Ashley said, grabbing onto my arm just outside of the theater. "I'm going to have nightmares all night long," she said with a shiver. She was holding tightly to my arm. Maybe this could work in my favor even better than a scary movie.

7

Read All About It

The next morning, Sunday morning, well, actually, just a little before noon, I went to Ashley's front porch to retrieve her newspaper and I saw us—all of us. It must've been a slow news day, 'cause we were front page news. *Murder in the Round*, the headline screamed, which was total hogwash, since it wasn't in the round. We used a three-quarters thrust stage.

My cell was already ringing. I answered it.

"Have you seen the paper yet?" Jamie asked. "We're the *it* kids, Irish! Nat wants everyone at the theater this afternoon for a special rehearsal and to get ready for next weekend."

"But . . . but . . . next weekend's quite a while away. And everyone already knows their parts."

"Folks have already been ringing Nat's phone off the hook, reserving tickets for next weekend. We'll be sold out the rest of the run. Might even add some extra nights and actually make some money on this one—if not a killing." I don't know where Jamie got her maniacal laugh from, but that was definitely what her laugh was, *maniacal*.

"Who was it?" Ashley asked, coming up behind me and wrapping her arms around me just after I hung up.

"Jamie. Apparently we're having a special meeting/rehearsal today at four at the theater. All the news coverage has really sent ticket sales through the roof."

"Then I'd better take a shower and make us some breakfast," Ash said, giving me a quick peck on the cheek before dashing to the bathroom.

I briefly thought about joining her. After all, I was the only way her back ever got good and thoroughly washed, but then I saw I had a pullout quote when the story was continued on page A12.

"Nobody knew, at first, if it was part of the show or if there really was a problem," they quoted me as saying. Almost all of us were quoted throughout the article, and apparently, the police were treating it as a homicide, a poisoning, in fact.

I found out even more by reading the article. Colin Hardy, thirty-six, was born and raised in Massachusetts, but no one knew why he was in Michigan. His mother, who was still alive and living in Boston, had been notified, but hadn't seen her son in several years.

Police had found no usable fingerprints on the timing device supposedly used to turn off the lights in order for the murderer to slip the poison into his drink.

So . . . nobody knew him. Nobody knew he was in Michigan. Nobody knew *why* he was in Michigan. But, obviously, someone was lying. Someone knew, someone knew well enough to kill him, and more importantly, had a reason, motive and ability to kill him.

My cell phone rang again.

"Oh my God! Can you believe it?" Kelly practically screamed

over the phone. "We're all over the newspapers!"

"We were just in the newspapers," I said. "People are gonna start talking about us."

"But talk is good. It sells books!"

"Are you sure you're not just staging all this crap to sell books?" I glanced through the rest of the newspaper, looking for anything related to our little murder. Nada.

"Positive, but what a great idea that would be! So okay," she went on. "Everyone from work who was there's already been calling me."

"Why were so many folks from work there last night anyway?"

"Well, they didn't want to be there on opening night, because they figured we'd still be working out the kinks, which we obviously were, but they figured night two would be a good show. So anyway, they've been calling me, and I've been talking with them. Apparently our man Colin came to Michigan—to our little show—with a purpose. At least two people heard him say something about someone needing to pay something, and that he seemed *quite* pleased with himself."

"And you're telling me this because . . . ?"

"Well, we're like a team. Crime-fighting partners!"

"No, not so much. I just keep getting sucked into this stuff. It's like a disease or something, always creeping up on me and shite." I went to the fridge to grab a soda, my morning Diet Pepsi. En route back to the dining room I saw that the message light on Ashley's machine was blinking. Repeatedly. We hadn't checked it the night before when we'd gotten home. We'd been rather, er . . . preoccupied.

"Well, I think you, me, Jamie and Ashley ought to get together before the rehearsal to start working the case. For instance, I mean, the fact that a timer was used means the murder was premeditated."

"Duh," I said. "He was poisoned. Normal folks don't just

wander about with poison." The light was blinking rapidly, like there were a few messages. More than one, two or three.

"Well, unless they're exterminators or some such." I went over to Ashley's desk, to grab a pen and paper to start writing notes down. Since I seemed to be becoming a regular detective, I really needed to start keeping notes of pertinent facts, like the mention that Hardy had an ex-wife. And, just like the very worst of all the dyke-drama detective novels I'd ever read, a picture fell out from underneath the pad, a picture of Ashley in a wedding dress. And her groom was last night's murderee.

"Well, there is that," Kelly said, about the exterminators.

"Um, Kel? I gotta let you go. Things just got really stupid here."

"What do you mean?"

"If you think about how my friends just set me up thinking about a serial murderer being among us, and then I thought a coworker *was* a serial killer."

"Technically she was," Kelly said.

"I was talking about you."

"Oh, okay, so you were wrong there. But there was another coworker who was. You just had the wrong one."

"Yeah, but you get the drift of the stupidity of my life of late, right?" I went through the rest of the desk, looking for anything else of import. I didn't find anything.

"Yeah."

"So it's taken another turn for the weird." I wondered what was on the machine.

"How so?"

"It's so unbelievable I don't even want to say until I'm sure. Gotta go now, talk to you later, 'bye." I hung up and hit *Play* on the machine.

"*Why the fuck did you think I'd just let you go, babe? You owe me, and I'm coming to collect.*"

"*Hey, babe, it's me, and I'm in town. If you want me to keep quiet,*"

Mrs. Hardy, *you'll be ready like I told ya. This time, I want a hundred grand. You got it, and I want it.*"

Funny, he hadn't looked as much a slimeball as he sounded.

"God, honey, why'd you have to go and do that?" Ashley said from behind me. "Raise your hands and turn around real slow."

Well, if this wasn't anticlimactic, I didn't know what was. I turned around and saw Ashley holding a gun on me. It wasn't a big gun, but I was sure it could do the trick.

"I hadn't planned on this," she said. "He tracked me down, *yet again*, and I had to do something about it this time. It couldn't keep going on and on."

"What was going on, babe?" I said. "Why'd he come after you for a hundred grand?"

"Oh," she said. "This is the part where you keep me talking until help arrives. Let me just quickly bottom-line it for you. I married Colin soon after college. I was scared and . . . I was scared of how I felt about you. So I married him when I moved to Boston and joined a bank. I embezzled some money, he found out about it, I divorced him and have been moving around trying to lose him since. He's been blackmailing me ever since, whenever he could find me."

"Hold on, you were never caught with the embezzling?"

"I paid off an auditor, or three, and when the government started coming down on us, they went after the bigger fish. I just stole a few mil, so I was small potatoes. I only worried that I hadn't paid enough of the right folks enough money. If any investigations ever get too close, I'll leave the country."

"You're kidding, right?" This was so stupid it had to be true.

"No. I'm just surprised Colin managed to keep tracking me down and all. He's the one who's been keeping me from you of late—having to discuss it on the phone with him at all hours. It was beginning to look like he wanted all the money, though he didn't take any of the risk."

"So now you're going to kill me?"

She shrugged. "I don't know. I didn't expect him to show up here, but I've been ready for him at all times." She raised the gun a bit, as if indicating that it was for him.

"You didn't answer my question. But I thought the *cyanide* was for him."

"Well, it was. If I had to kill him in public. If he broke in here, I'd have this waiting for him. But I guess now I'm going to have to use it on you and then chop you up into little pieces and either bury you all over, flush you, dissolve you in acid, or dump you in the Detroit River. Which might have the same effect as acid on you."

"Maybe might, but why don't you just hand over that gun, instead?" I lowered one of my hands to reach for the gun.

"Whoa, there, Speed Racer. I love you, but I don't trust you to not turn me in." She brought the gun up just a bit, so as to more assuredly point directly at me, as if ensuring I knew she meant business.

I shrugged. "Not that it matters, since that gun's empty and all."

She got this questioning look on her face, even as she tilted the gun slightly, as if she could judge whether or not it was loaded based on the weight of it.

I went low, so if she shot, the bullet would go over my head, and tackled her midriff. She pulled the trigger as we went down, but fortunately my greater weight and strength were enough to keep her down.

I slammed her hand against the floor so she couldn't use the gun as a weapon against me. "I am *so* glad I didn't take you to meet my grandmother," I said, looking down at her in disgust. "She'd've been *so* disappointed."

"But my dear, sweet little Shawn, what you need to know is this—this is what comes of being related to Lir, of coming from his blood: You will live long, but great injustices will come to you. Your life might be filled with the stuff of legends, but know that the impossible can right well be possible in your years.

"Oh, and yeah, women of our clan and blood tend to know the future. Or at least have some indications of it. We also like whiskey. Quite a lot, actually." She took another sip of her whiskey-ladened tea. "And that, my dear, is all you need to know. Well, and how to read and write and all that other nonsense, I suppose."

About the Author

Therese (Reese) Szymanski is an award-winning playwright.

She's also been short-listed for a couple of Lammys, Goldies and a Spectrum, and made the Publishing Triangle's list of Notable Lesbian Books with her first anthology.

She's edited a slew of books, worked on some team books, written a bunch of books on her own, and had a few dozen shorter works published in a wide variety of books. She's also written reviews, humor columns, feature pieces, interview stories and a bunch of other things for a lot of different publications. After all, she *is* a writer. (Just please never ask her about that particular bad commercial for a used car lot.)

You can e-mail Reese at tsszymanski@worldnet.att.net, and she keeps a very silly Live Journal about totally nonsensical things at http://reeseszymanski.livejournal.com.

Oh, and also, friends are betting that she and her girlfriend, Stacia, who is really quite the thing, will move in together sometime real soon . . .

Reese enjoys sending conventions up and having fun with things. She thinks Shawn enables her to meet the requests she used to oft receive (that she write a theater-based story), and to have some real, silly fun, while working hard to become an even better writer. And, now that the first Shawn has seen the full light of day, Reese will get back to writing Brett, with *When it's all Relative* due out in 2008.

WHISKEY AND OAK LEAVES by Jaime Clevenger. Meg meets June, a single woman running a horse ranch in the California Sierra foothills. The two become quick friends and it isn't long before Meg is looking for more than just a friendship. But June has no interest in developing a deeper relationship with Meg. She is, after all, not the least bit interested in women . . . or is she? Neither of these two women is prepared for what lies ahead . . . 978-1-59493-093-5 $13.95

SUMTER POINT by KG MacGregor. As Audie surrenders her heart to Beth, she begins to distance herself from the reckless habits of her youth. Just as they're ready to meet in the middle, their future is thrown into doubt by a duty Beth can't ignore. It all comes to a head on the river at Sumter Point. 978-1-59493-089-8 $13.95

THE TARGET by Gerri Hill. Sara Michaels is the daughter of a prominent senator who has been receiving death threats against his family. In an effort to protect Sara, the FBI recruits homicide detective Jaime Hutchinson to secretly provide the protection they are so certain Sara will need. Will Sara finally figure out who is behind the death threats? And will Jaime realize the truth—and be able to save Sara before it's too late? 978-1-59493-082-9 $13.95

REALITY BYTES by Jane Frances. In this sequel to *Reunion*, follow the lives of four friends in a romantic tale that spans the globe and proves that you can cross the whole of cyberspace only to find love a few suburbs away . . . 978-1-59493-079-9 $13.95

MURDER CAME SECOND by Jessica Thomas. Broadway's bad-boy genius, Paul Carlucci, has chosen *Hamlet* for his latest production. To the delight of some and despair of others, he has selected Provincetown's amphitheatre for his opening gala. But suddenly Alex Peres realizes that the wrong people are falling down. And the moaning is all to real-istic. Someone must not be shooting blanks . . . 978-1-59493-081-2 $13.95

SKIN DEEP by Kenna White. Jordan Griffin has been given a new assignment: Track down and interview one-time nationally renowned broadcast journalist Reece McAllister. Much to her surprise, Jordan comes away with far more than just a story . . . 978-1-59493-78-2 $13.95

FINDERS KEEPERS by Karin Kallmaker. *Finders Keepers*, the quest for the perfect mate in the 21st century, joins Karin Kallmaker's *Just Like That* and her other incomparable novels about lesbian love, lust and laughter. 1-59493-072-4 $13.95

OUT OF THE FIRE by Beth Moore. Author Ann Covington feels at the top of the world when told her book is being made into a movie. Then in walks Casey Duncan the actress who is playing the lead in her movie. Will Casey turn Ann's world upside down? 1-59493-088-0 $13.95

STAKE THROUGH THE HEART: NEW EXPLOITS OF TWILIGHT LESBIANS by Karin Kallmaker, Julia Watts, Barbara Johnson and Therese Szymanski. The playful quartet that penned the acclaimed *Once Upon A Dyke* are dimming the lights for journeys into worlds of breathless seduction. 1-59493-071-6 $15.95

THE HOUSE ON SANDSTONE by KG MacGregor. Carly Griffin returns home to Leland and finds that her old high school friend Justine is awakening more than just old memories. 1-59493-076-7 $13.95

WILD NIGHTS: MOSTLY TRUE STORIES OF WOMEN LOVING WOMEN edited by Therese Szymanski. 264 pp. 23 new stories from today's hottest erotic writers are sure to give you your wildest night ever! 1-59493-069-4 $15.95

COYOTE SKY by Gerri Hill. 248 pp. Sheriff Lee Foxx is trying to cope with the realization that she has fallen in love for the first time. And fallen for author Kate Winters, who is technically unavailable. Will Lee fight to keep Kate in Coyote?
1-59493-065-1 $13.95

VOICES OF THE HEART by Frankie J. Jones. 264 pp. A series of events force Erin to swear off love as she tries to break away from the woman of her dreams. Will Erin ever find the key to her future happiness?   1-59493-068-6 $13.95

SHELTER FROM THE STORM by Peggy J. Herring. 296 pp. A story about family and getting reacquainted with one's past that shows that sometimes you don't appreciate what you have until you almost lose it.   1-59493-064-3 $13.95

WRITING MY LOVE by Claire McNab. 192 pp. Romance writer Vonny Smith believes she will be able to woo her editor Diana through her writing. 1-59493-063-5 $13.95

PAID IN FULL by Ann Roberts. 200 pp. Ari Adams will need to choose between the debts of the past and the promise of a happy future.   1-59493-059-7 $13.95

ROMANCING THE ZONE by Kenna White. 272 pp. Liz's world begins to crumble when a secret from her past returns to Ashton.   1-59493-060-0 $13.95

SIGN ON THE LINE by Jaime Clevenger. 204 pp. Alexis Getty, a flirtatious delivery driver is committed to finding the rightful owner of a mysterious package.
1-59493-052-X $13.95

END OF WATCH by Clare Baxter. 256 pp. LAPD Lieutenant L.A. Franco Frank follows the lone clue down the unlit steps of memory to a final, unthinkable resolution.
1-59493-064-4 $13.95

BEHIND THE PINE CURTAIN by Gerri Hill. 280 pp. Jacqueline returns home after her father's death and comes face-to-face with her first crush.
1-59493-057-0 $13.95

18TH & CASTRO by Karin Kallmaker. 200 pp. First-time couplings and couples who know how to mix lust and love make 18th & Castro the hottest address in the city by the bay.   1-59493-066-X $13.95

JUST THIS ONCE by KG MacGregor. 200 pp. Mindful of the obligations back home that she must honor, Wynne Connelly struggles to resist the fascination and allure that a particular woman she meets on her business trip represents.
1-59493-087-2 $13.95

ANTICIPATION by Terri Breneman. 240 pp. Two women struggle to remain professional as they work together to find a serial killer.   1-59493-055-4 $13.95

OBSESSION by Jackie Calhoun. 240 pp. Lindsey's life is turned upside down when Sarah comes into the family nursery in search of perennials.   1-59493-058-9 $13.95

BENEATH THE WILLOW by Kenna White. 240 pp. A torch that still burns brightly even after twenty-five years threatens to consume two childhood friends.
1-59493-053-8 $13.95

SISTER LOST, SISTER FOUND by Jeanne G'Fellers. 224 pp. The highly anticipated sequel to *No Sister of Mine.*   1-59493-056-2 $13.95

THE WEEKEND VISITOR by Jessica Thomas. 240 pp. In this latest Alex Peres mystery, Alex is asked to investigate an assault on a local woman but finds that her client may have more secrets than she lets on. 1-59493-054-6 $13.95

THE KILLING ROOM by Gerri Hill. 392 pp. How can two women forget and go their separate ways? 1-59493-050-3 $12.95

PASSIONATE KISSES by Megan Carter. 240 pp. Will two old friends run from love? 1-59493-051-1 $12.95

ALWAYS AND FOREVER by Lyn Denison. 224 pp. The girl next door turns Shannon's world upside down. 1-59493-049-X $12.95

BACK TALK by Saxon Bennett. 200 pp. Can a talk show host find love after heartbreak? 1-59493-028-7 $12.95

THE PERFECT VALENTINE: EROTIC LESBIAN VALENTINE STORIES edited by Barbara Johnson and Therese Szymanski—from Bella After Dark. 328 pp. Stories from the hottest writers around. 1-59493-061-9 $14.95

MURDER AT RANDOM by Claire McNab. 200 pp. The Sixth Denise Cleever Thriller. Denise realizes the fate of thousands is in her hands. 1-59493-047-3 $12.95

THE TIDES OF PASSION by Diana Tremain Braund. 240 pp. Will Susan be able to hold it all together and find the one woman who touches her soul? 1-59493-048-1 $12.95

JUST LIKE THAT by Karin Kallmaker. 240 pp. Disliking each other—and everything they stand for—even before they meet, Toni and Syrah find feelings can change, just like that. 1-59493-025-2 $12.95

WHEN FIRST WE PRACTICE by Therese Szymanski. 200 pp. Brett and Allie are once again caught in the middle of murder and intrigue. 1-59493-045-7 $12.95

REUNION by Jane Frances. 240 pp. Cathy Braithwaite seems to have it all: good looks, money and a thriving accounting practice . . . 1-59493-046-5 $12.95

BELL, BOOK & DYKE: NEW EXPLOITS OF MAGICAL LESBIANS by Kallmaker, Watts, Johnson and Szymanski. 360 pp. Reluctant witches, tempting spells and skyclad beauties—delve into the mysteries of love, lust and power in this quartet of novellas. 1-59493-023-6 $14.95

ARTIST'S DREAM by Gerri Hill. 320 pp. When Cassie meets Luke Winston, she can no longer deny her attraction to women . . . 1-59493-042-2 $12.95

NO EVIDENCE by Nancy Sanra. 240 pp. Private investigator Tally McGinnis once again returns to the horror-filled world of a serial killer. 1-59493-043-04 $12.95

WHEN LOVE FINDS A HOME by Megan Carter. 280 pp. What will it take for Anna and Rona to find their way back to each other again? 1-59493-041-4 $12.95

MEMORIES TO DIE FOR by Adrian Gold. 240 pp. Rachel attempts to avoid her attraction to the charms of Anna Sigurdson . . . 1-59493-038-4 $12.95

SILENT HEART by Claire McNab. 280 pp. Exotic lesbian romance. 1-59493-044-9 $12.95

MIDNIGHT RAIN by Peggy J. Herring. 240 pp. Bridget McBee is determined to find the woman who saved her life. 1-59493-021-X $12.95

THE MISSING PAGE A Brenda Strange Mystery by Patty G. Henderson. 240 pp. Brenda investigates her client's murder . . . 1-59493-004-X $12.95

WHISPERS ON THE WIND by Frankie J. Jones. 240 pp. Dixon thinks she and her best friend, Elizabeth Colter, would make the perfect couple . . . 1-59493-037-6 $12.95

CALL OF THE DARK: EROTIC LESBIAN TALES OF THE SUPERNATURAL edited by Therese Szymanski—from Bella After Dark. 320 pp. 1-59493-040-6 $14.95

A TIME TO CAST AWAY A Helen Black Mystery by Pat Welch. 240 pp. Helen stops by Alice's apartment—only to find the woman dead . . . 1-59493-036-8 $12.95

DESERT OF THE HEART by Jane Rule. 224 pp. The book that launched the most popular lesbian movie of all time is back. 1-1-59493-035-X $12.95

THE NEXT WORLD by Ursula Steck. 240 pp. Anna's friend Mido is threatened and eventually disappears . . . 1-59493-024-4 $12.95

CALL SHOTGUN by Jaime Clevenger. 240 pp. Kelly gets pulled back into the world of private investigation . . . 1-59493-016-3 $12.95

52 PICKUP by Bonnie J. Morris and E.B. Casey. 240 pp. 52 hot, romantic tales—one for every Saturday night of the year. 1-59493-026-0 $12.95

GOLD FEVER by Lyn Denison. 240 pp. Kate's first love, Ashley, returns to their home town, where Kate now lives . . . 1-1-59493-039-2 $12.95

RISKY INVESTMENT by Beth Moore. 240 pp. Lynn's best friend and roommate needs her to pretend Chris is his fiancé. But nothing is ever easy. 1-59493-019-8 $12.95

HUNTER'S WAY by Gerri Hill. 240 pp. Homicide detective Tori Hunter is forced to team up with the hot-tempered Samantha Kennedy. 1-59493-018-X $12.95

CAR POOL by Karin Kallmaker. 240 pp. Soft shoulders, merging traffic and slippery when wet . . . Anthea and Shay find love in the car pool. 1-59493-013-9 $12.95

NO SISTER OF MINE by Jeanne G'Fellers. 240 pp. Telepathic women fight to coexist with a patriarchal society that wishes their eradication. 1-59493-017-1 $12.95

ON THE WINGS OF LOVE by Megan Carter. 240 pp. Stacie's reporting career is on the rocks. She has to interview bestselling author Cheryl, or else! 1-59493-027-9 $12.95

WICKED GOOD TIME by Diana Tremain Braund. 224 pp. Does Christina need Miki as a protector . . . or want her as a lover? 1-59493-031-7 $12.95

THOSE WHO WAIT by Peggy J. Herring. 240 pp. Two brilliant sisters—in love with the same woman! 1-59493-032-5 $12.95

WHEN THE CORPSE LIES A Motor City Thriller by Therese Szymanski. 328 pp. Butch bad-girl Brett Higgins is used to waking up next to beautiful women she hardly knows. Problem is, this one's dead. 1-931513-74-0 $12.95